Seeing Red
Copyright © 2019 by B. S. Todd.

Printed in the United States of America

Editing by Teri@editingfairy.com
Book Formatting by Derek Murphy@Creativindie.com
Bookcover image@pixabay.com

Paperback ISBN: 978-0-9991169-7-5
Ebook ISBN: 978-0-9991169-8-2

Library of Congress Control Number: 2019915249
First Edition: 2019

10 9 8 7 6 5 4 3 2 1

Seeing
Red

Seeing *Red*

A CLOVERLY WOLVES NOVEL

B. S. TODD

Prologue

Tracy

It was just after midnight when Tracy jolted awake, her eyes searching the pitch-black room. The thumping of her heart vibrated through her body and she quivered while listening for movement downstairs. Randy was asleep on the sofa, had he knew she was having nightmares, he would insist on sleeping in the chair next to the bed. She reached up and moved the curtains to the side, allowing moonlight to brighten the room.

Since moving to the farm with Randy, Tracy could envision a life that didn't include being an alpha female. That was never her ambition, but the primary reason her uncle was so adamant about raising her after the death of her parents. Travis was the only blood-kin that survived that night. The night Alpha Hudson—her grandfather—destroyed the pack.

"The pack belongs to me, and you will right the wrong," Travis warned with little concern for the trauma she had already suffered. She was only five years old at the time.

Growing up in a dysfunctional family, Tracy learned at an early age to keep her head down and her mouth shut. She wasn't allowed to mourn the death of her parents, or even mention their names, for fear of being locked in a closet, or worse, chained up in the cellar. Most of her time was spent learning the ways of the Hudson pack, while dreaming of a normal life. She despised what she was and envied humans, wishing she could be more like them. *They are beneath you. Trouble, always trouble.* Travis's words echoed in her head, another reminder of the brainwashing she was ceaselessly compelled to endure.

Even now, her body tensed when she thought about Travis's plan to take down Alpha Cooper. She never really wanted to be Jack's mate, and maybe she should have been more upset the day Travis died in a brutal battle with Jack's wolf, but she wasn't. With his death came her freedom, along with the rushing torrent of memories that now haunted her dreams. A tear slipped free, and she released a shuddering breath.

Tracy thought the whole concept of sharing a bond was a fluke, and animal lust was the law of attraction. But after bumping into Randy in the woods, she understood what it meant to have a soulmate, and there wasn't another male on earth that could compare to him.

Travis, however, never saw things her way, being

cruel like his father, her grandfather, and all the Hudson males. She didn't think her dad was as ruthless as the rest since he had bonded with her mom. He must have had some redeeming qualities, or so she wanted to believe, until the repressed memory replayed in her head.

She pulled the blanket to her chin, visualizing the willow branch high above her head and the sting as it snapped across her backside. She was no match for the monster that held her tiny frame over the back of a chair as she struggled to escape his wrath. She reached back and warily rubbed the still sensitive area.

Being a Hudson female and the last shifter to carry the family name, she believed herself cursed. Worse still, she would always be as long as Hudson blood flowed through her veins. So maybe the nightmares that frightened her were happening because her heart was tainted and her subconscious mind enjoyed tormenting her. That sounded better than calling it a harbinger, presaging that her now happy life with Randy was about to turn to shit.

It's a stupid dream, she told herself, but late at night when she awoke, frozen in fear and unable to even breathe, she sensed trouble looming.

One

Tracy

"Is this blindfold necessary?" Tracy grumbled, reaching up to touch the material strapped around her head. Randy was constantly springing silly surprises on her, but this was the first time he insisted she cover her eyes. And the way he rushed her out the front door, just after lunch, she couldn't help feeding off his energy.

She cringed, thinking Randy's parents were watching as she cautiously followed behind him, unable to suppress her giggles. "If I fall... so help me." She giggled again, guessing he was leading her around the lake to his parents' house, but she couldn't imagine why. "This is so awkward! Your dad will never let me live this down."

"Only because he loves you." Randy chuckled, squeezing her hand.

Recalling that first night when Randy took her to

meet his parents, Tracy felt out of place and unsure of what their future together would be. But when Randy's mom complimented her earrings, their love of jewelry blossomed into a friendship that even she couldn't foresee. Sharing their day around the dinner table at night was the perfect way to unwind. They were supportive of Randy, listening and laughing, everyone having a story to tell. And being accepted by humans in their home and made to feel like part of the family, Tracy knew her life would never be the same.

After that night, Tracy settled into a routine, wanting to learn everything she could about his family and eager to fit in. Admittedly, she wasn't a country girl, but the longer she was on the farm, the more at home she felt— even splurging on a pair of cowboy boots so she could work in the barn.

No longer alone, she found peace in her life with Randy... The cherry on top would have to be the little Oliver he promised that night not so long ago. Being an only child, she wanted at least three little ones of her own running underfoot. And because she knew how horrible loneliness was, her children would never go through life without the strong support of their siblings.

Now she was grateful for the bandanna tied around her head, absorbing the tears overflowing her eyes. *Shake it off!* She inhaled and slowly exhaled a breath, squeezing the remaining moisture from her eyelids. Channeling Randy's nephew, Oliver, who always got excited to go anywhere, she asked, "Are We There Yet?"

"Not even close." Randy's laughter filled the air, and she rolled her eyes as if he could see them. Then she felt the gravel underfoot and heard the truck door open. "Step up," he said and goosed her when she climbed into the front seat.

She swatted his hand. "Where are you taking me?"

"You'll see when we get there." Randy fastened her seatbelt and shut the door. His leather and soap scent never failed to send delightful, little shivers to her toes. She fanned herself, causing him to chuckle as a playful grin stretched across her face. She was beginning to question his motives, but whatever he planned she knew she would love it. He climbed into the driver's seat and fastened his seatbelt before starting the truck.

Being blindfolded and in a moving vehicle was somewhat enticing if Tracy were being totally honest. The roar of the tires and heavy breathing from her teasing mate—who kept reaching over to run his finger up her side, her arm, and her thigh—she could only imagine his mischievous grin. Her heart thumped with anticipation and goosebumps formed on her skin. She bit her lip as the urge to scoot closer to him caused her eyes to flare. Then Randy turned right, heading into Cloverly and she frowned. Oh, he was up to something, all right, and she could almost hear the cogs turning in his head. Then he chuckled as if he could read her mind, more proof he was enjoying her uncertainty.

"Damn, babe, you look hot in that pretty, little blindfold. We should do this more often." He reached over and poked her ribs and she squealed as a fresh layer of goosebumps appeared on her arms. "Imagine all the fun we could have." She was doing just that; apparently, they were both thinking the same thing. She forced the dirty thoughts from her mind and tucked her arm against her side, trying to thwart his tickles. He was having way too much fun.

"Why are we heading into town?" she asked, but he didn't answer. He turned up the radio instead, avoiding her question. She listened to the light tap of his fingers on the steering wheel and the soft murmur as he sang along with the song playing on the radio. By the time the truck slowed to a stop, she realized they were at the stoplight in Cloverly and she quickly cranked the window down halfway.

"You should probably roll that window back up or Officer Riley might think I kidnapped you." His teasing tone made her chuckle.

Scenting the air as the truck moved forward, she wasn't about to roll the window up. Randy thought he was being slick, and maybe he was, but she had a terrific sense of smell and would know where they were before they even got out of the truck.

Passing the café, Randy clicked on the turn signal, and her eyebrows shot up past the blindfold. She listened as he pulled the truck over to the side of the road, next to the Lucky Leaf Boutique. She wondered what was up with that, but it being her favorite store, she wouldn't complain. Then he parked the truck and got out, his booted steps sounding on the pavement as he rushed around to the passenger side and opened her door. Reaching past her, he unfastened the seatbelt and took hold of her hand. Her ankle twisted when she stepped down on the curb and she quickly latched onto Randy to keep from falling.

"Careful," he said, scooping her up and cradling her against his chest.

"Put me down, goofball!" She giggled, trying to wiggle

out of his hold. "We're in public. What will people think?"

She buried her face against his shoulder as his voice dropped to a whisper, "That's what makes it so appealing," and her entire body turned to mush.

"You're only doing this to further my humiliation." She inhaled an exaggerated breath when he growled into her hair.

Randy carrying her was a definite turn-on, and the afternoon sunshine added to the heat traveling to her ears. She could imagine what someone walking past probably thought. *You're a lucky female.* Okay, so maybe that's what she would think, seeing him in all his gorgeous glory. She snickered and Randy squeezed her tighter while standing her next to the building so he could press the doorbell. Her brows knitted together, but she didn't want to ruin his surprise so she pretended she didn't know they were at the boutique.

"I should probably remove the bandanna before we go inside," Randy said, swiftly working the knot at the back of her head. As the cloth fell from her eyes, it was hard to hold her excitement and she lifted up on her toes, wanting to squeal. Randy took hold of her hand when the door opened and Lori motioned them inside.

The huge grin on Lori's face was telling, and apparently, she was in on Randy's surprise, which could only mean one thing. *New underwear!* Tracy eagerly followed them through the warehouse and into the storeroom, where Lori stopped and handed Randy a key. Her brow furrowed when he turned and placed the key in her hand and said, "Don't lose this."

Tracy shoved the key into her front pocket before looking up to meet their grins. She waved when she noticed Hayden sitting in the lounge area, surprised that even he seemed amused. "What's going on?"

"Congratulations! You are now the proud owner of Lori's Lingerie," Lori said, causing Tracy's eyes to round.

If it were a joke, she would probably cry. And if it were real, she would probably cry. Her heart raced and her breath hitched as she forced herself to calm down. "Are you serious?" She expected someone to yell April Fool's, or sike, or whatever humans did when they pranked their friends.

"Well, I couldn't take the store to the mountains with me, so my only option was to sell everything at a discount and close it. But Randy thought you might be interested in taking it over." Lori smiled and wrapped her arm around Hayden's waist when he walked over and stood beside her.

Happy tears rimmed Tracy's eyes as she turned and took in the small overhead sign that proudly advertised Lori's Lingerie. Then she scanned over the various colors of lace and smiled. "This is all mine now? I can't believe you did this for me." She turned into Randy's chest, unable to hold back the tears streaming down her face.

Randy laughed at her muffled chuckles and slipped his fingers into her belt loops to pull her closer. "So, does this mean you...?" She nodded before he could finish the question. "Then let's pay the lady."

Tracy took the bandanna Randy offered and blotted her face as she followed him over to the lounge area and sat next to him, facing Hayden and Lori. Listening to them talk; it amazed her when Randy worked out the numbers in his head, saying, "It's been nice doing business with you." She knew her mate was sharp, but a savvy businessman? She never would have guessed.

"You can start on Monday if you want. You decide what hours you prefer to work and everything else you need to know is all written down, so you shouldn't have any problems. But if you do, you can always call me," Lori said, her smile widening as she took the check from Randy.

That was Friday afternoon, and needless to say, the weekend passed at a snail's pace.

Two

Jesse

Scrubbing nonexistent fingerprints from the enormous glass windows, Jesse struggled to deal with the loss of her best friend. It was less than seven hours since she last saw Lori, yet tears still flooded her eyes. There would be no more girls' night or smut-talking at the boutique. It was something she absolutely loved, but would never admit, the smut-talking part, that is. Lori always had a flair for making her laugh or cringe, depending on who was near enough to overhear their conversations. That was perhaps what she would miss the most. So keeping busy was her way of breathing until she could come to terms with not seeing Lori every day at the store.

She stared out the window, searching for the area where the two rivers came together. It really was beautiful there at the cabin and she could hardly wait until she and

Tucker moved to Berkley, but that would only happen after he completed his alpha training. She glanced up, following Tucker's reflection on the glass as he moved across the room in her direction, his curly brown hair, now much longer and in need of a trim. She tilted her head as he drew her into an embrace and sighed when he peppered kisses down to her shoulder.

"You know, you can go visit Lori anytime you like." Tucker tapped her nose and she nodded.

"It's just... I always thought she would be in Cloverly with me. She's the sister I never had and I already miss her so much." Jesse blinked to clear her eyes. She was being a silly girl.

"Yeah, but even you won't be in Cloverly much longer, and she's a seer—so you know it was too dangerous for her to stay." He tugged on the knot that twisted up her flannel shirt. Other than sleeping clothes, Jesse was never a fan of flannel until after she met Tucker. His mountain lifestyle showed in the rugged clothes he wore, and it didn't take long before she was swiping shirts from his side of the closet.

"But she's so far away," Jesse whined.

Lori's clairvoyance was a recent development that no one saw coming, other than her family. Her accident, which put her in a coma, somehow brought out an ability to have visions like—believe it or not—her great aunt, Brid. It was a hushed secret to keep them both safe. Having two seers from the same family, living in the same area, put a target on both of their backs. Lori's dad had also been a seer and he and Brid had shared visions, which was probably the reason for his fatal auto accident. Since there was never any proof, it still seemed odd that Lori, coming into her own ability, would crash her car at that exact location. Still, Tucker had a point, and because they wouldn't be living in Cloverly, she would most likely be worrying non-stop if Lori had not gone to Tennessee with Hayden.

Regardless, Jesse didn't like it and no matter how hard Tucker tried to reassure her, she couldn't shake the unease that settled in the back of her mind. There would be plenty of females upset to learn Hayden had bonded with a human, and what if one of them took revenge on Lori? She shuddered and untied the knot of her flannel shirt, then buttoned it up—the chill in the air suddenly colder.

"I missed my family when I moved here from Tennessee. It was a hard adjustment, but Hayden is only a phone call away and between the two of us, we've worn a path between Cloverly and the mountains."

Jesse smiled, remembering the story of Hayden bringing a tuxedo to the border. Twice! Maybe that's what she and Lori could do. *Yeah, fat chance.* She didn't think the guys would allow them to travel that far away alone and mentally, she rolled her eyes. "I guess because she's hours away instead of minutes is what bothers me most. Do you think we could visit them once they're settled in?"

"Anything you want, if it will take the sadness from your eyes." He hugged her tighter, swaying from side to side. "Mom would love to have us back, and you all did make plans for a spring visit."

Jesse pushed back and looked up at Tucker. "We did, didn't we? Can you call her tonight and make sure they have room?"

"There's always room if you don't mind hanging out

with the family. My old room is big enough for both of us. And we won't have to share the bathroom! So anytime we want to visit, we can; just don't expect Hayden to give up the cabin just yet."

"But they haven't even had their ceremony," Jesse grumbled, unsure how she felt about staying in the family's cabin—and being around so many people. Where was the privacy in that?

"Maybe not, but it's not required for two people to bond, and since they've already crossed that line, there's no way Hayden will give that up. Especially not so soon after."

"Yeah, I guess. It's been three months and still, I want our privacy."

"What we need are soundproof walls." Tucker tweaked her nose and pulled the vibrating phone from his pocket, saying, "I'll take this outside."

Jesse cocked her head as Tucker walk to the door—boy, was she enjoying the view! The way his washed-out jeans hugged his butt she was past drooling and practically swooning until Seth cleared his throat, reminding her they weren't alone.

She glanced back at Seth, who winked before he continued installing the newly built kitchen cabinets—her face now flushed. What a little hottie he was with his long, blond braid, hanging down his back and silver eyes that always suggested he was up to something. She turned back to the window, the constant hammering a reminder she and Tucker would soon live in Berkley and manage their own pack. That didn't sound as bad as Lori moving to the mountains, and the upside? Jesse could still work at the boutique. She sighed, knowing fate would lead her in the right direction if she were brave enough to allow it.

Returning to her window-washing duty, Jesse couldn't help being distracted by Tucker when he crossed his arms over his chest, nearly ripping the seams of his shirt. And judging by the way she was salivating, she could have probably licked the window clean faster than washing it with a squeegee. Gazing at him and the way his muscles flexed... *sweet mercy!* It would be a long day. Then she noticed the frown on his face when he moved to the edge of the porch. Deep in conversation, his brow furrowed as he stared out across the yard. She knew whatever was troubling him would soon be revealed when he shoved the phone into his pocket. And in three strides, he was walking through the door.

"That didn't look like a very pleasant conversation. Dare I ask?" She intended to wait until Seth and Brayden were outside, but curiosity killed the cat when Tucker bounded across the room like a man on a mission.

"Pack a bag. It looks like we're going to the mountains."

That was four hours ago, and after rushing back to Cloverly to pack her bag and calling Megan to explain why she wouldn't be at the boutique for Tracy's first day—Monday morning—they were already headed to Tennessee.

"I've run through every possible scenario as to why Hayden would call us to Tennessee, and still, I get nothing." Jesse wrung her hands and stared out the windshield, her mind a chaotic mess.

"All he said was Lori had a vision."

"Yeah, but it's not the first time she had a vision, and

that hardly seems reason enough to rush off to the mountains. I mean, she could have called." Jesse chewed her lip, unwilling to admit she was a little troubled. Lori's visions were new to her and at times, she wondered if she were having a vision or just recalling a dream. But if Hayden was the one calling, then without a doubt, it was a vision, and probably not one Jesse wanted to know about. Her life had just settled down and she was looking forward to her last few weeks in Cloverly being uneventful. But it was Cloverly, and the one thing she could say about that was there was never a dull moment.

"From what I gathered, Lori's been on the phone with Brid since they arrived and it worried Hayden. He didn't go into detail because he didn't know the specifics, but he asked that we come because apparently, the vision has something to do with you," Tucker finally admitted as he reached over and took hold of her hand.

"It's Lori and probably another one of her dreams." She dismissed it with a slight eye roll. If he thought for one minute she were in danger, he would turn around and head back home, which was why she changed the subject. "I can't wait to see everyone. Has Alyssa decided if she's moving to Berkley when she graduates? I hope so. She's so much fun!" Jesse grinned at Tucker, who apparently disagreed by the look on his face.

"Little sisters are never fun. Especially since said sister became an adult."

"Oh, it can't be that bad. Plus, she's pretty and she'll need a big brother to curb all the male attention, especially with Hayden so preoccupied." Jesse couldn't help bouncing her brows, causing a low growl to rumble in his chest. "Overprotective much?" She chuckled.

"Not overprotective, just not wanting to go there. In my mind, she'll always be twelve with pigtails and freckles." He cracked a grin and she laughed.

What would it be like growing up in a family with older or younger siblings? It sounded like heaven to Jesse. She had a younger brother, but he lived with her mother and they rarely saw each other. The miles stretched, carrying her thoughts to her family. She was a daddy's girl, which was why she stayed with him when her mother remarried and moved to DC. And since she promised to visit DC later in the summer, it seemed the perfect time to make plans for her little brother to spend fall break with her and Tucker at the cabin. He was the outdoorsy type and she longed for some much-needed time to catch up. And when he was older, he could spend the entire summer there. She was getting ahead of herself, by about five years, but picturing him wagging after Tucker, her eyes crinkled at the corners.

"What put that pretty, little smile on your face?" Tucker asked as he turned off the highway and onto the narrow mountain road.

"I was just thinking how cool it would be for my little brother to spend a summer with us, once he's a bit older. You know, he's about the same age as Lily Rose." She laughed at his groan.

"Please, whatever you do, do not repeat that to Lily. She'll want to meet him and if I recall correctly, he's entering the cootie stage and all girls have cooties. He won't want to be her best friend; heck, he'll be afraid to even look her way."

Jesse's mouth hung open and her brow creased. "Cooties? Really? I thought little boys that age flirted with little girls by chasing after them with live frogs. Or at least that's what Randy used to do. He was a bit older, but still." She smiled and batted her lashes and he grunt-snorted.

"Knowing Randy, I'd say the frog was supposed to eat the cooties so the boy could have the girl. It seems Hayden was quite fond of frogs at that age too." Tucker waggled his brows, and she swatted his arm.

"And you weren't?" She turned in the seat, his grin widening.

"No, I didn't care much for frogs," he said and she smirked, expecting that. "I preferred toads. They're not as slimy."

"You are so bad! But it'll probably be best to save the introductions until Joey's older. I'm thinking the Wilson boys might be a bad influence."

"Whatever. I could never be a bad influence." He sounded serious, but the gleam twinkling in his eyes said otherwise. He most certainly would be a bad influence, but not nearly as bad as Hayden. To hide her grin, she rolled down the window and inhaled the crisp mountain air as they continued up the road.

The Smoky Mountains was the most beautiful place she had ever visited, and she imagined it was hard for Tucker to leave. Of course, if he really wanted to stay on the mountain, she would gladly do so, but she would miss Moose. And her grandmother who unfortunately, wasn't getting any younger. After the feline took to her grandmother so fast, Jesse left Moose behind to keep her company. *It's the little things.* That was true, and since Moose wasn't a fan of the wolves, except for her and sometimes Tucker, he was better off staying in Cloverly.

"It's so beautiful here," Jesse said when she noticed

Tucker lost in thought. Was he thinking about his family and everything he left behind in Tennessee? Was he regretting the decision to move to Cloverly? She flashed an understanding smile when he glanced her way.

"It is, but nowhere near as beautiful as you." He lifted her hand and kissed her knuckles, pointing as the roofline of his family's cabin came into view.

Jesse would always consider the Wilson cabin her second home, the place where she and Tucker officially sealed their bond. She sighed, taking it all in as he turned off the narrow road, following the drive that snaked around to the back of the cabin. Just being there set her mind at ease even though it wasn't really a social visit. She would take whatever she could get, and wouldn't complain.

Three

Jesse

Expecting a swarm of siblings to rush out the backdoor, it was safe to say Jesse was a little disheartened to see only Sawyer waiting on the deck. He hurried across the yard to greet them, his worried eyes locking onto hers the instant she got out of the truck. He was on edge and she glanced around for Lori while zipping up her jacket.

"Where is she?" Jesse asked, catching sight of Lily Rose waving from an upstairs window. She waved back. Obviously, the alpha must have told them to wait inside because it was unusual for Lily not to rush Tucker anytime he came home. She nudged Tucker and nodded to the window, hating that Lily couldn't meet them, but Lori had to come first this time.

"She's at the cabin. We thought you two could use some privacy," Sawyer said and Jesse wrapped her arms around her body to ward off the sudden chill. Why was there a need for privacy if Lori weren't in danger? The only threat to Lori was Katherine and her snotty attitude as far as Jesse knew. Then she wondered how long it would take before Katherine started more of her nonsense. She would put an end to the she-wolf if she so much as ruffled a single hair on Lori's head, and she intended to fully make sure Katherine got the message as soon as she talked to Alyssa. Needless to say, she was more than eager to see Lori, much more than when they first pulled into the drive.

"You should probably go see Lily, and let Sawyer walk with me to the cabin," Jesse said, and Tucker grinned up at the window. He was a sucker for the little dimples that matched his, just as Lily was to his.

"Yeah, it would upset her if I didn't. Go on and I'll catch up," Tucker promised as he took off in a jog to the house. Jesse chuckled when the curtain dropped and she could almost hear Lily Rose bounding down the stairs to meet him in the kitchen.

Walking with Sawyer gave Jesse a chance to get to know him a little better since she didn't have the opportunity back in December. He was the spitting image of his two older brothers, but being younger, had yet to fill out and bulk up. His dark-brown hair was more like Hayden's, having more wave than curl. She smiled when the breeze danced through his hair. He would definitely be a favorite with the ladies in Cloverly, and she assumed he was there as well.

"So..." She glanced around conspiratorially and asked

when he looked her way, "With Tucker and Hayden spoken for where does that leave you?"

He flashed a shameful grin and pushed the hair out of his face. "Well, with both of them off the market, all the female attention will be fastened on me this year. So, I suppose this could be my summer to remember." His wink spoke volumes, and although he was almost twenty, and clearly a man in his own right, he still blushed. *How cute.*

"I think you might be right. I spotted several girls strolling down the street when we pulled into the drive. Is that what they do to get your attention?" Again, he blushed, and she grinned.

"Yeah, they like to gather in front of the house, or at least they did when Tucker was here. With Hayden, it was different. He never paid much attention to the girls that walked past the house. He was more interested in the ones that sought his attention in the woods. I'm sure I don't have to tell you why."

"Oh!" Jesse blushed with understanding and he chuckled. "I assume Hayden is with Lori now," she said, changing the subject because the last thing she wanted to do was talk about Hayden's sex life.

"Yeah, and I would suggest knocking before you enter. Some things never change." The grin on his face told her why, and her blush deepened. But he was also there at the apartment when Lori accepted Hayden's bond, so he already knew what they were more than likely up to.

"I guess that means we'll be bunking with the family tonight."

"Well, since Mom already aired out Tucker's room, I'd say that's a good sign we'll be camping under the same roof. She's thrilled to have you and Lori both here together, but if privacy is what you seek, you might want to take it to the woods." Jesse's face flamed a vivid red and he laughed. "Hey, I'm just sayin'! I know my brothers well enough that... yeah, you should take it to the woods."

"I don't think that's necessary. I'm sure we can survive the family for a few nights," she said although she would have definitely preferred the cabin. Hearing how much Lucia was looking forward to her being there, though, made her day. Secretly, she was afraid once Lori moved there, the family would forget about her. "I could be very happy living here."

Sawyer leaned sideways and whispered, "I wouldn't let that get out or Mom will scheme and pull strings until she relocates you here. If it were up to her, all her kids would stay under her roof, you included."

She chortled and peered out over the mountainside, a warm glow replacing the red on her cheeks. Waking up to such a spectacular view every morning and not being able to count her family members on one hand, it seemed almost worth moving to Tennessee. But she had to remember Gramma was getting up in years and Berkley was as far as she was willing to travel. *For now.* She glanced over when Sawyer stopped walking.

"You're on your own. Duck after you knock." His laugh echoed across the mountainside, and she glanced over at the door, wishing she had waited for Tucker.

How embarrassing would it be if Hayden came to the door wearing nothing but a sheet? *If that.* Thankfully, she didn't have to knock when Hayden greeted her as he stepped outside the door. Fully dressed. "She's inside," he announced before taking off down the pathway after

Sawyer.

Jesse knocked lightly as she opened the door to the one-room cabin. "I hear somebody wishes to see me." Lori turned, holding out a large cup of coffee.

"Thought you might need one," Lori said as she suppressed a yawn. She looked exhausted with dark shadows under her eyes, or maybe she was just stressed.

Jesse gladly took the coffee and sat down on the bed, the memory of her stay in that very cabin with Tucker still fresh in her mind. She would never forget how gentle he was, or how magically his large hands worked over her body. And if she closed her eyes, she could still feel the kisses that he trailed down to her thighs. That was perhaps what she loved the most—his teasing touch.

"So, are you and Hayden staying in the cabin?" she asked, temporarily banishing the images of her bonding night from her mind. She took a sip of coffee, allowing the dark brew to warm her as she glanced about the room. There was no sign Lori and Hayden were planning to stay there and it seemed odd at first, until she noticed Lori's bra behind a chair in the corner. She glanced back at Lori, noticing the low-cut shirt that was laced up over her cleavage, impressed that she had actually ditched the bra. It was the first time she'd ever seen Lori wearing anything that remotely suggested she had boobs.

"Yeah, I think we'll be here for a while." Lori flashed a cunning grin and leaned against the narrow counter. "Lucia was hoping we would stay at the house and since she was nice enough to throw me a Welcome Home party, I feel kinda bad that we aren't. I really like being here, in the mountains, with his family. I feel safe. Wanted."

"I know what you mean. I could be happy here. I so

want a big family." Jesse grinned impishly. "I also want your shirt. But don't you think it's... dangerous?" She arched an eyebrow and Lori grinned even more. Her faded jeans hugged her hips and for the first time, Jesse caught a glimpse of her as a young woman, no longer the teenage girl wearing baggy britches. She was a definite knock-out.

"Nope! I finally have something to flaunt, and these babies are sure to garner attention." She loosened the lace, revealing even more cleavage. "Plus, Hayden picked out the shirt."

"I bet he did." Jesse laughed and patted the spot on the bed beside her. That was when she noted the uncertainty in Lori's eyes. "You're supposed to be happy, so what's with all the doom and gloom?"

"I am happy! Hayden is unbelievably wonderful. I've never had a guy dote on me, and I know he doesn't look the type, but he is. He warms my bath towels and rubs my feet; he even brushed my hair for nearly an hour this morning while I yakked on the phone. Do you know how relaxing that is? Oh, and when he kisses me awake in the middle of the night..." Jesse held up her hand to stop Lori, making her chuckle. "Just know I am immensely happy with my life."

"Then what's the problem?"

Lori chewed her lip, her expression now troubling. "It wasn't a dream," she eventually said, meeting Jesse's eyes. "He watches from a distance, but it will be you that reveals his identity. I know it sounds crazy, but..."

"Who watches?" Jesse asked and Lori shrugged.

"I don't know who *he* is, but he's watching Tracy. Brid had the same vision for me, and I assumed it was Nigel, but now I'm not sure it was about me at all."

Jesse couldn't hide her scowl as Lori shrugged again. If Lori talked to Brid, it positively had to be a vision. "Is Tracy in danger? I mean, you weren't actually threatened since Nigel was watching you in order to keep you safe."

"I don't know. The visions don't include such specifics but it was Tracy, and that much I'm sure of. But you can't tell her. If you do, it will alter the vision, and you saw what happened to me. Just keep an eye out."

"So you saw me in a vision?"

"No. I saw Tracy. It was Brid that saw you. Which is another reason to keep it quiet. Sharing visions could be dangerous; not only for me but also for her."

Jesse glanced out the window, seeing Tucker and Hayden walking towards the cabin. "So, what now? Can I at least tell Tucker?" She set her cup on the counter and turned back to Lori.

"I notice the glazed look in your eyes, so I'd say he probably already knows."

Stupid eyes!

Lori got up from the bed and tossed her cup in the trash. "I don't really like having visions. They scare the hell out of me and give me a huge-ass headache. But right now, I'm starving, and Lucia's been busy cooking for us most of the day."

Jesse's stomach growled at the mention of food. "Good. I skipped lunch and I'm so hungry, I could eat a horse."

"Careful, your wolf is showing," Lori teased as she pulled open the door. "You know, you still owe me a run in the woods."

"Yeah, because you could keep up with my wolf," Jesse scoffed.

"Sure I can. I plan to put a leash on your ass and if that doesn't work, I'll ride bareback." Lori snorted as they joined Hayden and Tucker on the trail.

The first thing Jesse noticed when she looked up at Tucker was the little crease between his brows. Taking hold of his hand, she didn't miss the subtle squeeze and her heart fluttered. It was growing dark with the low setting sun, and she glanced up at the sky. *Beautiful.*

Jesse's attention returned to Hayden and Tucker who were talking about the eastern ridge, and she looked back to see where Hayden was pointing. It appeared miles away, and that's when she realized how large the Smoky Mountain Pack actually was. Could Lori really be safe there if everyone knew she was a seer? She hadn't even thought to ask when she was talking to her. "So, I assume we're keeping Lori's ability a secret, right? I mean, this is a huge pack."

"Yeah, only the family knows," Hayden said over his shoulder. "Why?"

"No reason. I just think it's best to be discreet. The less who know, the safer she'll be." Jesse didn't want to drag Lori back to Cloverly, but if she felt she were in danger, that's exactly what would happen.

It was after supper before Jesse had a chance to talk with Tucker alone. Sitting on the front porch swing, she scented the air, enjoying the hint of pine mingling with the smoke from the chimney. The untouched blanket of white stretched to the road where she could see a trail of footprints in the snow. She silenced a snicker as she relaxed back in his arms. It was so quiet; the only noises she could hear were the beating of their hearts, and her own thoughts driving her mad, about Tracy.

"Hayden told me about the vision," Tucker said so low she wasn't sure he actually uttered the words. Maybe he didn't and what she heard was in her head, but when the low growl rumbled in his chest, it was a sign that even his wolf wasn't happy.

"I'm not in danger," she whispered, but that didn't make him feel any better since there was still Tracy to think about. "Do you have any idea who would be watching her?"

He shook his head, his eyes scanning the lawn.

"Did Travis have any other family?"

Again, he shook his head no.

Her mind searched for an explanation, but there was none. "I don't like this at all. Why does it have to be me?" Being new to the shifter world, too many things still confused her, and she had to depend on Tucker for his guidance.

"Well, apparently we're not going to figure this out until we get back to Cloverly." Tucker lifted her chin, his slight smile comforting. "We'll keep our eyes and ears open without saying anything to Tracy. She'll become paranoid, and whoever is watching her will know she knows."

"Yeah, and Lori said she had the vision of Tracy; while Brid had the vision of me. So if anyone finds out, Brid will also be in danger."

"Then let's keep this off the record. It's not something we want others to overhear. It can't leave the mountain."

With Tucker at her side, Jesse felt better, but not completely. "Right now, Tracy is a sitting duck, unaware of what's going on, so I think we should head back to

Cloverly as soon as possible."

"I was hoping you would say that. I know under normal circumstances Randy can protect her. He has a shotgun and he isn't afraid to use it," Tucker informed her with a smirk.

"What!?" That bit of information stunned Jesse because even though Randy tried to project a bad-boy persona, she couldn't actually picture him harming anyone.

"He pulled it on us the night we questioned Tracy about changing you. He was certain she didn't do it and refused to let her take the blame." He laughed, and she could tell he was recalling the memory.

"You're joshing. You actually thought Tracy was the one that changed me?" Tracy was confrontational at times, even slightly bitchy, but if she intended to cause harm, she would have done so the first day they faced off in the woods.

"I knew she wouldn't, but she brought up something to that effect at a pack meeting once, so Alpha Cooper had no choice but to question her."

"So Randy pulled a gun on Alpha Cooper?" Admittedly, she had gotten snippy with the alpha the night of Hayden's accident, but to hold a gun on him was virtual suicide. Jesse snuggled against Tucker as the realization settled in her mind. Both times when she'd been attacked, it was by a member of Tracy's family. Still, it was sad to know both Travis and Vivian got killed because of their actions. A light quiver worked through her body when she recalled how Vivian was ruthlessly gunned down. It was terrifying to know the hunters were aiming in their direction, and not something she ever wanted to experience again.

"Oh, yeah. It was probably one of the scariest things I've ever witnessed, and funny-as-hell at the same time. Not only did he demand our attention, but he also put everyone on notice. He would do whatever it took to keep Tracy safe, regardless of whom he was up against."

"Well, suddenly I'm seeing Randy in a whole new light." She chuckled, trying to imagine the alpha with his hands in the air, looking down the long barrel of a shotgun. "Thank you for saving me that day in the woods," she said as she tilted her head up to kiss his chin.

"Don't thank me. It's my job to keep you safe." With that, he held her a little tighter, instantly melting away her anxiety.

Four

Jesse

That night in bed, Jesse listened to the whispered giggles and envisioned herself as a kid, snickering beneath the blankets when her parents assumed she was sleeping. She chuckled low as she realized what a large family really meant. No privacy, ever! Constant noise and having to share the bathroom. She wanted it all. She curled into Tucker whose eyes were shut and he had a lazy smile on his face. "I want this."

His eyes opened in surprise and his smile turned to a grin. "Right now?" He seemed hopeful, to her disbelief, and she rolled her eyes, moving her hand up to his stomach. She should have clarified what she wanted, especially considering where her hand was resting.

Shaking her head against the pillow, she giggled. "I was referring to the family, not... you know... I want a large family with all its chaos, craziness, and clutter." Her body heated when his hand moved to her thigh.

"And you want to start working on it now?" He rolled over and tickled her sides. The rumble of his voice was soothing to her wolf, and she melted against him just because she could.

"No, silly! Not here." He didn't understand, and she chuckled. "I want all this, A-sap but in Berkley." Nothing could compare to the beauty the mountains offered, but their cabin in Berkley wasn't a pigsty either. Surrounded by a river on three sides, the view was great, and the privacy it provided, even better. She sighed, thinking what it would be like to cuddle beside him with the balcony doors open as the water lapped the riverbank and the sunset painted the sky. So many romantic nights, it was something she couldn't wait to take advantage of.

"Darn! And I thought you were getting frisky." He trailed kisses along her shoulder, and she shrugged him away when she heard a light tapping on the bedroom door. Needless to say, there would be no sleeping anytime soon.

Shushing and giggling while trying to be as quiet as possible proved extremely hard to do once Tucker set the mood. He was a blast with his silly antics and had a flare for storytelling. And since Lily Rose and Paige snuck into their bedroom, she was certain the older sibling's mind stayed in the gutter until the early morning hours. The low giggles and squeals would make anyone suspect their late night activities; and the sexual overtones at breakfast would have her beaming beet-red.

Jesse stretched and yawned as she glanced over at the hunky wolf man that took up three-quarters of the bed. Wearing nothing but a soft smile on his face, she debated whether to stay there and lick his dimples, or crawl out of bed at the crack of dawn, freezing her tail off, just to get a jump start on breakfast. It would be a quiet morning, just the coffeepot and her. Then her stomach rumbled, sounding more like a lion's roar in the early morning silence. Biting her lip to keep from laughing, she quietly slipped out of bed and tiptoed down the stairs.

The large cabin was spacious, and the low flames from the front fireplace cast the family room in a soft, golden glow. *The perfect place to have a cup of coffee,* and with that thought, she scurried into the kitchen.

Wearing a long, pink, flannel gown, she shivered from the chill as she hastened over to the oven and set the temp to pre-warm. Another quiver rocked her body, but she didn't think it was from the cold. She turned and slowly examined the massive kitchen. *It is you who will reveal his identity.* She mentally rolled her eyes. That vision would have to play out in Cloverly, not there in Tennessee.

Jesse continued over to the sink and peered out the window while filling the coffeepot. The sun had just topped the horizon, and she expected the house would be awake with chatter within the hour. As the coffee brewed, she opened the refrigerator and began sorting through the breakfast food possibilities, *yum, strawberries.* She clutched the bowl to her chest as a hard body pressed against her backside. Believing it was Tucker, she did a little wiggle, prompting a deep-throated groan. But when his hands seized her hips, she jerked up, bumping her head on the freezer door. Her eyes widened as the unfamiliar scent drifted to her nose, and when she turned, bile rose in her throat and she covered her mouth to keep from throwing up.

"Well, now, aren't you just full of surprises?" Strange eyes wandered down to the strawberries and then to her hips, his sly smile indicating he liked what he saw. "An early morning bump and grind gives a man something to think about when he's alone on the ridge. If you know what I mean." He licked his lips and adjusted something, but fearing what it could be, she didn't look down.

She couldn't identify the foul-mouthed man: tall, broody, and beautiful in a rugged sort of way. His sun-tanned skin and golden-blond hair reminded her of Brian, especially the green hue in his eyes. His one-sided grin teased with a slight dimple. She narrowed her eyes, still bristling from where his hands had grasped her hips.

"Sorry, I didn't mean to frighten you." He closed the refrigerator while reaching for the strawberries and placed them on the counter, caging her in the corner of the cabinets. His breath fanned across her cheek, causing her eyes to glaze over. Apparently, he mistook her silence for fear, but she didn't mistake the bump against her rear for an accident.

"One more step and I'll neuter you where you stand." A low growl worked up her throat and her eyes flared red. "Who are you?" The room darkened with her rage and she was sure he moaned.

"I can be anyone you want me to be." He scented the air and stepped back, lifting his hands. "Whoa, you're the new-blood."

She wasn't buying his fake assertion and suspected he

heard the heavy footsteps thundering down the stairs.

"Jesse!" Instantly relieved that she and whoever-the-perv-was weren't the only ones awake in the house, she slumped back against the counter and nearly knocked the strawberries to the floor. She was rubbing her head as Tucker entered the room. "What's going on here?" Tucker asked not so nicely as he stepped between them and shoved the jerk back against the bar.

"My mistake. I didn't mean to startle the little lady. Does she belong to you?"

Ignoring the question, Tucker whipped around, his hand touching where Jesse was holding her head. "Are you okay?" Anger flashed in his eyes, something she seldom saw. "Did he hurt you?" He scanned down her body and she knew he was a breath away from tearing into the stranger.

"No," she whispered as if the man couldn't hear, moving behind Tucker and suddenly feeling overly exposed in her nightgown. "Who is he?"

"This is Tony, dad's beta." She glanced over Tucker's shoulder and Tony had the audacity to wink after she had just saved his ass. What a piece of crap! She scowled, knowing her first impression of him was correct.

"I came down to start breakfast. I didn't realize anyone else was here. I need to get dressed." She slipped past Tucker and headed up the stairs as fast as her feet would move. She didn't bother greeting Tony because she didn't like him.

Her hands trembled when the bedroom door closed behind her. She should have told Tucker what really happened, but decided to give the creep the benefit of the doubt if only because he was the beta. Sorting through her bag, she pulled out a pair of jeans and a turtleneck sweater—spring on the mountain was still chilly. Hastily, she pulled her hair up into a loose bun and slipped on a pair of boots before going back downstairs to make sure Tucker hadn't mauled Tony in her absence.

Passing through the family room, the little ones were still sleeping while the adults gathered in the kitchen. She smiled and greeted Alyssa who had just sat down next to her mother. It was unusually quiet, compared to the normal chatter from the night before. *Awkward.*

She tried not to look over at Tony, the elephant in the room, but knew she'd eventually have to face him. She half-ass nodded, her smile more like a smirk. That was all she could give him, and better than her initial urge to waylay the scumbag.

"Sorry about earlier. I like ice in my coffee."

Jesse glanced down at Tony's mug, and sure enough, it was full of ice. She chuckled and said with a slight sneer, "Don't worry about it. I promise it's not that big…" She coughed into her fist, her excuse for not completing the sentence. Perhaps it wasn't the right thing to say, but if he had the balls to bump up against her, she had the balls to shoot him down. Moving over to the counter where Tucker stood holding a mug of coffee, he was still pissed based on the tick of his jaw.

"So if you're the new-blood, who's the female at the cabin?" Tony asked just as the backdoor opened and Lori and Hayden walked in. "That's her."

Hayden nailed Tony with a glare, apparently overhearing his question. "Don't be mistaken, we're at the cabin together." A low growl echoed through the room and Hayden pulled Lori back against his chest. "She's my bond mate." Lori leaned into Hayden to hide her now reddened face. Jesse would have hidden her face too if her husband just admitted to the entire family that they were having sex before their formal ceremony.

"Hmm, I didn't know." Tony stared longer than necessary, prompting another growl from Hayden before glancing over at Jesse. "A lot has changed since I've been gone." He turned toward Sawyer and grinned. "So, where's your mate hiding?"

"Not going there," Sawyer replied, getting up from the bar, the blush on his face suggesting he didn't want any part of the discussion.

"Well, I hate to leave such delightful company, but I should probably head home. I'm sure Liv is wondering where I am. I'll call you later," Tony said, nodding to Alpha Wilson as he got up from the stool. Casually, he walked over to the counter, brushing against Jesse's arm as he placed his mug in the sink.

But before Jesse could jerk her arm away, Tucker had both hands on the beta, his threatening words thundering off the walls. "Touch her again and you're dead."

"Tony," the alpha said, his eyes tightened in warning, "go, while you can still walk out on your own."

Jesse looked up at Tucker, who was staring down the beta. "He has a mate," she whispered, trying to defuse the situation, but Tucker pushed Tony away and followed him out the back door.

"Why is he still here? I thought you were sending him away for the summer." Hayden looked over at the alpha as he sat down, pulling Lori down in his lap.

Jesse cut a glance to the backdoor, wondering if someone should follow Tucker to make sure he didn't rip into Tony, but no one seemed concerned. She leaned back against the counter to see out the window while the others returned to their breakfast.

"Liv is having an issue or something," Lucia said, reaching for a biscuit. "He got back yesterday afternoon, but apparently, didn't see the need to go home until now. I don't understand him."

"You need to replace him. I mean, he's not really your beta," Tucker replied when he walked back into the kitchen, a scowl on his face. Joining Jesse at the sink, he wrapped his arms around her waist, pulling her back against his chest—his anger dispersing as she squeezed his hips.

"It would be more trouble than it's worth. I'll be retiring before long, and Hayden will have Sawyer. Until then, I'll just keep him busy out-of-town or off the mountain," Sam said, but it was clear he wasn't happy about the situation. From the frown that marred his otherwise smiling face, Jesse expected he would have words with Tony before the day was over.

"So, what are we doing today?" Jesse asked and Lori grinned. She didn't want to hear anything more about the beta; she'd already made up her mind about him.

"I thought maybe we could take a quick stroll downtown, and browse the stores. There's a little coffee shop along the way and they serve the best hot chocolate and whipped cream."

Jesse was quick to take Lori up on her offer since she and Tucker would be leaving later in the day. It would give her a chance to clear her thoughts before Tucker sensed them and finished off the beta. "Let me get my coat and we can go now if you want." She gave Tucker a quick peck on the cheek and said, "We won't be gone long." He nodded tersely, unable to stop the grumble rattling his chest. He was determined to protect her, and she suspected he wouldn't be far behind them.

To say walking through town wasn't nerve-wracking was like saying walking over hot coals won't burn your feet. Jesse instantly sensed when the locals noticed them, but she wasn't sure if they were more interested in her or in Lori. She nudged Lori when a group of girls waved and quickly whispered something she couldn't hear. Okay, maybe it wasn't a friendly-friendly gesture, but at least they had acknowledged them. That was a start.

"I know Hayden won't let you out of his sight for long, but promise me you'll watch your back and not go anywhere alone, or at least not until after your bonding ceremony. I'd hate to have to come back to the mountains and open up a can of whoop-ass." She glanced over at the group of girls who were now giggling, and her eyes flared, causing them to look away. *Good.* She wasn't there to make friends. She was, however, putting them on notice. Lori would be well-protected.

"You did not just say whoop-ass!" Lori tittered. "My baby girl is all grown up and ready to take on the world."

"Like I said, just watch your back." As they rounded the corner, Jesse glanced up to see a small stone building, rustic, with large windows and the word Coffeehouse painted in white lettering across the windowpane. "I think I died and gone to heaven," she said, inhaling deeply.

"You and me both." Trudging across the parking lot, Lori kicked the snow off her boots and pulled open the door as Jesse followed her into the building. Waiting as

Lori placed their order, Jesse turned to the front window to study the little mountain town. It was similar to Cloverly, but much busier with more stores and people on the streets. She smiled warmly when a young woman and a little boy walked through the door.

"Here," Lori said, handing Jesse a large toffee-nut coffee. As they walked out of the building, she took a sip while Lori lapped up the whipped cream that topped her hot chocolate.

"So, which way do you want to go?" Jesse asked heading back across the lot. But seeing Tony now huddled with the group of girls, his arm draped over the shoulder of a little blonde, she whispered, "I don't like him. He gives me the creeps."

Lori wrinkled her nose and pulled Jesse in the opposite direction. "Yeah, I know. Hayden said he's a big blow-hard and most of the pack keeps their distance."

"He's worse than that. Just don't go near him, alone," Jesse said, causing Lori to look over her shoulder.

"Why? What happened this morning? It had to be something for Tucker to escort him out of the house the way he did. And the whole time he was gone, I swear, Hayden's chest rumbled."

After confessing to Lori, Jesse shook her head. "Obviously, his lame excuse of coming back because of Liv was a lie, or he'd already be at home with her, not out feeling up the locals." Her skin crawled with the thought, but she refused to look back and acknowledge the jerk.

"His mate is human," Lori said finally glancing over her shoulder. "It ticked Hayden off when he scented him outside the cabin last night. He doesn't trust him either and said he was a big flirt."

"Well, he needs to take his flirty ass home, and learn some manners. I swear if I were his mate, I'd wring his neck." Jesse blew across her cup to warm her nose. "Speaking of..." She nudged Lori and nodded at Tucker and Hayden who had just turned the corner and were heading their way.

"Come to Mama," Lori said as she seductively licked her lips.

From half a block away, Jesse swore she heard Hayden groaning. "Horn-dog much?" She snickered and Lori laughed. "I swear you and Hayden were meant for each other."

Five

Tracy

Parked alongside the Lucky Leaf Boutique, Tracy glanced up at the building, excited to start the work week. She got out of the car and strolled to the front door, greeting everyone she passed with a pleasant smile. It was something she didn't dare do a year ago. And was amazed at how much life had changed since then. Free from Travis dictating her every move, and finally being able to breathe, she didn't dare ask for more. *Mom, I wish you were here to see this,* she sighed, recalling her mother's smile. Her dad wasn't as generous, which was why she was never a daddy's girl. But someone up above must have been watching out for her, and having Randy as her bond mate thawed the hardness that surrounded her heart.

Being the proprietor of Lori's Lingerie was something Tracy didn't believe possible before moving to Cloverly. Or ever! The store was her favorite place to shop since it opened in December, and now she could afford to splurge at a discount. A win-win if you asked Randy. The drawback to owning the business meant Lori wouldn't be there, and she truly liked Lori. They had become good friends over their passion for frilly bras and lace panties. So much so that anytime there was a new shipment, Lori would call her. But she also knew that once Lori accepted Hayden's bond, she wouldn't be sticking around Cloverly. She admired her for that, being able to walk away and start a new life elsewhere. However, when Randy suggested she take over the store, offering to buy Lori out, her envy only went so far. She would miss the fiery brunette and do everything she could to fill her shoes.

Just holding the key in her hand was confirmation she had done something right in her life. And imagining what her mother might think of her made her beam as she unlocked the front door. Randy would argue that he was what was right in her life. She would have to agree with that as well.

Tracy pushed open the door and hauled her roll-along case inside, parking it behind the dividing wall that separated Lori's Lingerie from the lounge area, centrally located inside the Lucky Leaf Boutique. Sniffing the wonderful lavender fragrance that wafted in the air, she removed a large lidded bowl from the case and placed it on the short wall.

Rushing into the warehouse, she switched on the lights and took off her sweater while scanning the row of shelves that held everything from Jesse's clothing supplies to Megan's beauty products. She cocked her head, listening to the rattling noise beneath the metal staircase. It was creepy and she shuddered until she realized the noise was coming from the heat unit. That ancient appliance seemed as old as the building, which was probably why it sounded like it was on its last leg.

Shrugging off the unease on her way back through the store, she picked up the bowl and placed it on the large wooden table that separated two sofas in the lounge area. One glance at the overhead clock told her it was eight thirty-five, which gave her plenty of time to get the coffee brewing. Tracy wanted everything perfect when Megan and Jesse arrived, and after filling the pot, she took a seat on the sofa that rested against the wall. She opened the plastic container and looked back up at the clock. Being there alone for the first time was unsettling with all the nooks and crannies. She slowly glanced around the store. The door was locked, and although she was the only one there, she couldn't shake the feeling of being watched.

Tracy was on her second cup of caramel coffee when the overhead bell dinged and Megan entered the store. "Morning," she said as she hurried to the front counter.

"Look at you! All business-like. It fits," Megan gushed.

Tracy guessed perhaps she did fit the image by wearing the green floral dress that brushed her knees. It was the one dress she had to have, and by wearing it, she would also advertise for the boutique. Jesse was exceptionally talented when it came to designing dresses, and she expected to add a few more of Jesse's designs to her wardrobe.

"Do you like?" Tracy turned and the skirt flared.

"I think you look lovely." Megan pulled her jacket off and placed it on a small hook behind the counter. She was all business too, wearing a pair of khaki pants and an olive green sweater, and proof that if you wanted something bad enough, you could make it happen. "What is that wonderful smell?" She sniffed the air, making Tracy grin.

"Just a little something Randy's mother sent from home. Come on back. I also have hot coffee waiting." Tracy motioned and Megan followed her to where the plate of caramel-pecan cinnamon rolls waited on the table.

"Oh, my, those look delicious!" Megan scooped up a roll and took a huge, enthusiastic bite. "Mmm, Jesse will be so disappointed she missed these."

Tracy looked toward the door, her smile wavering. "Jesse's not working today?"

"No, Tucker got a call from Hayden and they left yesterday for Tennessee. She didn't say why but I assume it probably had something to do with Lori and her anxiety around a new pack. But she wanted me to apologize for not being here today. She was so looking forward to it." Megan picked up the large styrofoam cup Tracy placed on the table in front of her.

"I hope Lori's all right. Even Randy is sometimes overwhelmed and our pack is tiny in comparison." Tracy carried her coffee over to the sofa and sat down beside Megan. Her knee bounced and she blamed that on the caffeine.

"Yeah, with everything that happened, I can understand if she's intimidated by the pack. I assume that's all it is, but with Hayden there, she'll be all right."

"I'm surprised anything intimidates her. She's the one person that could hold her own against me. She's cocky like Randy, and once she gathers her confidence, look out Smokies because Lori is on the mount." Tracy chuckled, remembering the first time she met Lori in the woods. She was quick to let her know she had overstepped her bounds, and when she elbowed Steve in the stomach, it was hilarious.

"Yeah, I think she'll make her stand within the week. She's not one for staying in the background too long, and with Hayden cheering her on, things are sure to get interesting." Megan placed another roll on her napkin. "Speaking of mates, where's Randy? I figured he would be here with you this morning."

"He had to make an emergency trip to Buffer County to get a part for his bike. And since he gets up with the roosters, he let me sleep in." Tracy did a slight roll of her eyes, but secretly she was as eager as Randy, and couldn't wait to get the motorcycle back on the road.

"Well, it looks like it will be just the two of us today, but I can already tell we're going to have a blast. I can't wait to see how you shake things up." Megan tipped her cup and took a drink. "Jack's coming by later to bring lunch. Whitney's treat."

"That sounds great considering I didn't bring anything. I was so excited, it totally slipped my mind."

"Well, there's always the café, but at lunchtime, it's so crowded. I don't know how many times Lori came in swearing because the wait was so long. But when that girl was hungry, waiting wasn't an option, which is why she always carried candy in her pockets. I don't think her stomach knows what it feels like to be empty."

Tracy laughed. "I sure am going to miss her antics around here."

"Yeah, she was a hoot, but I think you are just what this place needs. We could even use you as a live mannequin. That should kick up the sales, at least for Jesse."

"I'm sure that could be arranged." Tracy grinned against her coffee cup. "Which reminds me... I have something I wanted to run past you and Jesse." She placed her cup on the table and rose to retrieve her case from behind the dividing wall. "It was an idea I had last night and thought I'd run past you this morning. Although, at the time I thought Jesse would be here as well." She rolled the case over beside Megan and popped open the top. "Do you think it would be okay if I sold some of my jewelry here? If not, that's perfectly fine. Like I said, it was just a thought." She picked up her cup and sat down beside Megan as she opened the first box filled with earrings.

"Oh, my word, they're gorgeous!" Megan moved closer to the case and picked up another box. "We could always use more bling in the store." She glanced at the rest of the boxes in the case. "These are nice."

"Really? Do you think they're good enough to sell?"

"Definitely! If you want, I have an empty display case you can use. We can place it in the front window for everyone to see when they walk by. It might bring in a few new customers; and just like the lingerie, jewelry always sells," Megan said and Tracy was quick to take her up on the offer.

The morning passed in a flash and within no time, Tracy had settled into Lori's routine, thanks to the many notes she had posted on nearly everything. There was a lot to do, sorting and stocking merchandise, and greeting the customers that came into the store to meet the new owner of Lori's Lingerie. It wasn't until Jack showed up with their lunch that Tracy finally stopped to take a break.

She pinched herself as she moved over to the sitting area to join Megan for a quick bite to eat. The plate lunch Whitney prepared looked delicious and she couldn't wait to dig into the cheesy chicken and broccoli casserole. But before she could take the first bite, the doorbell jangled, signaling another customer.

Tracy stretched to see an elderly woman standing in the doorway holding a large vase of flowers. She seemed familiar and probably came from the flower shop directly across from the boutique. She listened when Megan hurried to the front of the store as the woman placed the vase in the window and carefully rearranged a few of the blooms.

"Tracy," Megan called out, motioning her to the front of the store. "I have someone I want you to meet."

Setting her plate on the table, Tracy stood and straightened her dress, tentatively sauntering to the front counter.

"Tracy is the new owner of Lori's Lingerie," Megan said, smiling when Tracy came to stand beside her. "Tracy, this is Brid. She owns the flower shop across the corner."

"It's so nice to meet you," Tracy said, suddenly feeling a bit shy. "The flowers are beautiful." Standing before Brid, Tracy felt exposed in a way that didn't include taking off her clothes.

"Yes, after the doldrums of winter, it's nice to have a spring bouquet to liven up the place." Brid patted Tracy's arm, her way of shaking hands, Tracy assumed. "These are for you, from Lori."

"Me?" Tracy's hand landed on her chest and her mouth hung open. Had anybody ever sent her flowers? Randy brought flowers home occasionally, but nothing like the riot of blooms that filled the window.

"She said they would look great on the wall, but I'm not sure how these would go on a wall. I'll leave that up to you." Brid glanced up and around before looking back at Tracy. "Good luck." With that, she walked out the door, leaving Tracy speechless.

"The dividing wall," Megan said. "That's what Lori was talking about, not the actual walls." Tracy chuckled as they watched Brid walk down to the corner. Regardless of where Lori wanted the flowers placed, it was sweet of her to send them.

Six

Randy

Leaving early for Buffer County and allowing Tracy to sleep in was Randy's way of avoiding the unwanted questions that would surely catch him in a lie. He mentioned picking up a part for his motorcycle the night before, but she was stressing about her first day at the boutique, a distraction that worked in his favor. It would be her time to shine, and knowing how clever she was, he expected she would jump right in and rock it. She wasn't as confident though.

So keeping his bike under tarp, in the back corner of the barn, Randy wanted her to assume it was out of commission. Even if that meant they couldn't ride it over the weekend when the weather forecast was predicted to be warmer. And by making the excuse of needing a part for the motorcycle, which was a total lie, kept his stomach in a constant knot.

So maybe sneaking off to Iretta's house wasn't the smartest thing to do. She was pretty cool for a girl. Short and slender with almond eyes the color of gold, and her signature spiked hair—darker than night—stuck out in all directions and complimented her biker chick attitude. She wore carpenter jeans and black, steel-toed boots, along with tank tops that exposed her toned upper body. Randy never saw her dressed any differently, except during the cold months when she traded out the tanks for tees. And even though she was stunning in her own right, there was never anything between them besides their love of bikes. However, as soon as he returned home, he would have to jump in the shower to prevent Tracy from picking up her scent. That was the downside to having a mate with a remarkable sense of smell. She could practically sniff out a lie.

As Randy turned off the highway, he sucked in a deep breath to calm the rapid rhythm of his heart when the large pole barn came into view. He was there to purchase a motorcycle, not to rob the Pope, and yet his guilt overwhelmed him. He'd been to Iretta's a hundred times although this was the first time he considered turning around and going back home. He assumed it was because he wasn't truthful about where he was going. Intuition? Did guys even have that? He hit the horn and waited for the garage door to open before getting out of the truck.

Iretta wore a variety of hats from mechanic to dealer to supplier of parts. Teacher could also be added to the list since she was the person who taught him everything he knew about motorcycles. She was also the best mechanic in the area, and he had yet to meet a man that could do a better job. Plus, she was nicer to look at than some beer-bellied biker that constantly spat wads of tobacco on the ground. That alone was nasty, and he didn't have a weak stomach.

"Hey, pretty lady. Long time no see," Randy said, nearly biting his tongue once the words slipped out of his mouth. Tracy would be upset at the greeting, but Iretta was his best friend for years, and that was how he always greeted her.

"Where the heck have you been? I thought you dropped off the face of the earth." Her narrowed eyes said she was pissed, but the twitch of her lip said she wasn't.

"Oh, you know me, just trying to stay out of trouble." He rushed over to where she waited and drew her into a hug. "I've missed you." She stretched back and scrunched her nose, making him think his deodorant wasn't working. As he followed her into the building, he sniffed his underarms but detected nothing other than the powdery fragrance.

"So, what has you in my neck of the woods without your bike?"

"Since when do I need a reason?" He quirked a brow and she tittered as he moved to the opposite side of the motorcycle from where she had just squatted down. "I need a bike. Another bike," he quickly clarified when she blinked up to meet his eyes. "It's for my fiancée." His face flushed when she paused and grinned. He didn't know why, but suddenly, he felt he should have replaced fiancée with soulmate as if it would make the statement truer.

"The wild child has been tamed. I'm impressed." She smiled and held out her hand. "So when do I get to meet the lucky lady that stole you away from me? Or is this you sneaking out the back door?" She winked when Randy handed her a ratchet.

"Yeah, uh... sorry. I've been pretty busy lately." Stumped by her comment, he couldn't very well tell her he'd been hiding out from a deranged werewolf. Where was the sanity in that? He chuckled nervously, but allowed her to think whatever she wanted.

"The fiancée?"

Randy nodded and again she grinned.

Falling into their normal routine, he missed hanging out with Iretta and working on bikes. But her saying, "stole you away from me" was the first time she had ever insinuated there could've been something more between them. He never looked at her as a girlfriend since she always reminded him of his older sister. Then he frowned, thinking maybe he was wrong not to tell Tracy where he was going. Hearing something like that could definitely give her the wrong impression about them.

"So, how did the reunion go? Did you get everything worked out with your parents?" His change of subject drew an uneasy chuckle from Iretta and she turned back to the bike. Rarely did she visit her family in South Dakota, and when she did, it was usually during the big bike rally held in Sturgis every year. This past visit, though, had nothing to do with bikes, and everything to do with her refusing to move back to the Black Hills region.

"Not exactly." She stared across the garage, a slight crease marring her forehead. "It went about as bad as I expected." She sighed and turned back to the bike. "I'm still black-balled, if that's what you're asking."

"Yeah, I guess I was."

"So, about this motorcycle, did you want a rebuild?" Now, she was changing the subject, but he expected as much. She wasn't one to talk about her family and usually kept a tight lip where they were concerned.

"No, I need one quicker than that. By the end of the month."

"That's doable. I'll make a few calls and see what I can arrange. Anything particular, or did you want a bike like yours?"

"She has her heart set on a Sportster." He handed Iretta a shop towel and she wiped her hands. "Green is her favorite color."

"She has good taste, I'll give her that, but then again, she did snag you." Iretta stood and walked across the garage, a slight tinge of pink on her cheeks. He didn't know what to say to that, his own face blushing with the compliment. Then she tossed him the keys to the bike and motioned for him to take it out the door. Finally, a welcome distraction he could work with.

It was half-past two when Randy headed home that afternoon. He stayed at Iretta's longer than planned, but anytime he had the chance to work on a motorcycle, time just slipped away. Overall, the visit was a success and by the end of the month he would be picking up Tracy's new bike. His gift to her so they could ride together on their bonding night. He beamed, knowing she would be overjoyed, and in turn, he would get lucky.

He cranked down the window, the sunny afternoon reminding him of the day he first met Iretta. He was sixteen and all ego. She was twenty and badass. He grinned at the memory. *Driving out the highway in the old farm truck, he had the windows down and the music up, on his way to the farm store to pick up seed. It was supposed to be a quick trip, fifty-five minutes tops, until the radiator hose busted. Stranded on the side of the road, with no other option but to walk, he set out on foot heading back home. But as luck would have it, Iretta pulled over on the side of the road and offered him a ride. Watching her petite frame manhandling the big-ass bike was the start of his bike obsession.*

It was nearing three that afternoon when Randy pulled into the drive and followed it around to the back of his parents' house. Parked in the driveway, he got out of the truck and headed to the barn, hearing his dad call his name.

"Could you give me a hand?" His dad was working on an old 1930s tractor and needed help to hoist the motor into place. Forgetting about the bike momentarily, it didn't take long before Randy was elbow deep in grease. His dad liked tractors as much as he liked motorcycles and had restored three tractors to like new. That was what he did on his downtime, and something Randy hoped to do with motorcycles. "Did you get the bike?" his dad asked, wiping his forehead with an oil-stained rag.

"I'll have it by the end of the month." He could have driven another forty-five minutes and picked up the bike from a dealer, but Iretta was always having shipments delivered to her house. By ordering through her, he also got her discount. Plus, he didn't want Tracy to see the motorcycle before their ceremony. It was hard enough keeping her away from his bike, and hers would be twice as tempting. But he couldn't tell his dad that, not yet. So far, his parents had no idea Tracy was a shifter, at her insistence, but eventually, he would have to tell them. He bit his jaw to keep from grinning, imagining a little boy running across the yard, chasing chickens and growling. He was looking forward to that day.

Pulled from his thoughts, when his mom's car pulled up and parked behind the truck, he looked back over his shoulder to see Tracy's smile. He didn't realize it was so late and he couldn't wait to see how her first day went. He ran out to meet her when she got out of the car. "So, how did it go?" He tried to hug her, but she made a face and pushed him away.

"Ew! You smell like you've been rolling in cat piss."

He looked down at his greasy hands and tapped her nose, leaving a smudge of dirt behind. "Yeah? You wanna help me shower?" She giggled when he bounced his brows. He couldn't wait until the day when she would actually agree to that.

"No, but as soon as you get rid of that funk, I might be persuaded to dry you off."

"I'll take whatever I can get," he said, planting a quick kiss on her cheek before she could jump away.

Seven

Tracy

Tracy stood against the counter, staring up at the loft with tears in her eyes. She wanted to have a quiet dinner and surprise Randy, which was why she stopped by the café on her way home from work and purchased a cherry pie. It wasn't much, considering all he'd done for her, but it was his favorite, and she knew he would appreciate it. She could picture him poking his finger into the thick syrup before licking it clean. It was quite a turn-on, just watching that, and she assumed he did it for that reason. Now, though, all she wanted to do was to shove that damn pie down his throat!

Randy had just stepped into the shower and dropped the soap, something that normally made her giggle, but she wasn't in any laughing mood. She wanted to go upstairs and confront him about who he was with earlier that day, but fearing his reply kept her pacing downstairs in the kitchen. Her wolf was on edge, and the incessant rumble in her chest resounded like thunder rolling in the distance.

Scowling at the table and the sweet-smelling pie, she'd show him. She dug into the pie and shoved a handful of the sticky goodness into her mouth, letting the syrup and crust smear across her face. Too bad they couldn't enjoy it together because it tasted every bit as good as it smelled. She grunted her frustration and turned to the sink to clean herself of the sugary mess.

Tracy wouldn't have suspected a thing if only had Randy had thought to uncover the bike, thereby at least giving the impression he was working on it. But with no sign of anything bike-related inside or outside the truck, and the telltale odor of a female on him, Tracy could only question their bond. Where did he go and why would he lie about it? She trusted him with her life, but now she wasn't sure she could trust his word.

Swallowing hard, she dried her face while mulling over what to do next. She loved Randy more than she loved herself, but perceiving the unfamiliar and undeniable scent of another female, where should she draw the line? Glancing around the small cottage, the place she called home, she wanted to vomit. If he tossed her away after everything they'd been through, it would devastate her wolf. She needed time to think and figure out what was going on with him. She had to find out where he went and who he was with. Fear gripped her insides. Had she forced him into the arms of another by not completing their bond? *Stupid, stupid, stupid!* It seemed like her entire life had been a series of one stupid mistake after another.

"Tracy," Randy yelled down from the bathroom and she all but growled. "Would you please bring up some shampoo?" She assumed he used that as an excuse to get her upstairs since he always tried it. He was playful that way and liked to tease her with wet kisses.

"Give me just a minute!" she yelled back and heard the bathroom door close. It would take more than shampoo or soap to rid his body of the piss smell. She glanced back down at the pie and then up at the loft. He could get his own damn shampoo!

Quietly, she dashed up to the bedroom, grabbing a few items and cramming them into the largest handbag she could find—while yelling to Randy she would be right there. If she were quick enough, she could be long gone before the water ran cold. It was the only thing that made sense to her disillusioned mind. Just a few days, or at least that's what she told herself, but honestly, she wasn't sure when she would be back.

It was nearly dark when Tracy tiptoed down the stairs and out the back door. Sneaking around to the back of the barn, she stayed in the shadows, well beyond the view of his parents' house. Taking advantage of the darkening sky, she quickly pulled off her dress and hung it on a hook next to the motorcycle. A place Randy would surely see it. The heels she would also leave behind; they were a gift from him for her nineteenth birthday back in September. She placed them on top of the tarp and closed her eyes, inhaling briefly to drive out her anxiety. Taking one final look back at what she thought would be her forever home, she phased.

Her wolf was equally stressed but clamped onto the

bag, skirting the field to race along the tree line. She had no clue where to go. She just knew she had to leave before facing Randy or he would invariably tempt her to stay.

The darkened field went on for blocks and when she slowed and stepped behind a tree, Randy still hadn't come out of the house from what she could tell. That was a good sign; it meant he didn't realize she was gone. *It doesn't matter now*. Especially since she now knew why he was so secretive lately.

Deciding not to tempt herself by seeing Randy run out the door, *as if that would happen*, she darted across the field to the back of the animal shelter. It was secluded and a safe place to gather her thoughts before moving on to where? She didn't know.

She phased and sat down between the trashcans. And for the first time in years, she bawled like a baby. She wasn't the confident person everyone thought she was, just a mere shell of a young female determined to survive a reality so twisted, even her worst nightmares couldn't compare. Beaten down for most of her life and broken by the iron rod of harsh discipline, she did whatever was necessary to protect herself. Now she wondered if she could shield her heart again before she mentally broke down.

Everything right in her world revolved around Randy, the only male that ever mattered. She wanted more than anything to share his life and his family. She wanted what he had and brought to their relationship, everything he offered her that afternoon standing beside the lake. She wanted his name.

But who was she kidding? She had nothing to give in return. No family, no home. She was a shifter, a freak, and stupid to think she could ever be anything more. Then she thought about Jesse's description of Vivian, *a muddy, brown mutt.* That would be her in a few days if she didn't find shelter.

Tracy pulled herself together as best she could behind the animal shelter. Fear, anxiety, and dread flowed through the bond, taking with them, her breath. She stilled, pushing the thought of going back to comfort Randy out of her mind. If he rejected her, it would destroy her entire world. A constricting pain belted around her chest and in that instant, she knew Randy was on the move.

She didn't know where he went early in the day and failed to recognize the scent that lingered beneath the grease and oil smeared on his arms. The one thing she did know, which shattered all aspects of her sanity, the female he was with was a shifter. She jumped to her feet, her anger returning as she pulled a pair of jeans and a sweatshirt from the bag. *Trouble, always trouble.* She spewed a few choice words at the voice in her head and quickly dressed before slipping on her running shoes.

The cool breeze that cut across the field made her shudder as she shifted the bag up over her shoulder and started around the building. Beneath the waning moon, she walked in the darkest shadows, ducking behind trees when cars passed, managing to keep out of sight. But she knew it wouldn't be long before Randy came looking for her.

She continued through the neighborhood with her head down, wishing she could escape the morbid thoughts that taunted her. *He deserves better. You are a freak!* As she neared Main Street, she heard the farm truck before she saw it turning onto Cabin Run Road. Randy was heading to Tucker's, the first place he knew she would go. He didn't know Tucker was out of town but he'd find out soon enough. That posed another problem: she had totally forgotten about that herself. *Damn!* It was just her luck.

Tracy chewed her lower lip and adjusted the bag as her stomach rumbled. Why didn't she think ahead to bring some food? Silently cursing, she pulled the bag off her shoulder, remembering the cinnamon rolls at the boutique. She pushed her hand into the side pocket and blew out a slow breath when her hand touched the key. Breakfast food wasn't her idea of supper, but it was better than nothing, and if she could make it to the store without being seen, no one would be wiser. It was the perfect place to hide until morning. And before Megan arrived at work, she could slip upstairs to the apartment and take a shower. That was actually a good idea, and maybe Megan would let her stay in the apartment for a day or so, or at least until she could get her life straightened out.

Hair stood on her arms as her wolf stirred, suddenly becoming more aware of the surroundings. It was crazy and she was a wolf, so what the heck was she afraid of? A low vibration settled in her chest. She needed Randy to chase away the boogeyman, but Randy didn't need her. With no other choice but to backtrack through the neighborhood, she turned in the direction she came, without giving much attention to the car traveling towards her. It was probably someone on their way home from work. She picked up her pace, only to slow to a stop when she heard the familiar voice.

"Tracy, is that you? What are you doing on this side of town?"

"Well, excuse me. I didn't realize I was out of my territory," she flippantly said when Officer Riley stopped his vehicle next to her. She cut a fleeting glance over her shoulder, hoping Randy didn't drive past and find her talking to Riley. That would definitely not go down well. She squirmed and shifted her weight from one foot to the other.

"Is everything all right? You seem on edge." He put the SUV into park, apparently, not in any hurry to leave.

"I wasn't until you stopped me. Now I'm going to be late." He raised a brow and she rolled her eyes. "Tucker's waiting for me." That should've shut him down, except she was going in the wrong direction and of course, he noticed.

"You don't say. The last I checked, Tucker lived that way." His finger lifted off the steering wheel to point as a troubled look fell across his face. He was mulling something over in his head, something that puzzled him.

"I said he was waiting for me, not that I was going to his house," she explained, refusing to give him anything more. "So, if you'll excuse me, I really have to go."

"I can give you a ride if you're in such a hurry." The smirk on his face said he wasn't that easily fooled, and she narrowed her eyes with his next question. "Although, I'm surprised you're not with Boyfriend. I haven't seen him around town lately. Did you two break up?"

"Uh, I don't know what you're talking about." Again, another lie, but she felt like she was facing Travis and almost expected his ghost to step out from behind a tree. She stuffed her hands into her pockets to hide her nervousness. Only a handful of people knew she lived with Randy, and that's the way she preferred it. Riley wasn't one of those people.

His grin widened as if reading her mind. "The male you were hanging out with over the summer. Dark hair, cocky, rides a motorcycle? I'm actually quite surprised you let that one get away."

Her eyes flared and she quickly averted them as irritation roiled beneath her skin. Biting her tongue to keep from telling him where he could go, she tasted blood. "I didn't let anyone get away, and he does have a name if that's any of your business." She wasn't trying to piss him off, but really? She shifted on her feet when a call came across his radio. *Thank the moon.* She would use his distraction in her haste to escape his interrogation. "Have a good night," she said, turning to ignore him when he put his finger up for her to wait.

Seizing the moment, she took off in a jog, which ended up becoming a full-out sprint as she looked back to make sure he didn't turn around to follow her. He was the officer that caught her the night she stole Travis's car, and she would never forgive him for taking her home. Although that wasn't fair. He had no idea how Travis treated her. She never told anyone.

He's human. He's trouble. Always trouble. Hearing Travis's words echoing in her head, she wanted to scream. Travis was dead, and yet he still had a way of disrupting her thoughts. She didn't want to think he had been right all along.

By the time she arrived at the boutique, her body was covered in a thin sheen of sweat. Releasing an exasperated sigh, she clutched her chest, her heart one beat away from exploding. It was too much. She needed seclusion, a dark cubby, a closet like the one she hid out in when she was younger. The darkness soothed her soul, a place she felt most comfortable, where no one could see her scars.

Standing at the side door of the boutique, she could easily slip into the building without being seen. However, there was no way she could get across the warehouse and shut off the security lights before they clicked on. With no other choice, she hurried around to the front of the store, casually approaching the front door while scanning the park across the street. Certain no one would see, she quickly unlocked the door and stepped inside the building as a car rounded the park and turned toward the river.

Moving back to the lounge area, the exit light atop the warehouse door dimly lit the room and she dropped onto the sofa and pulled the bag off her shoulder. She eyed the plastic container sitting next to the coffeepot—but was no longer hungry. With nothing else to do, she rested her head on the cushion, allowing herself to relax as her thoughts drifted to Randy.

He was the closest thing she'd ever had to family and now she was pushing him away. It hurt like hell and that nasty, little voice in the back of her mind was a constant reminder he was a human and she was a freak. Unfortunately, it would be a daunting night, and she prayed sleep would come easy.

Eight

Randy

Randy had to admit he was a little disappointed when Tracy didn't bring up the shampoo. Using all that he had, the water ran cold before he finished rinsing the suds out of his hair. His body quivered with goosebumps as he stepped out of the shower and wrapped a towel around his waist before heading into the bedroom. The room he and Tracy would share after their bonding ceremony. He glanced around the room and reached over to close the open dresser drawer.

Since Tracy moved in, everything in the house reminded him of her. The selection of shower sponges in a wicker basket on the bathroom counter, the jewelry box on the dresser, even the throw pillows lined neatly across the headboard of the bed. She had turned the small house into a home, and he loved spending time with her there.

"Tracy," he called out as he opened the closet door and grabbed a tee shirt and a pair of sleep pants off a shelf. Expecting she would yell back, he quickly dressed and hurried out of the room when she didn't respond.

Randy glanced across the open floorplan as he raced down the stairs. The small two-bedroom cottage was nice, but eventually, he intended to build Tracy the house she deserved. He walked into the kitchen and noticed the mangled cherry pie on the table, which stopped him dead in his tracks. His brow furrowed, wondering why and sensing something wasn't right. He ran his fingers through his hair and glanced back across the room—the silence was deafening. Maybe it was a gut feeling, or the heavy thud of his heart pounding in his chest, but in that instant, the house felt terribly... *empty*.

"Tracy," he yelled again and when she didn't answer, he rushed over and yanked open the front door, knowing she wasn't there. Greeted by a blast of cool air, he shook off a shiver. It was mid-March, and although the famous groundhog of Philadelphia had already predicted an early spring, the night air still clung to the winter's chill.

Unable to suppress the fear that knotted in his stomach, he took off in a jog as a flood of moisture blurred his vision. He was misreading the bond; he had to be, and Tracy was with his parents. At least, that's what he told himself as he ran up onto the back porch, heading toward the door.

The first thing he noticed was his mother standing at the counter, talking to someone on the phone. Then he spotted his father asleep in the recliner as he pushed open the door. If Tracy were there, he wouldn't be sleeping. His stomach knotted tighter.

His mother warmed to Tracy the first day they met and ever since then, Tracy had become her shadow. Wanting to learn everything she could about cooking, and apparently, him, she would sit and visit his mother for hours. Still, sometimes his heart freaked, and the fear of losing her literally took his breath away. As he walked into the kitchen, his mother scowled when he asked, "Have you seen Tracy?" The knot in his stomach climbed up his throat and he rushed out the door, gagging.

There had to be an explanation, he knew, and yet his thoughts were frantic as he sped around the yard, checking the cars, the truck, and eventually, the barn. But when his eyes landed on the floral dress hanging on the hook next to his bike, along with her red heels sitting on top of the tarp, a crushing pain ripped through his chest, causing his jaw to clench. He grabbed his shotgun from where it hung on the back wall, never bothering to remove her dress from the hook.

Randy flew to his truck and tossed the gun onto the dash before backing out of the drive, knocking the mailbox down along the way. It was unlike Tracy to go anywhere without telling him, so maybe it wasn't by choice. *If anyone touches her.* Had he been a wolf, the growl that reverberated through the cab would've been mighty impressive.

His bond with Tracy wasn't the same as the connection Jesse shared with Tucker, and because it was Tracy's bond, he couldn't track her. He slammed his fist down on the steering wheel as a wave of devastation threatened to consume him. *She left you. She just walked away.* His temper flared when he turned onto the highway, leaving a strip of rubber in his wake. *But where would she go?* He shut off the radio to concentrate on his driving. It would be his luck to end up with a ticket, although it wouldn't be his first. Taking the chance, he topped the hill at highway speeds and blew through the stoplight before attempting to slow down. Just up the road, a few more blocks, and he would be at Tucker's cabin.

The traffic on Main Street was light and as he passed the boutique, he scowled, wondering if something happened there earlier in the day. It was possible, he guessed, but Tracy didn't seem put out when she arrived home that afternoon. Anger boiled beneath the surface and he clenched his jaw tighter at the thought of anyone treating her poorly. She'd been through enough hell in her life. And after vowing to protect her, he had every intention of keeping that promise. He hit the brakes and jerked the wheel sharply to the left, fishtailing onto Cabin Run Road.

The area was dark beneath the large pine trees, and once he had parked in Tucker's driveway, he sat for a good five minutes before venturing to the door. Unfortunately, he knew Tracy wasn't there even before he walked up to find the door locked. He marched around to the backyard, confirming his original thought as prickling pine cones dug into his bare feet—Tucker was also gone. His teeth gnashed at the thought of Tucker taking Tracy away from him. He liked Tucker, probably better than most of the pack, but as his thoughts wandered, he feared he had misplaced his trust.

His mind recalled the hours after Tracy came home from work and parked behind his truck. He was helping his dad work on his tractor when Tracy got out of the car.

Seeing how beautiful she was, wearing the green floral dress and the heels he bought for her birthday, it was hard to keep his eyes off her. He ran over and met her in the driveway, wishing he didn't have grease on his hands. He ached to pull her close and inhale her spicy scent. It drove him wild just being near her, but she scrunched up her nose and said something about cat piss. After that, she accompanied him into the house, and...

His heart dropped to his stomach and he spewed a few profanities when the realization coldcocked him upside the head. Being distracted by his dad, he forgot to shower! *Dammit! It's your own damn fault.* He was the reason she left, and if anything happened to her, he could never live with himself. *She trusted you!* The voice in his head taunted as if he needed the reminder.

He climbed back into the truck and rested his forehead against the steering wheel as he closed his eyes, picturing Tracy. Her brilliant green eyes stared back at him, and her flowing red hair—he groaned. He loved her shapely body and long legs, but her hair was his kryptonite. What he wouldn't do to fist his hands in her hair, and hold her against his chest, to capture her breath...

Tracy, I'm sorry, he pleaded through the bond while remembering how it felt when he thought she was leaving him for Jack. *Sitting with her on the wagon, he swore he would do whatever it took to keep her in his life.* Admittedly, when it came to her, he was a weaker man, and maybe a little obsessive, but never a jerk. He loved her and intended to do everything in his power to make her see that. What she held over him couldn't be explained, and a life without her was unimaginable. He wanted to breathe her in, basking in her warmth, and hold her until the end of days. She was his sun, the center of his universe, his soulmate. His eyes shot open, and he jumped out of the truck, wincing with each step as he dashed out from beneath the pine trees. He glared up at the crescent moon and yelled, "She's mine," before dropping to his knees.

Randy didn't know how long he stayed on the ground, holding his head in his hands, but he knew it couldn't be the end for them. Tracy had to know he would never do anything to destroy the bond they shared. Still, as the night engulfed him, he would take full responsibility for her abrupt departure. Had he been upfront about where he was going, she wouldn't have thought anything about Iretta's scent. Then he questioned his own agenda. He knew it would upset Tracy, which was why he planned to shower before she came home. *But why?* Did a part of him secretly want Iretta's attention? He shivered, trying to imagine it, but she was a friend. *Only a friend.*

"What the hell is your problem? You trying to wake the dead?" Seth's voice broke through the darkness and Randy opened his eyes.

"I fucked up. Tracy's gone." Confessing his sin out loud crushed his spirit and shattered any hope he had of finding her. Never had a girl walked away from him before, and Tracy doing so felt like a double-edged sword slicing straight through his heart.

"Dressed like that, I can see why," Seth criticized and Randy looked down, forgetting he was still wearing the tee shirt and blue-plaid pajama pants.

"Just be glad I was dressed before I realized she was

gone, or you'd be staring at my bare ass," Randy sarcastically replied as he glowered up at Seth who pulled a face.

"Well, unless she's dead, your bond will stay intact. 'Til death do thee part, and all that good stuff," Seth countered with a smirk. "Doesn't mean she has to stay with you though."

Randy definitely didn't like the sound of that and he jumped to his feet, getting into Seth's face. He wasn't a wolf, and he damn sure wouldn't take any shit from one of them either.

"Whoa, hold up! What's going on?" Brayden asked, rushing across the yard and stepping between them. "What the hell?"

Seth grinned, and Randy scowled. "Nothing! Just me, being stupid enough to think I could confide in this jackass," Randy hissed and as he walked away, he shoved Seth with his shoulder.

"That's right. Get pissed! And then go find Tracy. Use your damn bond."

"As if I could," Randy shot over his shoulder. Again, Seth smirked.

Determination set his pace as Randy headed back across the yard, paying no attention to the prickling damn pine cones. *I'll show him pissed.* After starting the truck, he backed out of the drive, mad enough to kick a cat. He would find Tracy, despite Seth. He blasted the horn as he passed the asshole and yelled, "Get out of the damn road!" Then he glared through the side door mirror at Seth who had the balls to laugh. *Use your damn bond.* What did he know about a bond? He was single. Then Randy chuckled, knowing it was Seth that pushed him into action, and if he hadn't provoked him, he would probably still be sitting on the ground, scowling at the moon.

Randy slowed but didn't stop when he approached the corner as he continued across Main Street, heading toward the animal shelter. Seth made him angry, but Officer Riley pulling out in front of him pushed the limit by tenfold. His body jolted forward when he slammed on the brakes, nearly T-boning the white SUV. He had the right of way and Officer Riley was an ass. Fighting the urge to cuss Riley out when Riley slowly pulled alongside the truck, Randy bit the inside of his jaw. His grip tightened on the steering wheel and he glared when Officer Riley turned and sneered, "Careful boy," before slowly driving up the road to the corner.

Normally, Randy would have shot back with a smartass remark, but since Riley didn't notice his shotgun on the dash, he decided not to push his luck. He huffed loudly, but in that brief encounter, the hostility radiating off Riley was like ice water in his veins. He never cared for the officer, but this was something altogether different. They had moved to a higher level of hate and Randy knew, given the right opportunity, Riley would hang him with something. That man was evil; there was no doubt of that in his mind. *Dirty ass cop.*

Nine

Randy

Looking through the side door mirror, Randy watched Officer Riley turn onto Main Street, heading toward the only stoplight in town. Half expecting he would drive around the block to further harass him, he kicked the truck in gear and shot up the road. Riley thought he was being slick, but it wasn't Randy's first rodeo. He pulled in behind the animal shelter to hide his truck.

It wasn't unusual for Riley to follow him anytime he was out. Especially if Randy was heading toward the river. He had left his mark beneath the bridge several times, but in his defense, the bland concrete needed a facelift. So by adding what some considered graffiti, it looked sweet, and almost everyone liked it. Except for Officer Riley.

Randy seized a flashlight from beneath the seat and got out of the truck. Quietly closing the door, he started across the lawn to the field that ran behind the shelter. Tracking across the farmland was the only other way to leave the farm without traveling by car down the highway. He had no clue what he was looking for, but as the flashlight beam skimmed over the grass, the light reflected off a silver hoop that he recognized as Tracy's. He snatched it off the ground and shoved it into his pocket before scanning the darkened field. Maybe she was there watching him, or maybe not. He had no way of knowing because he wasn't a wolf.

Use your damn bond. Could he actually do that? He stilled his thoughts and focused entirely on Tracy. At times, he could sense her emotions, so why not now if she were there? The scent he loved faintly drifted past his nose and vanished just as quickly. It was impossible to track Tracy using the bond, and Seth had to know that. He cursed as he got back into the truck, thinking maybe Seth knew more than he let on. Frustrated, he drove back towards Tucker's but pulled into Seth's driveway instead. He scowled when Seth walked out the door with a cunning smirk on his face. "You're wasting my time, now get in. I need your help." Tucker was by far the best tracker in the pack, but Seth came in at a close second.

"I guess that means you didn't find her?" Seth flashed a knowing grin.

"Hell no, but I found this." He pulled the broken earring from his pocket. "It was behind the shelter." He didn't like the frown on Seth's face, making him think something worse might have happened to Tracy and perhaps she didn't just run. "What's wrong?"

"I don't know. Go get Jack and I'll meet you all at the shelter."

Randy nodded and backed out of the drive as Seth undressed in the front yard and phased, taking off toward Main Street. He glanced through the rearview mirror and then turned onto the narrow gravel road, which led to Jack's cabin. Following the drive, he pulled up beside Jack's car and put the truck in park but kept the motor running. He climbed out of the truck, the darkness overtaking him until the porch light came on, lighting the way. He jumped up on the porch, meeting a confused Megan at the door.

"Where's Tracy?" Her voice was soft, but when Jack stepped up behind her, panic flashed in her eyes.

Randy ran his hand over his jaw, wishing it was only Jack that came to the door. Not wanting to explain, but having no other choice, he sighed. "I don't know. She took off just before dark and I haven't seen her since. She's upset with me and I need to find her."

"Where was the last place you saw her?" Jack asked, stepping past Megan.

"At home, but I was in the shower so I didn't see her leave. I found this behind the shelter." He pulled the piece of jewelry from his pocket and Megan confirmed it belonged to Tracy.

"She was wearing those today."

Randy nodded and gave Jack a worried glance. "Seth is on his way to the shelter to see if he can track her. Can you help?" He didn't think he had to ask since Jack was the Cloverly alpha, but it seemed like the right thing to do.

"We'll ride with you," Jack said, and then hollered through the house for Mason.

By the time they arrived at the shelter, Randy had explained everything to Megan. To say she was pissed was putting it mildly, but she was also the one that looked out for Tracy when the pack questioned her about changing Jesse. And apparently, she wasn't giving him a pass either. He appreciated it more than she knew.

"There's Seth," Jack said when they got out of the truck.

It was pitch-black behind the shelter, and if not for the flashlight, Randy wouldn't have seen Seth's wolf when he looked where Jack was pointing. He didn't have their keen eyesight, and the moon was but a sliver. Huffing in frustration, they waited on Seth who made one last lap around the field before joining them behind the shelter.

"Did you find anything?" Randy asked as soon as Seth phased. Seth didn't seem bothered to be standing there with no clothes on, but he was a wolf and modesty was never an issue for them. Ordinarily, Randy would have prattled on with an off-color joke, but there was nothing funny about the situation.

"She's alone. She phased at the barn and crossed the field before crossing back and then phasing again here." Seth pointed to the trashcans. "She's on foot or at least she was when she took off down the street."

"Is it safe for him to track her through town?" Randy asked Jack and he nodded.

"Stay in the shadows and we'll follow behind you," Jack said and Seth phased and took off down the road. "It's late, and most people will assume they saw a large dog."

Randy was nervous for Seth and a little annoyed that Tracy just up and left. He understood her being jealous, but at some point, she had to trust him. Following Seth through the neighborhood, he turned and drove past the boutique. He stopped at the corner and Seth jumped into the bed of the truck and phased, pointing toward the building.

"Does she have a key?" It was a stupid question, considering he was the one that gave it to her Friday afternoon. Randy pulled over to the side of the road and parked next to the building and got out of the truck. Come morning he would make an extra key, but for now, his only mission was to find Tracy.

Knowing she was inside the building, his nerves calmed but only a little. He had no idea how angry she was. She was clever; an expert at hiding her emotions. Megan handed Randy a key and insisted he used the side door. Why? He didn't know, but he was thankful she waited outside with the others to give him time alone with Tracy. He would do whatever it took to get her home, and he didn't need any witnesses watching him grovel.

Randy took a deep breath and unlocked the door, whispering a silent prayer that Tracy wouldn't turn him away. Inching his way inside the building, if he were quiet enough he could sidle up on her before she could escape. Then the security lights clicked on and he glanced up, knowing it was Megan's way of taking Tracy's side.

"Tracy," he called out. If she were inside, she already knew he was there. "Tracy, please hear me out." He walked between the shelves and across the warehouse, stopping at the entrance to the storeroom. With a perfect view of the front and back door, if she were there, she wouldn't be able to leave without being seen. "I know you're here. Seth tracked your scent and Jack and Megan are outside." He waited for what seemed like thirty minutes when in reality, it was only three.

"Go away! I don't want to see you."

Randy leaned against the warehouse door and inhaled through his nose. *Be glad she's here.* The thought should have reassured him, but he didn't like knowing she was unhappy, especially when it was his fault. "I'm not leaving until you give me a chance to explain."

"There's nothing you can say that will change my mind. So do us both a favor and just go." The last part came out so low, he almost missed it. The pain in her voice and her determination to push him away without a second thought had him clenching his fists and his anger flared.

"NO!" he shouted, irritated that she was being so damn stubborn. "I'm not leaving without you. I'm here to take you home."

"I don't have a home. I never did. Just leave me alone."

Her words shattered his heart and his gut twisted with fear. She had a home. They had a home. "Please don't do this. Don't destroy what we have over a simple misunderstanding. I wasn't with another girl. I was with a friend. I promise on our bond. It's only you that I love."

"Our bond? Yeah, you would promise on something that means absolutely nothing to a human. Only a wolf could make that promise actually stick." The growl in her voice angered him more, and he squeezed his eyes shut, seeing red.

"Tracy, stop it!" He released an exasperating sigh, hating how she caused him to lose his temper. He had never spoke to her in that tone, but if that's what it took to make her listen, so be it. "I may not be a great, all-powerful wolf, but I know what love is. Bond or not, you and me? We were destined to be together. I knew the moment you plowed my ass down that life would never have any meaning without you." He paused, hearing a small chuckle and his voice softened. "Stop pretending like it's only a wolf thing because it's not."

"Would you stop yelling and come over here and sit down?"

He assumed she wanted the others to hear him pleading with her as her head popped up from behind the sofa. But he couldn't complain. At least she was giving him a chance to explain, and he wasn't about to blow it. He casually strolled over to where she was hiding, aggravated that she had planned to sleep on that damn sofa all night. She deserved better, more than he could give her, and damn, if he didn't want to give her the world. He spun around and dropped to his knees. "Hey, sexy she-wolf," he sang out of tune, bringing a smile to her face. He reached up to wipe the tears from her eyes and then moved over to the sofa, leaving plenty of space between them. "Don't leave me. Please." That was all he could get out before he choked up and quickly blinked back tears. "I swear on my bike, I will love you forever. Only you!"

Randy looked down at his hands, wanting so badly to pull her into his arms, but it was her move to make, and he would never force her. He swallowed hard, struggling to hold back his emotions. He needed to hear her tell him they would be all right. That she still wanted him in her life. She had no idea what she meant to him. For her, he wanted to be a better person, to raise a family, to build a future. Everything was because of her and without her at his side, it wouldn't be the same. She shifted and dropped her feet to the floor as he glanced up, bracing for what was to come.

"I love you. I do." She pressed her fingers to her lips and hot tears rolled down her face. "You could have your choice of females, I've always known that, but sometimes it's hard having to compete with every girl that crosses your path." She looked down when he reached over and took hold of her hand.

"Wow, I feel the same way about you. I want you to have a bonding ceremony with the pack because I think your wolf needs it. But I would be lying if I said it didn't bother me. I mean, take Seth, for instance. He's a good-looking guy and he turns into this magnificent wolf. I can't compete with that. I'm just a guy with a motorcycle who causes a little trouble, breaks a few laws, but I would never, ever run out on you." He looked down when she pulled her hand from his before throwing herself into his arms, causing him to fall backward and both of them landing on the floor.

"You have exactly one minute to explain where you were today or I'm not leaving the store." She stared into his eyes, not the least bit worried they were caged between a sofa and a table. He stretched up and planted a quick kiss on her lips.

"I admit I didn't buy a part for the motorcycle. I kinda lied about that. But only because I wanted it to be a surprise," he quickly added. "Iretta is a friend of mine that lives in Buffer County. She's the reason I have the bike. She taught me everything I know about them. She's just a friend and I greeted her no differently than Tucker would greet you. It was just a hug for a friend that I hadn't seen in almost a year."

"Then why didn't you tell me about her? I'm not that controlling! Granted, I don't like females hanging all over you, but I would have trusted you if you had only told me the truth to begin with."

"I'm telling you the truth now. Iretta is my friend since the day she picked me up on the side of the highway and gave me a ride home. I only went to her house because that's where she works. I wanted to surprise you and I needed her help. I ordered a bike for you and she'll call when we can pick it up."

Tracy shot up off the floor like someone had lit a firecracker under her ass, backing away, and practically tripping over the table. "You bought me a bike? My own bike?" Her hands trembled when she covered her mouth. "My very own bike?"

"Yeah, your very own bike." He pulled himself up against the sofa and stood.

"I think I'm going to be sick." Tracy sunk down on the sofa and bent at the waist, her muffled words barely audible to his ears. "I'm so sorry."

Admitting he was as much to blame for her confusion, Randy held Tracy in his arms until she cried herself to sleep. She felt foolish, but it was only a misunderstanding, he told her, if for no other reason than to ease her mind. He leaned down and lightly kissed her hair. They were together and he could finally breathe normally again.

Ten

Tracy

Tracy was unusually quiet as she held Randy's hand the
entire drive home. She put him through hell for most of
their relationship, and still, he fought to be with her. *He
loves us.* Her wolf reminded her, but how long would he
put up with her bullshit before he eventually told her to
hit the road?

It was midnight when they pulled into the driveway
and parked beside the barn. Randy quietly got out of the
truck and led her across the yard to the small house on the
far side of the lake. How many times had she and Randy
sat by the lake, staring up at the stars? She glanced up.
She loved the way the stars sparkled like glitter scattered
across the sky. Shuddering, she didn't realize the night air
had taken on a chill, but Randy wrapped his arm around
her because that's what he always did.

Without Randy, she would be completely lost. Travis would say she was weak, and maybe she was. Maybe that was how he managed to manipulate her for so many years—incessantly beating her down. In that regard, she assumed she deserved it. *You're not weak!* Her wolf argued, and from her point of view, she was right. Tracy escaped Travis's clutches before he could damage her mind, and although there were times when she didn't think she would live to see the next moonrise, she did survive. It cost her dearly, the primary reason she never trusted anyone or believed anyone could ever love her. The mind games Travis played were exasperating, and she all but gave up on any dreams of a future where she could find peace. Despite lacking the guidance of her parents, she longed to believe she was still somehow worthy of a happy ending. She wanted that happy ending. It was within her grasp. Now, though, she was mentally exhausted and so damned ashamed. She had broken Randy's spirit, and for that, she would be eternally sorry.

Tracy quickly blinked the tears from her eyes as they walked into the house, but Randy didn't turn the lights on, so thankfully, he didn't notice. He led her up the stairs to the small loft bedroom where he kicked off his shoes. "Get in the shower and I'll find you something to eat," he said.

Her stomach wouldn't allow her to eat. Not even the chocolate cake that was sitting on the table waiting for them when they got home. Randy's mother must have brought it over. Humiliation plagued her, dragging her back to a world where she was nothing more than a pawn in the game of power. "I'm not hungry. I just want to shower and go to bed." She tried to smile, but the lights were still off so... Leaving him standing in the bedroom, she hurried into the bathroom and closed the door.

Tears ran freely when she turned on the water and stepped into the shower without bothering to remove her clothes. She needed time to calm the constant tremble that shook her to the core. Sliding down into the tub, she allowed the warm spray to wash away her remaining tears as her thoughts traveled back to the boutique. It was an eye-opening experience being there with Randy. He held her on the sofa and allowed her to cry. Something she didn't dare do growing up with her uncle. *An alpha doesn't show weakness.* Apparently, she wasn't alpha material. She sat there until the water ran cold before finally peeling off her wet clothes.

"I'll be out in a minute," she yelled, hearing Randy moving about the bedroom. She was in the shower an easy twenty minutes, so she quickly washed and shampooed her hair before shutting off the faucet. She was freezing from the cold water, but the icy chill that numbed her heart was justified. Like it or not, Randy deserved better than her, a shifter that was raised to despise humans. She stared at her puffy eyes in the mirror, determined to make things right between them. After quickly towel-drying her hair, she wrapped another towel around her chilled body.

When she walked out of the bathroom, Randy looked up from the book he was thumbing through. He would often sit there at night, reading to her when she had a stressful day. "Sorry it took so long." It seemed every time she turned around, she was apologizing for something.

She pulled a nightgown from the dresser drawer and slipped it over her wet head. Once the gown dropped to her knees, she pulled off the towel. Usually, that would be where Randy cracked a Houdini joke, but he kept his eyes trained on the floor. *Not good.* She carried the towel to the bathroom and hung it over the shower rod, running her fingers through her hair to remove the tangles. She would fix it better come morning. She yawned and walked back into the bedroom where she expected Randy would gather his blankets and head downstairs to the couch, as he did almost every night since she moved in.

He was fidgeting, a little unsure, but finally asked, "Can I stay with you tonight?" His pleading eyes tore at her heart and another tear trickled down her cheek. She nodded and pulled back the blanket while he pulled off his shirt and jeans. It wouldn't be the first time they slept together. He was always the gentleman, never pressuring her to do any more than light touching.

Just lying there in his arms calmed her wolf and she snuggled closer, needing to feel his body next to hers. "I'm sorry," she whispered, running her hand over his chest as his body shivered beneath her touch. "Do you think we could...?" Her words were cut short as her hand slipped down beneath the waistband of his boxers. It was time she surrendered to the bond, binding them together, making her his forever. His eyes fluttered shut and he drew in a sharp breath as she continued the slow, torturous motion. He moaned in response, sending a wave of heat to her toes. "I think it's time to complete our bond," she finally said, nipping little kisses along his chin.

His eyes shot open. "No." He pulled her hand away and rolled her over, pinning her to the bed. "Not like this." She didn't understand as she searched his eyes, until a small smile turned up his lips. "You know I've been with other girls, but you? You are my soulmate. I've waited for you my entire life and taking you now would be no different from the others. Our bond night will be special, and when I make love to you for the first time, I want you to know it's only you, and will only ever be you that holds my heart." His lips lightly brushed over hers and she sighed. "It will be me promising to love you forever." Then he rolled over to his side of the bed and closed his eyes. And for the second time that night, Tracy was blown away by his heartfelt confessions.

The following morning, the somber mood lifted and Randy returned to his normal playful self. Waking her with kisses as his hand traveled down to her waist, she stared into his eyes, the sadness gone. "Hey, beautiful, you're gonna be late." Her eyes widened and she jumped out of bed, his laughter following her across the room. Gosh, she loved hearing him laugh.

Randy was beside her when she made the walk of shame later that morning. Tracy expected Jack to be at the boutique with Megan, if for no other reason than to check on her. Still, thoroughly embarrassed by her actions, Tracy wouldn't allow Randy to take all the blame. He explained everything to them the night before, making it sound like it was his fault. She would make sure Megan knew better though. That nasty little voice that crept into her mind anytime another female showed him attention was the real source of the blame.

"Good morning," Megan said, moving out from behind the counter when they walked into the store. Megan was adorable with her bouncy curls and short frame, reminding Tracy of a little pixie. Her cream-colored sweater hung off one shoulder, and the front tucked into the waistband of her black-stretch jeans. She looked amazing, especially with the black knee-boots that screamed fashion. "Are you okay?" Her concern was endearing, but when Tracy smiled, the anxiety disappeared from her face.

"Yeah. I hope I wasn't too much trouble." Her ensuing blush rose to her ears, but since it was Megan, she hoped she would understand.

"Not at all. We're here for you no matter what. Just promise the next time you'll come to us. We'll help in any way we can," Jack said, stepping past Megan to pull Tracy into a hug.

Her body stiffened but when she looked over at Randy, he was grinning. He didn't say, "I told you so," or "that right there is what I'm talking about." No, instead, he headed back to the lounge area as if it were just another day.

"This is a nice place," Randy said as he poured a cup of coffee, adding caramel creamer and a packet of sugar. He brought the mug to Tracy and she smiled sheepishly. He was way too good to her. She took a sip, watching him as he turned and walked back to Lori's Lingerie.

Tracy excused herself and left Jack and Megan to join Randy as he sorted through the different colors of lace-wear. She'd never seen him concentrate on anything as much as he was right then and she wondered what was going through his mind. "Can I help you, sir?" she asked, trying not to laugh at the intent expression on his face. The only thing missing was the way he rolled his tongue in his cheek when he was deep in thought.

"Do you have this in white?" He held up a blue satin

bra and matching panties, and she set the mug down on the dividing wall to assist him.

"I do. I also have it in cream." After pointing out the two colors hanging on the back wall, she grinned when he reached for the white but just then, noticed the pale green.

"I'll take both of these."

A soft, rosy tint covered Tracy's cheeks when Randy took the items to Megan and placed them on the counter. She fought off a giggle and her face heated up even more when she noticed Jack shifting uncomfortably on his feet. He was looking anywhere except at the undergarments on the counter—his blush matching hers.

"Will that be all?" Megan asked cheerfully. She carefully placed the items in a small bag, along with a free sample of her latest perfume and winked at Tracy as she grinned.

"No, actually, I need one more thing." Randy turned and walked to the back of the store, scanning the dress racks until something caught his eye.

Tracy peeked over at Megan, who was still grinning and waiting for Randy to return. Jack quickly made an excuse to leave and kissed Megan on the cheek. He was out the door in a flash, throwing his hand up to wave without looking back. Tracy could hear him chuckling when the door closed behind him. She was glad he was gone and sucked in her jaw to stop the ache. Then Randy walked past, holding the most amazing dress she'd ever seen. Her mouth dropped open when he strutted to the counter and she had to lean a little to the left to get a better view. *Damn!* He really knew how to fill out a pair of jeans.

"You're going to make some lucky lady very happy,"

Megan said when Randy delicately placed the floral dress on the counter.

"That's the plan."

Tracy couldn't take her eyes off the maxi-dress as Megan placed in a box. Soft white with pale pink flowers and pastel green leaves... What female wouldn't love getting that for a gift? Sipping the caramel coffee, she hid her smile as Randy pulled his billfold from his back pocket and paid for his purchase. Then just like Jack, he walked out the door without looking back.

"It's nice to see you two have worked everything out," Megan said as she walked to the lounge area to refresh her coffee.

"Yeah." Tracy sighed dreamily. "I know Randy told you everything was his fault, but it wasn't. I just get... sometimes I'm afraid he will realize his mistake and tell me to leave. I don't know what I would do if he did. I was the one being childish last night, not him."

"Everyone has secret doubts. You? Maybe more than most. You went through a lot of crap growing up with Travis but look at you now! You're a beautiful businesswoman who's ready to bond with the man of your dreams. Could life get any better?" Megan stirred in a spoon of sugar and picked up the cup. "If there was ever any doubt about how Randy feels about you, these should put that to rest." Megan sat down on a sofa and patted the seat beside her. Placing her cup on the table, she picked up one of Jesse's dress books and laid it across Tracy's lap. "These were taken by the security cameras here in the store." She pointed up at the camera overhead.

Tracy didn't know what to expect, but when Megan opened the book, she teared up. Staring down at the black-

and-white photo of her and Randy, she traced over his image with her finger. In the first picture, she was asleep and Randy was kissing her hair. The next picture showed him tucking a strand of hair behind her ear, a sad smile on his face. And the third—she couldn't hold back the tears— his eyes were closed, and she was staring up at him from where her head rested against his shoulder, her fingertips tracing his jaw. "Can I keep these?" she asked wiping away a tear.

"You can have them all." Megan flipped the page and Tracy smiled, quickly scanning the remaining six pictures.

Eleven

Jesse

Arriving in Cloverly just after midnight, Jesse was dead to the world as soon as her head hit the pillow. She woke up early the next morning to get breakfast and coffee before heading off to work. She could honestly say she missed all the noise of the alpha house in Tennessee. She wouldn't miss the beta, though. She had a good feeling Tucker and Hayden took him down a notch or two. And after spending the previous day with Lori and discovering the role she would play in the latest vision, she was eager to get to the boutique and see how Tracy was doing.

She quickly dressed in a pair of designer jeans and a blue, long-sleeved, button-down shirt before pulling her hair up into her signature bun. With one last glance in the mirror before rushing out the door, she grabbed a lightweight ivory sweater to finish the look.

Tucker would be in Berkley most of the day; and she would resume working on Tracy's wedding dress, the one Randy had designed. It was a secret, but with Tracy working at the store, she could get her input and make any necessary alterations. She smirked, knowing for once, she had a secret that even Megan knew nothing about.

As Tucker pulled the truck over and parked in front of the boutique, she glanced across the sidewalk to the door. It would be different without Lori there, but Tracy had her own quirks, and she was looking forward to being entertained by the redhead. Tracy was feisty, a hell-raiser on her own, which was probably why she and Lori got along so well. Giving Tucker a quick peck on the cheek, because anything more would have been considered inappropriate in view of the customers, she pushed open the door and said, "Call me later and let me know how things are going."

Tucker flashed a dimpled grin, and she nearly melted into a puddle. Oh, to lick those dimples! She had half a mind to go back home and call in sick. Sighing wistfully, she practically glided across the sidewalk, watching his reflection on the window glass. She turned at the door to wave when he pulled onto Main Street.

"What is that glorious smell so early in the morning?" Jesse asked when she walked into the boutique. She didn't care about the time—be it day or night—she adored the smell of fresh-brewed coffee.

"It's not that early and it's your favorite brew." Megan stretched from where she was sitting on the sofa and grinned. She was probably having her first coffee of the day, Jesse assumed. It was a nice way of preparing for the day and catching up on anything pack-related or otherwise. A little girl-time was just what she needed.

"Who ordered the flowers? They're beautiful." After removing her sweater, Jesse moseyed over to take a quick sniff, fanning the fragrance to her nose. She smiled contentedly.

"Aren't they a gorgeous burst of spring?" Megan said at the same time Jesse noticed the display rack in the opposite window.

"Hey, when did we start selling jewelry?" Jesse moved over to the rack, her fingers lifting the chandelier earrings that dangled so prettily. "Oh, I like these." Her eyes raked over the various shapes and sizes, before drifting to the matching necklaces. "I know where I'll be shopping for Mother's Day. Just sayin'." Her words were songlike, and she could hear chuckles coming from the lounge area, so she hurried back to join in.

"Tracy made them; aren't they great?"

"They are, and they fit right in with the boutique, as do you," Jesse said, admiring Tracy's soft green sweater and the dressy black slacks she wore. "Sorry I missed your first day. How did it go?"

"Great. Lori left me plenty of notes, so it wasn't hard to pick up where she left off," Tracy said.

"Speaking of, why are you here so early? Lori usually never came in before ten. Wait; am I still on mountain time?" She actually glanced up at the clock.

"If so, you're late by an hour." Megan laughed and handed her a cup.

"Anything's possible when I switch time zones. I swear, daylight savings... oh, don't forget, we spring forward next weekend. Yay!" Jesse tipped her cup as she took a seat across from Tracy and draped her sweater over the back of the sofa. "So, what gives? What did I miss, and who sent those beautiful flowers? They'll give me something to do later, by the way." She laughed; her third cup of coffee was kicking in and she was rambling.

"Meaning, she'll spend most of the day with her head buried in the blooms." Megan chuckled and rolled her eyes.

"The flowers were from Lori," Tracy said, mindlessly tracing the tip of her finger around the rim of her mug. "I miss her not being here, and a few times I slipped into customer mode and expected her to come out of the warehouse. It will take some getting used to; that's for sure."

That was conformation to Jesse that Lori had sent Brid over to scope out Tracy. Brid's visions were based on the people she interacted with, and apparently, she had never crossed paths with Tracy. Lori, on the other hand, was her friend and probably the reason she could place her in the vision. But Jesse wasn't a seer and didn't know the rules for having a vision, so any input from her could be disastrous.

"Yeah, it won't be the same without her smut mouth, but I look forward to working with you. I can't wait to see what you bring to the boutique and I'm sure we'll have a blast." Jesse grinned, feeling way too chatty so early in the morning. She glanced down at the dress book Tracy held in her lap. "Did you find something you liked?" she asked and Tracy quickly glanced over at Megan as warning bells sounded. "What's going on, Lizzy-bop?" She pinned her best friend with a questioning glare.

"Oh, nothing..." Megan lifted her brows and Tracy nodded, flicking her tongue out to wet her lips. "A misunderstanding, actually. Randy came home with another female's scent on his shirt and one thing led to another. Tracy left and came to the boutique. She needed time to think and be alone, but things are all better now."

"If I know Randy, I bet he was fit to be tied. You're going to cause that poor guy to have a heart attack one day," Jesse said, trying not to crack a grin. She noticed the way Randy looked at Tracy, and judging by the way his eyes lit up, he would never be interested in another girl. "He probably just bumped into some chick at the store; there's no way he would risk what he has with you. That boy is so far over the moon. I'm surprised his feet ever touch the ground." She snickered when Tracy grinned. She never imagined she would defend Mr. Lather-Rinse-Repeat, yet there she sat.

"Well, it's a good thing you didn't put money on it," Megan chimed in. "Because that's exactly what he did. Not for that reason, but still, he was hugging on another female."

Jesse cut a glance at Tracy who was chewing her lip. They may have worked things out, but it was obvious something was still bothering her. "So... was the female a friend? Or did he say?"

"He said she was a friend. She's from Buffer County and he was at her house." Tracy looked down when Jesse scowled.

"What was he doing at her house? Sorry, but you have to draw the line somewhere," Jesse said, remembering Gina at Tucker's cabin.

"Cool your jets. She's self-employed and works from home," Megan cut in.

"Oh, really? Let me guess... a masseuse." Jesse wasn't

helping the cause, but she also wanted Tracy to get pissed enough to fight for her bond mate. Ordinarily, Tracy would be in-your-face and ready to bite your head off, but for some strange reason, she seemed tamer, almost docile.

"Would you stop?" Megan laughed. "She's a motorcycle mechanic, dealer, or something like that. They've been friends for years."

Tracy confirmed it with a nod.

"But that doesn't mean her feelings couldn't change, or that she wasn't hitting on him." Jesse loved stirring the pot more than she should. Usually, she was the one thrown in the middle of a pissing match, so for once, she was glad to be a spectator.

"He bought me a new bike as a bonding gift," Tracy said, but still, something seemed off.

"Oh, wow! I get it now." Jesse's eyes squinted with her grin. "I don't believe it. You have cold feet."

Megan's eyes rounded and then, even she grinned— apparently agreeing with Jesse. "This is what you have to look forward to, working with Jesse, but she's right."

Jesse confused the brazen beauty completely to the point of not knowing if she were coming or going. It was bad for Tracy, considering she had no idea what they were talking about. Jesse chuckled when Tracy looked down at her strappy sandals and frowned.

"My feet aren't cold."

"Not literally." Megan snickered and rolled against Tracy's side. "It's another way of saying you have pre-wedding jitters."

"We all have them at some point especially with a guy like Randy. You know there are females that interpret his friendliness as flirting. Even I'm guilty of that, a long time ago," Jesse said, her lashes fluttering with the roll of her eyes. "He's quirky and cool, and he rides a frickin' bike. He's got the body and the facial scruff. He's a perfect ten. What girl wouldn't be tempted to rub up against that?" Okay, maybe she should have left that last part out, seeing the scowl on Tracy's face. "I guess what I'm trying to say... you've put your guy on a pedestal, and now you're questioning whether you're good enough for him. You are, but that little niggling in the back of your mind will constantly try to trick you into thinking you're not." Jesse reached out and took the photos Tracy held in her hand as she casually glanced up at the camera overhead. "Stop doubting yourself. You are his world."

"I know but..." Tracy drew in a shuddering breath and Jesse took that opportunity to glance at Megan who furrowed her brows. "He smelled like shit."

Jesse fell back against the sofa, her stomach bouncing with laughter. "Now there's the Tracy we love."

"No, seriously." Tracy chuckled and pushed back against Megan who fell over on her lap, snickering. "It's not funny. I couldn't place the scent, but from the whiff I got, he smelled like a fresh-rolled cat turd."

Jesse couldn't stop laughing to save her soul and neither could Megan until the first customer of the day walked through the door. "Good morning," Jesse squeaked as she got up off the sofa. Wiping her eyes, she assumed she was as red-faced as the other two. "See, I knew you would be a blast!" She released a final snicker and hurried to the front of the store.

Twelve

Tracy

The week flew by with Tracy looking forward to another early morning chat session at the boutique. Just being around Jesse and Megan on a daily basis put her at ease. Not only were they supportive of her taking over for Lori, but they also brought her closer to the pack, and that was something she never imagined. She quietly chuckled, standing behind the flower arrangement that still looked as fresh as the day Brid delivered them. She inhaled deeply, staring out through the large front window. It was another beautiful spring day, but that was about to change with the darkening clouds that began to drift overhead.

"So do you always leave early when there's a storm?" Tracy asked, glancing over her shoulder.

"If it's a slow day; and usually, only one of us leaves. I still have work to do, which is why Megan left. If you want to leave early, you can. I'll keep an eye on things here," Jesse said, certain there wouldn't be many customers that afternoon, once the storm set in. She had been working tirelessly for most of the day, even skipping lunch, and only picked at the tuna sandwich Megan brought her from the café.

"Randy dropped me off this morning and he won't be back until five." Tracy looked up at the clock to see it was three-thirty. She didn't mind waiting at the store because there was always work to be done, although she couldn't seem to concentrate for long. She glanced to the right, towards the corner, trying to glimpse something in her peripheral vision. She couldn't explain why she was so edgy every time she looked out the window, but she also couldn't shake the notion that someone was watching her.

It started early in the day, right after she and Megan returned from lunch. Intuition, or just being paranoid, she didn't know, but she didn't think it was all in her head. She scowled and rubbed down the goosebumps that prickled her arms as she moseyed back to where Jesse had just rolled out a dress form with the start of an ivory gown draped over it. Envy filled her eyes, knowing once it was finished; it would be the dress of her dreams. "Is there anything I can help you with?" She was happy with the gown Jesse had designed for her, and wouldn't complain. But something about the dress Jesse was currently working on spoke to her, pulling her in, and she reached out to touch it.

Jesse seemed unsure at first, but Tracy wasn't a dressmaker, so she understood her hesitation. "Sure, if you don't mind. I could use another opinion." Jesse pulled out several sketches and spread them across her table. "I have a customer that wants a casual gown, not an over-the-top, traditional wedding dress. Does that make sense?" Tracy nodded as if she knew exactly what she was talking about. "I've sketched a few designs from the description they gave me, and these two are my favorite of the five. Lace bodice with a three-quarter sleeves and chiffon skirt, or sleeveless, lace V-neck and chiffon skirt. I can't decide."

Tracy studied both of the sketches, and both gowns were beautiful in her opinion, but the sleeved gown had a simple elegance that took her breath away. "I really like that one." She pointed and Jesse nodded, agreeing. "It's breathtaking." As she said it, she tried to picture herself wearing something as elegant while standing next to Randy. A wistful sigh settled on her lips. It would be the perfect dress.

"That was my pick too. I like the lace bodice. It has a casual flair, elegant and feminine. I think any girl wearing it would be beautiful," Jesse said, moving back over to the dress form as the lights flickered overhead.

"Are they expensive?" Tracy had no idea how much a bridal dress cost, but she expected one like that would have to pull in a small fortune.

"This style runs between six and twelve hundred. But it really depends on the fine details. Jesse glanced toward the ceiling as if she could see the sky, and then walked to the front door to lock it. "The storm's here." Flipping the sign to *closed,* she walked back to where Tracy waited.

Twelve hundred dollars was a lot of money. No way could she ask Randy to foot the bill. The dress would be gorgeous if it looked anything like the sketch, and she lightly ran her fingers over the bodice.

The dress Jesse made for Tracy's bonding ceremony

didn't have all the fine details, but it was simple and elegant and designed to serve the purpose. She glanced over to where the dress hung on a rack in the corner of the store and tried to imagine what she would look like wearing it. She had yet to try it on and even though it was a lovely dress, she secretly envied human females that wore the flowing white gowns. *But you're not a human*, she reasoned every time she thought about her bonding ceremony. At other times, she still wished she were.

Startled by the rolling thunder, Tracy turned toward the front windows as lightning lit the sky and, for a brief moment, exposed a tall figure at the edge of the park. Her eyes narrowed as she looked past her reflection on the glass and sighed dramatically. "He must have a quota to meet," Tracy said, noticing the car Officer Riley drove apparently pulled over on the opposite side of the park.

"I think it comes with the job. It's a small town, and if he wasn't pulling over speeders, he would probably die of boredom." Jesse chuckled and looked toward the window.

"Yeah, I don't think I'd want his job." Tracy turned her attention back to the dress.

"Me neither. My butt would be as wide as a barn if all I did was sit in a vehicle all day. And Lord knows I have an ample enough butt as it is." Jesse glanced down, making Tracy laugh.

"Well, at least you have one!"

"That I do. Have you ever seen me haul ass? I have to make two trips." Tracy rolled with laughter when she glanced over to see the goofy grin on Jesse's face. "What? It's true. Ask Tucker. He even threatened to get me a beeper for this wide-load."

Tracy had no choice but to walk away. Her stomach

hurt from laughing and Jesse wasn't helping with her quirky comments. Standing next to the front counter, she clenched her jaw to quiet her chuckles. Finally, when she was certain she could breathe again, she wiped the moisture from her eyes just as lightning lit the sky again. "This is getting eerie," Tracy said, forgetting all about Jesse's butt problems.

"What is?" The sudden change in Jesse's demeanor had Tracy hurrying to the back of the store, her arms covered with chills.

"The windows. Lightning lit up the sky and I could see everything in the park, as plain as day, yet half a second later, I was staring at my reflection." Tracy motioned to the front of the store as the unease of someone watching her crept up her spine. "One second, it's a window, and the next, it's like a giant mirror. I wasn't expecting to see me staring back at me." Again, she rubbed the goosebumps on her arms and scolded herself for being foolish enough to think someone was watching her.

"Yeah, it takes some getting used to, but that's nothing compared to living in the apartment upstairs. This old building with its rattling pipes... talk about a nightmare. They make absolutely no noise until late at night and then it's like the whole building comes to life. With all the clinging and clanging, I can't say I miss it." Jesse did a little shiver and pulled a face, causing Tracy to snicker while holding her stomach.

"I can't believe we're having this conversation."

"Yeah, but it's funny though. I mean, I used to be afraid of the dark, but I'm not anymore. I'm not afraid of people or animals, but a little bump in a building? I practically jump out of my skin. There's actually a baseball bat in the upstairs closet and I've had plenty of practice swinging at nothing," Jesse said and again, Tracy laughed, easing her tension.

It was nice having friends to talk to and Lori's Lingerie to keep her busy while Randy worked on the farm. Owning a business and feeling like she was part of the community made her feel good about herself. Despite the way she was raised, she never wanted to be an alpha female or take on the drama of running a pack. Tracy did, however, want a family. A family was always something she grew up dreaming of, and something she would eventually have with Randy. She glanced over her shoulder at the tapping on the front door to see her sexy mate smiling. "I'll get it."

The grin on Randy's face as Tracy walked to unlock the door made her giddy. "Did you have a good day?" he asked as soon as he entered the building and she looked up at the sky, glad they were no longer alone.

"It just got better." Her body tingled with his nearness, and when he leaned in and nipped her lip, she shuddered with the feather-light kiss. "I don't know what I did to deserve that, but I hope I can do it again."

"You were here waiting for me." Randy blushed, making her smile as they walked back to where Jesse stood grinning. "I hope you're keeping her out of trouble," he teased as he moved around the table to study the drawings.

"They're good, aren't they?" Tracy asked, her head now leaning against his shoulder.

"Yeah, this one here is nice." Randy glanced up at Jesse's smile. "Is that what you're working on?" He turned

SEEING RED

and studied the ivory material while chewing his lip. "It's amazing what you can do with a little fabric. Is this a custom order?"

"Oh, yeah! A very picky customer. I'm surprised the bride and groom haven't made ten trips to the store to make sure I'm actually working on it." Jesse dramatically rolled her eyes. "While you're here, check out the bonding dress and make sure the color suits you. Tracy said you were wearing a matching tie."

Randy cut his eyes to Tracy and she quickly turned away to hide her grin. Seems she forgot to mention the tie. "That's probably a good idea." He winked and walked past, prompting Tracy to follow him to the corner.

"Have you decided what you're wearing?" Tracy asked as she took the dress from the rack, turning it toward the light and silencing a chuckle. Despite what he thought, a purple tie would look good on him. It would bring out the color of his smoky eyes.

"I've considered a blue-plaid kilt, or maybe leather chaps. Boxers with butterflies are also a possibility unless you think it's too extreme." Randy grinned when Jesse snorted from across the store. "But then again, if we're getting naked afterward, maybe I'll just wear a bathrobe." He flashed a sizzling smile and Tracy could have melted in his arms.

"Well, some of us will strip to run, but you don't have to." What was the point? It wasn't as if he could run with the pack. She grinned when he tugged on the purple satin ribbon that matched the purple and gold leaves trailing down one side of the skirt. It was the same as Megan's dress, only the colors were different. "You could wear your dress slacks and that black button-down shirt. A

106

purple tie would look nice." It was only a suggestion. He could wear a bathrobe if he really wanted to, but whatever he wore, he would have to include a tie. She remembered the commercials on TV where a man was fancily dressed, and his tie was loosened around his neck. It was sexy, the way he ripped it off, and she could imagine Randy doing the same thing.

Randy sat on the edge of the table while Tracy fastened the ribbon back into place. With his tongue rolling in his cheek, he was deep in thought. "Just so you know," he finally said, and she turned to meet the naughty gleam in his eyes. "Not only am I stripping down to my birthday suit. I will make that run with you, one way or another."

Tracy squeezed between his knees and pushed her fingers through his thick, black hair as he wrapped his arms around her waist. "Oh, yeah?" She lifted a brow at his cocky grin. "Then don't be surprised if you receive a few catcalls. Those she-wolves can be brutal." She grinned before planting a big smacker right in the center of his forehead. The smooching sound made him snicker, and even she couldn't hold back a laugh. He was silly. She could be silly too. He taught her many things since meeting him in the woods, like how to stop taking life so seriously.

Thirteen

Randy

"I'm glad you had a good day," Randy said after Tracy was buckled into the truck and they were headed home. Finally able to relax, now that he was away from the boutique, he would later admit Jesse nearly gave him a heart attack when he walked into the store. She was definitely creative and apparently sneaky as hell, which explained why she was working on the dress he had designed for Tracy right in front of Tracy's eyes. At first, he feared Jesse slipped up and his secret was out, but when Tracy asked his opinion, he knew that wasn't the case. He smiled at Tracy; her face radiating a soft glow. He could picture her wearing the dress for their bonding ceremony, and knowing her, it would be the only thing she wore. He rolled his tongue to stop a grin.

"Yeah, me too. I enjoy working at the boutique, and

Jesse is so creative," she said, her smile nearly causing his heart to triple beat.

He didn't realize how much of his world revolved around Tracy until the night she bolted, leaving him to question why. The emptiness that consumed him that night darkened his spirit and stole his breath. But after playing back the day's events in his mind and realizing he was the reason for her running, it was even harder to swallow.

"She's a master at dressmaking, that's for sure, but don't sell yourself short. You're pretty creative in your own right." He squeezed her hand when she blushed, adoring the way it highlighted her freckles.

"I hope you're right. There have been a lot of lookers but so far, no one has bought anything. I might have to reduce my prices." She reached up to touch the long, dangling earring—her latest creation.

Tracy liked pretty things, especially things that could only be purchased at Lori's Lingerie. She said they made her feel sexy, and he could see the appeal of wearing the lace undergarments if they made her feel better about herself, but she didn't need any of it. She was a natural beauty with long, flowing, red hair that drove him wild, and vivid green eyes that took his breath anytime he stared into them. Someone upstairs must have seen his worthiness to send her his way. *Fate,* that's what Tracy called it. He called it a miracle.

"Don't jump the gun. A lot of labor and heart go into your jewelry. Just give it more time." He kissed her knuckles and released her hand.

It was hard to hide his excitement, and the closer they got to home, the faster his pulse raced. But if Tracy noticed, she didn't say a word. Instead, she hummed softly to the music playing on the radio, the same music he drummed his fingers to, or maybe it was the rhythm of his heartbeat. At that point, he wasn't sure but it helped calm his nerves. Finally, when the farm came into view, he exhaled and dared to glance down at the white dress slacks that hugged Tracy's hips. Boy, did they demand his attention. *Soon*, he reminded himself, because if she suggested the same thing she did Monday night, he wasn't sure he could resist her again. He wanted the intimate relationship of knowing she would always be his and with him forever. "Had I known the store was closing early today, I'd have picked you up sooner."

"That's okay. I had fun helping Jesse, especially when she started talking about the rattling pipes." Tracy chuckled. "But it was kind of creepy once the storm blew in."

"Yeah? How so?" Randy cut a glance her way as he turned into the drive.

"I don't know. It felt like someone was watching me all day, and when the storm moved in, the front windows became like mirrors, and it was hard to see out. It was a weird feeling."

"Maybe people were looking into the store when they drove past. Maybe that's all it was." He didn't believe it even when he said it, and fully intended to mention it to Jack. He was always stopping by with Megan's lunch, so maybe he could keep an eye out.

Parked beside the barn, Randy jumped out of the truck and hurried around to the passenger side. Being the gentleman that he was, he held Tracy's hand as she stepped down from the truck. *Damn those white slacks!*

He squeezed his eyes shut for a brief second before looking over toward his parents' house. His mom was peeking out the kitchen window and smiling as they walked across the yard.

His mom really liked Tracy, and although Tracy was nervous about telling them she was a shifter, it wasn't necessary. He'd already sat down with them earlier that day and spilled his guts. He should have waited, but knowing how worried Tracy was, he chose to be the buffer between her and what frightened her the most. His dad was a little stunned with the news although he'd known about the wolves for years. His mom, however, just smiled. Growing up in Cloverly, she heard all the stories and even befriended a girl at camp that was a shifter. Her admission surprised him; even more so when he found out her friend was Jesse's step-mom.

"What are you grinning about?" Tracy asked and he giggled like a little girl.

"My parents." He bumped her shoulder, and her brows knitted.

"What about them?"

"They know you're a wolf." He chuckled and pulled Tracy to his side when her eyes rounded and her mouth dropped open.

"How?" Her voice cracked and her body stiffened as sheer panic filled her eyes.

"It's nothing you did, so stop worrying. I told them this morning. I also told them we're planning our bonding ceremony for the end of the month. I'm not ashamed of what you are, and they aren't either."

"But..." she pulled back and looked past his shoulder, smiling before raising her hand to wave. Randy glanced back to see his mom's grin stretch across her face. "She's okay with it?"

"Yeah, she was actually happy to hear we were making it official. She's looking forward to a lot more grandbabies." His brows bounced, and she blushed. Who was he kidding? He was as eager to start a family as she was and the thought made him beam with pride.

"I never... I... I don't know what to say."

"What's to say? We love you for who you are." Randy pushed open the front door and stepped back for Tracy to enter the house. He knew the instant she saw the first dozen roses. She reached back for his arm as if she needed his support to stand. Her eyes took in the candles, lit and placed randomly around the room.

"You did all this for me?" She turned, her fingers pushing through his hair, and drawing him into a slow, smoldering kiss. Randy would admit having kissed a lot of girls in his lifetime but this was the first time he could ever recall feeling the slow-burn all the way down to his bootstraps. The red-hot desire burning through his veins had him seriously rethinking of them completing the bond—like right that minute!

He pulled her tighter into his arms to feel her soft curves against his body. It was most definitely getting hotter in the room, and not because of the candles. "Of course I did. Everything I do is for you." His smoky eyes stared into her bright green ones and if he weren't mistaken, he could see her wolf staring back. It was amazing the way her eyes brightened and were proof her wolf approved. He kissed the tip of her nose. "Wait right here. I'll be back in just a minute." He darted up the stairs two at a time as soft laughter filled the room.

Paying attention as he walked into the bedroom, the first thing he noticed was the second vase of red roses—he hurried into the bathroom. Everything was going as planned, so he quickly lit the three candles he had arranged across the vanity, and pushed down the stopper on the tub. He turned the faucet to warm, and dropped two lavender bath balms into the water because his ginger girl deserved an extra boost of the soothing aroma. Satisfied she would love it, he laid two fluffy white towels on the tiled counter, and closed the door as he exited the room.

"You have about three-and-a-half minutes to get into the bathroom before the water runs onto the floor," Randy said, practically sliding down the banister. "I would suggest you go now." He swatted her backside as she took off up the stairs, giggling. "And take your time. Supper will be waiting when you're done." He listened... waited... and when he didn't hear the bathroom door shut, he reminded her, "The water." He laughed, picturing her in the bedroom, staring at the roses, until he heard the bathroom door shut.

Pushing thoughts of Tracy stripping down out of his mind, he gathered everything he needed to recreate their first dinner together, minus the alpha showing up on his doorstep. He chuckled and filled a pot with water before rushing over to lock the front door. *No unexpected visitors tonight.*

Forty-five minutes later, he looked up to find Tracy watching him from the loft. "Is that garlic bread?" she asked, and the urge to run his fingers through her hair had them flexing at his sides. He inhaled through his nose, trying to slow the beating of his heart when she lifted the front of her gown, the smooth silk caressing her skin as she descended the stairs.

"Uh, yeah," he cleared his throat of the raspy sound and met her at the bottom step, locking his fingers with hers. Leading her to the table where a single white candle was waiting to be lit, he pulled out her chair and then lit the candle. "I hope you're hungry." His fingers skimmed over her shoulders as he moved over to the sink, trying to maintain his composure. He washed his hands while staring out the window at his parents' house, anything to distract his mind. Once he regained control of his breathing, he shut off the water and dried his hands, silently thanking his mother for the freshly baked cherry pie.

"Do you need any help?"

"Not tonight." He placed the prepared plates on the table and then took a seat across from her. It was perfect, just the two of them, the way it was that first night. He grinned and she tilted her head curiously. "Tonight if anyone knocks, I'm not answering the door." She smiled shyly, and in that instant, he fell in love with her all over again. "I love you." He needed to convince her and make her understand exactly how he felt.

"I know you do and I love you." She twirled her fork into the spaghetti and offered him a bite.

Okay, it was obvious he had made a mistake. Just sitting at the table with her made it extremely hard for him to keep his hands to himself. The way she held the fork to his mouth, then licked her lips when he took the bite, signaled his inner beast and he fought the urge to growl. But when she reached over and wiped the sauce off the side of his mouth with her finger before licking her finger clean, he was ready to throw in the towel and go straight for the cherry pie.

"What?" she asked when his eyes darkened with a naughty gleam.

"It's amazing how sexy you are when doing absolutely nothing. I could stare at you all night. Well, maybe not all night. I'd probably have to take a cold shower or two, but still." His tone softened and he took hold of her hand. "After everything we've been through, I still can't believe you chose me."

His eyes followed her as she stood and walked around the table, hiking up her gown to straddle his lap. Mesmerized by her long legs and the feel of her fingers working through his hair, he closed his eyes, lost in the moment.

"With or without a bond, I would always choose you. You saved me from Travis. And from myself." She kissed his chin and his jaw, working her way to his ear where she whispered, "My life is better only because you're in it." Then she drew him into another toe-curling kiss.

Holy hell! His eyes shot open and he forced himself to pull out of the kiss. "How long before our bonding ceremony?"

"Less than three weeks. Why?" She nipped his lip and nuzzled his neck as his body sizzled beneath her touch.

"You need to go back to your seat." The way his body responded to hers, he didn't think he could bear three minutes of her teasing. His hands trailed up her legs, beneath the silky nightgown, his fingers digging into her waist. "Or I'll be spending the night beneath a spray of frigid water." The urge to make her his was overwhelming at times and the closer they came to their bonding night, the harder it was to control. He stood, locking eyes with her as he carried her back to her chair. He kneeled down and buried his face against her chest, his heart hammering as he drank in her spicy fragrance. "Tell me to stop," he wanted to say but he failed to utter the words.

"Just once. I need to feel..." With her arms still wrapped around his neck, she pushed out of the chair and pulled him down to the floor, her gown now up around her waist.

"We can't." His ragged breathing caused her to shiver as his hand slipped down to her lower belly, and she arched against his touch. "Damn!" he hissed, barely holding it together.

Fourteen

Tracy

It was early Saturday morning when Tracy awoke on the sofa, with her back pressed against Randy's chest. Inhaling deeply as his arm tightened around her waist, he drew her closer, his leather and soap scent delighting her wolf. She smiled and stared across the room to the kitchen, and a soft sigh settled on her lips. She would agree things had gotten a little heated the night before, and their spontaneous foreplay on the kitchen floor only made her want him more. She blushed with the memory of his hands bringing her to an earth-shattering release, and then wiggled back against him, wishing he would touch her again.

"You don't want to start something you can't finish," Randy said through a yawn.

"I would have finished last night, but you wouldn't let

me return the favor." She tilted her head as he peppered moist kisses along her jaw and gently nipped her chin. Her wolf whimpered. "Now who's starting something they can't finish?" she teased when his hand gripped her hip.

"Sorry, ginger girl, but if I start something this morning, I promise there will be no stopping until I'm finished." His gravelly voice made her giddy with the possibility until he licked her earlobe and added, "We'll just have to get your bike some other day."

Tracy squealed and jumped off the sofa, making Randy laugh as she rushed up the stairs. Facing off with Iretta wasn't her ideal way to spend the morning, but if that's what it took to get her motorcycle, she would face the devil himself. Plus, she wanted Iretta to know, friend or not, Randy was off limits, and she needed to keep her grubby, little paws to herself.

After a quick shower, she changed into a pair of jeans and a green tank top, adding a light gray cardigan to finish off the look. She slipped on her running shoes and brushed out her hair. It would be a lie to say she wasn't a little intimidated, but that was something neither Randy nor his friend needed to know. With one final glance in the mirror, she turned and headed downstairs to meet Randy at the door.

"Are We There Yet?" Tracy asked for the umpteenth time and they hadn't even left the county. Randy was very smug and constantly up to something, but usually, that meant good things for her. She cracked a grin at the smile she saw on his face.

"Has anyone ever told you, you have the patience of a

child?"

"Maybe a time or two, but you love me just the same." She batted her lashes and puckered her lips, kissing the air.

His grin widened. "I got something you can kiss." Stunned by his teasing words, her jaw dropped and she choked out a breath.

"I can't believe you just said that. Who are you? And what have you done with my boyfriend?" She giggled, her face now a pretty shade of pink, highlighting her freckles. Calling him her boyfriend almost made her sound human... *almost.*

"Well, your so-called boyfriend can't seem to get the job done, so I'm taking over now. You can call me The Beast."

Tracy bent over, laughing. "The Beast, as in your motorcycle?" His eyes sparkled, and she couldn't wait to hear what came next.

"Yeah, and if I recall correctly, you love riding my motorcycle." Again, his eyes flashed an impish gleam, causing her body to quiver. *Damn his naughty nature.*

She sat back in the seat and blew out a breath, fanning herself with her hand. They had yet to consummate their bond, but certainly not for her lack of trying. She claimed to be old-fashioned and wanted to wait until their bonding ceremony, but all that changed the night she ran. Since then, she had propositioned him twice, and both times, he shot her down. He wanted their night to be special although that didn't stop him from teasing her.

"So, what do ya say? You, me, and those luscious lips." He winked.

Grinning out the passenger window to avoid his wicked smirk, Tracy always thought the pack males were forward, but Randy was twice as bad. She bit her lip, thinking of all the things she would like to kiss, which made her chuckle, but she never looked his way. And as much fun as she was having, she really couldn't wait to get her new bike. She would have rather taken his bike instead of the truck, so she could ride hers home, but because it wasn't licensed or insured, he wouldn't allow it. If it were his bike, she was willing to bet, he would ride without any registration. She licked her lips, and for a mere second, she could almost hear the rumble of a motorcycle calling to her.

The image of her flying down the highway with Randy as her wingman drifted through her mind. She liked knowing she wouldn't have to peer over his shoulder as the miles flew past, but would gladly hug up against him if only to feel the way his body moved with the bike. She looked back at Randy, his tongue working his cheek. "We there yet?" But instead of getting a snarky reply, he reached into his shirt pocket and pulled out a cherry lollipop, and her eyes rounded.

Before meeting Randy, Tracy never ate hard candy; she never cared to, not until he snatched a few suckers from his nephew's Halloween bag. The fruity flavors teased her tongue when she licked over the hard surface— and cherry was her favorite. She waited expectantly as he pulled off the wrapper, but when he popped the sucker into *his* mouth, she scowled. "I can't believe you did that!" she said, dramatically shocked.

He plucked out the lollipop, licking his lips. "If you want it, come and get it." He shoved it back into his mouth and tapped the seat beside him.

Tracy unfastened her seatbelt and slid over to the middle of the bench seat and held out her hand. "Belt," Randy said, taking the opportunity to glance down at her lap and she grumbled. Tugging the center belt around her waist, she snapped it in place and looked up to meet his grin. He pulled the sucker from his mouth, and she snatched it from his hand.

"Cherry is my favorite!" she said excitedly, taking a big lick before shoving it into her mouth.

"Yeah, mine too." He bounced his brows, again with the teasing. "You know, we're alone on a deserted highway."

"Are you trying to get us arrested?" She nodded toward the rearview mirror.

"Damn," he groused as he hit the brake and Tracy looked down to check the speed. He was only going five miles over the limit but even that was enough to pull them over if the officer were having a bad day. She kept her eyes on Randy, who kept watching the mirror. The larger his frown, the smaller she tried to make herself without actually sinking down in the seat.

"Jackass," Randy grumbled when the SUV blew past.

"You don't like Officer Riley very much, do you?"

"No, and neither should you. I've had a few run-ins with him. The guy can't be trusted."

"But he's been patrolling Cloverly for years."

"I know. I haven't always been the outstanding citizen I am today. I was cuffed in the backseat of his car on more than one occasion."

"You mean I bonded with a criminal?" Tracy's stunned expression made him laugh and she swatted his arm.

"Do you regret it? Bonding with me?"

Tracy rolled down the window and tossed the sucker, deciding to chew her lower lip instead. "Well, I don't know. I guess that would depend on what you did." She adjusted her sweater to avoid his eyes. "I mean, I'm no saint, but I've never been thrown in jail."

"Me neither, but there were plenty of times when I thought I would be. It wasn't anything serious. Okay, maybe once, but in my defense, the punk keyed my bike."

"Who keyed your bike?" Tracy scowled her irritation. It was such a human thing to do. *Like taking a sledgehammer to Jack's car?* Indeed, she once considered bashing Jack's car, but it was more a fleeting thought and not something she would have actually done.

"Brian. He was obsessed with my sister and it pissed him off when I talked her out of dating him. She only knew him as the jock hero from high school. I, however, knew him as the dirt bag he truly was." Randy checked his speed and glanced ahead, but Officer Riley was long gone.

"So, he keyed your bike and got away with it?"

"No, I put sugar in his gas tank. He knew it was me, but he couldn't prove it. Officer Riley was hot on my ass for months afterward though."

Tracy couldn't hold back a laugh, although her opinion of Brian drastically changed. "If that's the worse you've done, you're an angel compared to me." Her eyes sparkled with her grin. "I stole my uncle's car."

"What the hell! That's a felony." He cut a quick glance her way.

"Yeah, but I would have taken prison over the hell-hole I grew up in. Travis didn't press charges. Instead, he locked me in my room for a month." Her eyes misted with the memory. Living with Travis and Vivian were the worst years of her life, and after several failed attempts to escape, she had no choice but to submit to his teachings. Travis was a know-it-all and criticized Alpha Cooper for not running the pack according to the tradition. He was always scheming to take down the alpha, which only proved he was borderline psycho.

"I stole his car to run away. I hated living with him and Viv," she said and he moved his hand to rest on her thigh. She leaned into his shoulder, staring out the windshield. "I'll never regret bonding with you." Randy saved her life that day in the woods, even if he didn't know it. She sniffled and cleared her throat. It was a happy day, and there would be no crying over the past. She looked up through her lashes and said, "Are We There Yet?" rolling against him when he groaned. "Can't you at least tell me the color of the bike? Give me a hint?"

"Nah, I like to watch you squirm." He reached into his pocket and pulled out another sucker. "This should keep you busy for a while."

Tracy laughed and snatched the lollipop out of his hand and pointed. "Is that Nigel?" Seeing the new alpha of Buffer County walking down the highway, she had to wonder why. She waited until Randy pulled to the side of the road before she unfastened her belt and slid over in the seat to finish rolling the window down. "Hey, Nigel, you need a ride?"

Nigel looked surprised to see them there and shook his head *no* as he neared the truck. "I was just out walking."

"Along the highway?" Randy questioned. "Good way

to get run over."

"Unless you're the one running me over, I haven't seen a car come this way in the past twenty minutes."

Tracy glanced down the road, seeing nothing but highway miles. "Yeah, it seems pretty dead. I figured Randy was taking me to some deserted location to have his way with me." She grinned when Randy choked on what she assumed was a sucker, and Nigel snickered, unable to hide a grin.

"I'm just scouting, trying to get a feel for the place," Nigel said with another snicker.

"Oh, you tell that story so well." She winked and again, Nigel shook his head but still couldn't hide his grin.

"So what are you doing in Buffer County?" Nigel was quick to change the subject.

"Randy bought me a motorcycle, and we're on our way to pick it up," Tracy bragged and Nigel groaned.

"No, not you too!"

"Yeah, me too. I love the sun on my face, the wind in my hair, and the revved up power between my thighs." She grinned and shoved the sucker back into her mouth. That would teach Randy to be perverted with her.

"Well, I think I've heard all I need to hear," Nigel said, a rosy tint covering his cheeks. She glanced back at Randy, whose face mirrored Nigel's. "Just try to keep the speed down, at least in my county." He stepped back from the truck and winked. "And enjoy the sucker."

Tracy watched through the side door mirror as Nigel jumped the ditch and ran into the woods. She chuckled and moved back to the middle of the seat, not wanting to venture far from Randy, especially since he had candy. She fastened her seatbelt and pulled the sucker from her mouth. "Are We There Yet?"

Fifteen

Randy

Teasing Tracy was Randy's way of taking her mind off Iretta. She hadn't mentioned Iretta since the night at the boutique, but now that they were on their way to her house, Tracy's nervousness overshadowed his excitement. She laughed and joked with him but still, he saw the discomfort in her eyes. Something about Iretta's scent triggered her. Maybe because it was a scent she didn't recognize; he only hoped that was the case. By tempting her with suckers, since hard candy was her favorite, he hoped to provide a sweet distraction at least for a little while. Glancing down to check his speed, as he continued down the highway, he looked over and she said again, "Are We There Yet?" That brought a smile to his face and eased the tension building in his shoulders. He rolled his eyes and turned back to the road, glad she had started to relax.

Tracy was an excellent driver, and as much as he loved having her on the back of his motorcycle, he knew she wanted to control the bike all on her own. And not only would she be thrilled to find out her bike was green, matching her eyes, but after their bonding ceremony, and their run with the pack, they would share a run together—his way.

Tucker offered them the cabin for a week, another surprise Tracy didn't know about, and wouldn't find out until they arrived in Berkley. The past week was busy with him sneaking clothes from her closet, buying a few things here and there, anything to make their stay in Berkley memorable. He glanced over and gestured with a nod, knowing she was getting antsy. "Just up ahead. The road to the left." He chuckled when she turned to scan the farmland. She was worse than Oliver.

Clicking on the signal, Randy checked the rearview mirror as Tracy unfastened her belt and slid to the edge of the seat, reminding him of a kid at Christmas. Their first Christmas together—the excitement that shone in her eyes when they first turned on the tree lights—she sat in the big-butt chair and stared at them for hours. Randy could only guess she was recalling childhood memories from when she was smaller and her parents were still alive. Tracy was a caring person when she let her guard down, but the heartache she held onto was always one tear away from a mental shutdown.

As the truck slowed, and Tracy's excitement grew, he turned and followed the blacktop drive to the pole barn that was set back off the road. "We're here," he announced. After he parked the truck, she slid across the seat to the passenger door. Her brow furrowed when he sounded the horn and hurried around the truck to open her door. Then the garage door lifted, startling Tracy, and a low growl worked up her throat.

"Whoa there, gorgeous, it's okay," he said, taking hold of her hand. "Your bike is inside there." He gestured toward the garage but didn't understand her hesitation. He looked over at Iretta, who was now standing outside, her face in a scowl. Even she was acting peculiar and unlike her normal docile self. Fairly shy, Iretta only warmed up to those she felt most comfortable around and having Tracy there seemed to agitate her.

"Maybe you should go in without me. I suddenly feel the urge to puke."

His frown said he didn't buy her story, but he didn't want to cause a scene, so he went with it. "Are you sick?" His smoky eyes revealed his concern, not about being sick, but why she would make up the story to begin with.

"No, I…" She looked over his shoulder, apprehension in her eyes. She was also agitated; something definitely had her on edge.

"It will only take a minute and then we're out of here. I promise," he whispered against her hair. It was awkward walking up to the building where Iretta stood, especially after she witnessed Tracy's near meltdown. "Hey." He smiled, pulling Tracy to his side, noticeably sidestepping his normal greeting. "Iretta, this is Tracy." He squeezed Tracy's waist when a low growl rumbled in his ear. He didn't know why she was being so standoffish.

With a slight frown, Iretta glanced up at Tracy and he wondered if she too heard the growl. "This way," Iretta said, leading them into the garage, but forgoing any pleasantries. "It's in the corner." The petite brunette moved over and stood behind the motorcycle she was working on.

"Did you get it running?" he asked, leading Tracy over to her bike.

"Yeah, it purrs like a kitten," Iretta said and Tracy snorted.

"So, what do you think?" Randy asked, hoping when Tracy saw the bike she would loosen up since Iretta was keeping her distance. It was the weirdest thing to witness, but maybe Iretta heard the growl and wasn't sure how to interpret it. "I hope you like it."

Tracy teared up as her fingers trailed over the gas tank to the leather seat before answering, "I can't believe you bought this for me. It's beautiful." Her words made his heart zing and his grin spread as he planted a quick kiss on her cheek.

"Oh, I'm just getting started." He pulled her into his arms, his breath tickling her ear. "You have no clue what's waiting for you," he whispered, inhaling her spicy scent. She seemed relaxed as she laid her head on his shoulder, but stiffened when Iretta moved into view."

"Can we take it and go? The stench in here is burning my eyes." Tracy aimed a glare at Iretta and holy shit! He wasn't expecting her to turn so vicious, but when she did, he had no choice but to take control of the situation.

"Will you excuse us for a minute?" Taking Tracy's hand, he pulled her outside while Iretta nodded from the door—her smirk visible for Tracy to see.

"What is wrong with you?" Randy demanded, standing Tracy beside the truck. "Why are you being so rude?" She hung her head and he instantly felt like an ass.

She deserved the scolding because she wouldn't give Iretta a chance; and he refused to give her any leeway. "She doesn't warrant your attitude. She's just a friend, so get over it."

"I wasn't being rude, just get the bike and let's go."

Oh, hell no! Randy scowled, done with her shitty attitude. She could have a meltdown when she got home, but not at Iretta's; it wasn't the place. "No. You tell me what's going on or we're getting back in the truck, and you can forget all about the bike." His intentions weren't to hurt her feelings, or to defend Iretta, but at some point, Tracy had to understand not every girl he was friends with expected something more than friendship from him.

Iretta cleared her throat and he glanced back as Tracy stepped away from the truck. "Would you like me to have it delivered?" She directed her question to Tracy, but something dark flashed in her eyes.

"No, we'll take it today," Tracy said with a slight flutter to her lashes. Her sudden change in demeanor left him speechless as she followed Iretta back inside the building.

What the hell? Randy stomped inside the garage, expecting to referee round two, but Iretta's next question, he assumed, was aimed for his ears. "Does he know?" Not recognizing the harshness of her tone, he frowned. She was defensive and standing toe-to-toe with Tracy, but being shorter, her attempt at intimidation only caused Tracy to sneer.

"Of course he does. We share a bond." Tracy's words rang pretty in his ears, and he moved over to her side as Iretta stared, stunned.

"If you're talking about me, I'm standing right here."

He glanced between the two with a questioning look on his face. Remembering how it worked out the day he stepped between Tracy and Vivian, the hair rose on his neck.

"She wants to know if you know I'm a shifter," Tracy scoffed, holding her stance.

"You knew she was a wolf?" His tone suggested he was caught off guard by the statement, and Iretta scrunched her nose, causing Tracy to growl.

"Yeah, I could smell her before she ever got out of the truck."

"I'm done. I don't even know how to process this." Randy threw his hands in the air, and took hold of Tracy's arm, pulling her back down the driveway. "I'll be back in a minute," he yelled to Iretta, but the low growl Tracy emitted told her otherwise. "I don't understand what's going on between you two. She's just a friend. This is where I get my bike supplies. I've known her for years." He sighed; their squabbling was getting them nowhere.

"Really?" Tracy jerked her arm away and narrowed her eyes. "Just how well do you know her?"

"Apparently, not as well as you." He ran his fingers through his hair. "Is she like a sworn enemy or something?"

"You could say that." Tracy flashed one last glare at the building. "She's a shifter."

Whoa, that was not what Randy expected to hear. Maybe Tracy was a little jealous, like she was around any girl that claimed to be his friend, but to accuse Iretta of being a shifter was by far the craziest thing he'd ever heard. Well, maybe not the craziest. Tracy played that card the night she offered him her bond and exposed her wolf.

"So, she's a member of Nigel's pack?" It was possible, he guessed. Since meeting Iretta five years ago, he hadn't noticed anything that would suggest she was a shifter. Then again, he didn't know there were such things until recently. He helped Tracy get in the truck and even fastened her seatbelt, which she quickly unsnapped. "Stay here while I put the bike in the back," he said. Surprisingly, she nodded and obeyed him.

It took a little doing but once Randy had the bike securely fastened in the bed of the truck, he turned back to Iretta. He didn't offer the normal hug before leaving, and she seemed to understand why. "We'll talk later." He waved as he pulled open the driver's door.

"If you need anything else, you know where to find me," Iretta said, turning and disappearing into the building.

"She's not one of us," Tracy said as they pulled out of the drive and he glanced at the side door mirror.

"What do you mean?" he asked; at that point, even he was confused.

"That place smells like a litter box, I'm surprised you didn't notice." His brow furrowed, but what she said next made his heart pound audibly. "She's a panther."

His eyes went wide, and had they not been on a straightaway, he would have probably driven into the ditch. The shock that rocked his body was anything but subtle, which made Tracy laugh. "Panther?" It wasn't really a question, but who knew?

"Alpha Cooper needs to know," she said, enjoying his cluelessness. But the rumble in her chest said she was still jealous.

Lost in thought, Randy wasn't looking forward to visiting the alpha. He had an obligation to the pack and Tracy, but Iretta was his friend. She hadn't done anything or tried to harm him, so why would he out her? He glanced over at Tracy. "I'm on your side, you know. And if you think talking to Alpha Cooper is what we need to do, I'll go with you."

"So you're not mad?"

"At you?" She nodded, and he took hold of her hand. "No. Iretta is my friend, but you are the one I want to spend the rest of my life with." That seemed to appease her, and she moved over in the seat and rested her head on his shoulder.

"She's really pretty. Your friend."

"Yeah, but she ain't you."

Sixteen

Tracy

There was only one way to balance out a stressful weekend, and that was with an early morning chat session offered only at the boutique. To say Tracy was a little ticked by the turn of events Saturday morning was like saying the Empire State Building was a little tall. And Randy scolding her in front of Iretta, for being rude or some shit, was pushing the boundaries of their bond. He was her mate, not her daddy, and she had her own opinion of the shifter whether he agreed with her or not.

So eager to get the bike, she caved and pretended everything was good, although deep down she still stewed. Randy was an artist though, so he, of all people, should have known what she said in front of Iretta wasn't rude, but rather, constructive criticism. She quietly chuckled. It was actually her way of setting the record straight and warning little Miss Piss Cat not to tempt her wolf. She'd had enough of every female floozy constantly hitting on him, and although he claimed Iretta was just a friend, Tracy noticed the way she eyed her, and knew she was checking out her competition.

So doing what Tracy did best, and because she could, she said something that may have sounded a little snarky, but it was the truth. In her opinion, the place stunk, and by the time they pulled out of the drive and were heading home, her eyes were burning and bloodshot. Luckily, Randy didn't have the keen sense of smell like she did, so he didn't notice. It was a territorial issue, and she had the right to defend their bond if she deemed another female was a threat. Iretta wasn't really any threat, but that was something she intended to keep to herself. Based on her hair alone, Iretta was nothing more than an overstuffed alley cat, scrounging for her next meal, which was another thing Tracy had over Iretta. Randy loved long hair—and fisting his hands through it when he got a little... spunky. Damn sure couldn't do that with two-inch spikes! But she had to give credit where it was due. The slinky shifter had good taste in men and motorcycles, and she sure wasn't butt-face ugly like Tracy originally hoped.

The super-sized cherry bomb that crowned what was almost an explosive day came later that night when Tracy and Randy met up with Alpha Cooper. She explained to him about Iretta, and he was quick to inform her that the timid feline was already under pack protection. That was by far the dumbest thing Tracy had ever heard, and unfortunately, she couldn't keep her mouth shut on the issue. "Well ain't that just peachy?" Tracy spewed in a deep country drawl. The alpha, however, didn't find it amusing, which was good; that was the point. Now, not only was she forbidden from scratching Iretta's eyeballs out, but she also couldn't even test the theory that cats had nine lives. She rolled her eyes, thinking the feline was pretty darn lucky for a black cat.

Tracy put on her newest pair of earrings, inspired by the color of her bike, and slipped on her flats as Randy yelled up from the front door, "You're gonna be late." She waved off his warning while standing in front of the mirror. She could picture herself on her brand-spanking-new motorcycle and grinned, knowing deep down, she had the adventurous heart of a speed demon. Riding solo, she could be at the boutique in a flash, but being allergic to road rash and unwilling to scuff her new bike, Officer Riley could hold tight to his ticket book for a little while longer.

Dressed in a pair of dark jeans and a pale blue sweater, she twisted her hair up and fastened it with the turquoise sunflower clip she had made the night before. "I'm coming," she yelled back and then hurried down the stairs.

Tracy couldn't wait to ride her bike to work, which was probably why Randy hid the keys. She longed to feel the power and knowing that made the ride in the farm truck seem longer than normal. She glanced over to check the speed, thinking he was going slow just to taunt her. Huffing out an annoyed breath, she stared out the windshield and continued counting the white highway lines. She hated how the two-mile drive seemed to crawl by, but her sulking only made Randy chuckle. Not once, but twice, he reached over and tugged on her bottom lip, causing her to scowl. If he grabbed her lip once more, she'd be calling him *Stubby*, after taking his finger off at the second knuckle.

Randy really enjoyed her pouty mood, based on his ridiculous grin when he pulled over in front of the boutique. "Perk up, I love you," he said causing her brain to short circuit. She smiled flirtatiously and actually blushed when he winked. That was what she loved most about him. He knew how to lift her mood and turn her insides to slush.

Inhaling his leathery scent made her dizzy and when she got out of the truck, she drifted to the door, her footsteps feathery light. She was blissfully happy and feeling a wee bit giddy. Then her smile widened even more when she pulled open the front door and was greeted by two large grins and a styrofoam cup. It was time for a little kiss and tell, minus the kissy parts.

"Of all days, you pick this one to come in at the last minute? Are you trying to drive us crazy or what?" Megan asked, handing her the cup of coffee. "So, tell us, how did it go?"

"It went great, in a disastrous kind of way." Tracy took a sip and set the cup on the counter.

"Meaning... you have a new friend, or Randy lost one?" Jesse chuckled and unbuttoned her sweater, revealing a paisley top that went well with the black slacks she wore.

"Well, I'm not sure about the friend part. She liked me about as well as I liked her." Tracy waved as Randy pulled away from the curb, preparing to spill her guts.

"Don't tell me you and she had words. Who'da thunk?" Laughter danced in Megan's eyes and she winked at Jesse. Those two were definitely bad influences.

"Yeah, sort of. She got a little offended when I said her place stunk, but seriously, the garage smelled just like a litter box." That had them rolling with laughter, and although Randy scolded Tracy for her attitude, she still found it funny. "She also seemed concerned that Randy didn't know I was a wolf."

"Oh, right, and how did she know that? Did Randy tell her?" Jesse questioned, suddenly suspicious.

"No. She knew what I was the instant I got out of the truck. I could see it in her eyes, and she wasn't happy about it either. She's a shifter, and not the wolfy kind." Megan spewed coffee, and Jesse's mouth hung agape. Both were equally stunned and at a loss for words. Tracy nodded, and added, "She's a panther."

Jesse slumped down on the stool behind the counter and Megan slid over to share the seat. They were still processing her words, speechless, something neither of them had ever been before. Then Megan finally asked, "Does Alpha Cooper know?"

"Not only does he know," Tracy said with a dramatic wave of her hand, "but apparently, she's under pack protection. She's originally from South Dakota but she moved to Buffer County when she was eighteen. Evidently, she refused to accept her pre-arranged mate, and the pack retaliated by blackballing her, so..."

"So she moved here to what... find another mate?" Jesse asked. Again, stirring the pot, something she was getting really good at.

"I don't know. Alpha Cooper said panthers were solitary animals that rarely mingled with other shifters. I think that's why she likes Randy. Him being human, she doesn't feel pressured to hook up with him. She seemed a little shy, but I'm no expert on body language, so take it for what it's worth."

"You know, I remember Alpha Cooper telling Jack about her, but he said she was a leopard." Megan tapped her chin in thought.

"Actually, they're one and the same."

"I don't think I like the sound of that," Jesse said, fighting off a shiver. "Wolves, panthers, the hillbilly beast. So the folklore that surrounds Sallee's Rock is all true?"

"Gosh, I hope not!" Megan shuddered. "I don't dare imagine what a hillbilly beast looks like. That's just freaky."

Tracy laughed at the sour expression on their faces. Randy told her the story of Sallee's Rock, but at the time, she thought he was being silly. Apparently not.

"No, what's freaky is being called to come down to the boutique before daylight this morning because Officer Riley was driving by and he noticed the side door standing open," Jesse said. "I was the last one here Friday and I know I locked that door unless one of you came in over the weekend."

Thinking back to Friday afternoon, Tracy frowned. "It wasn't me. I was with Randy all weekend."

"Maybe when you locked it Friday, it didn't latch, and the wind blew it open. It's in the suck zone," Megan reminded her with a soft chuckle. "Did you check the cameras?"

"Funny you should ask. It seems whoever was in here was smart enough to erase the footage. Officer Riley checked the store, but other than an overturned trashcan, nothing was missing."

Needless to say, Tracy remained on edge for the rest of the morning. Worrying about Iretta was problematic enough, but it didn't compare to someone breaking into the store. She shivered, recalling her first day at work, and the sensation of being watched. But Jesse informed them Officer Riley had secured the building earlier that morning and would run extra patrols in the area. It sounded great; now if only he would patrol the warehouse. With all the shadowy nooks, someone could jump out at her and she would more than likely scream. She rushed into the warehouse and grabbed a box of sale items, then hurried back into the store and sat down on the bench next to the dividing wall. "This is ridiculous. I frickin' scared myself."

Jesse leaned on the wall and snickered. "I know. I about jumped out of my skin when the backdoor buzzer sounded. I'm not sure what was moving faster, my feet or my arms. See?" She held up her arm and pointed out a visible scuff from her wrist to her elbow. "Concrete is pretty slick if you spill your coffee, so be careful."

"We really need to replace that doorbell with something a little less shrill," Megan added. "Are you sure you're all right?" She reached over to touch Jesse's arm.

"I'm fine. I caught myself before I hit the shelf, but the delivery man got an earful." Jesse snorted. "Until things settle down, I think it would be best if two of us were here at all times."

Tracy couldn't agree more, or shake the feeling of being watched again. She glanced up at the clock, but the day was only half over.

Seventeen

Randy

Randy found it impossible to play nice when he knew he was the target of bullshit. And the lingering stench between him and Officer Riley was becoming pretty foul. He didn't mind being pulled over when it was warranted, and a ticket? Psst, that was just a piece of paper.

But his outlook on life totally changed the day he met Tracy in the woods. Now he wanted to be the man she deserved, not the rebellious asshole that taunted the law. So he kept his speed down and stopped painting graffiti beneath the bridge, which coincidentally made the bridge look better. Building a life with Tracy was his top priority, but Officer Riley didn't seem to notice and continued to hassle him.

It was late afternoon and he and Tracy were hanging out upstairs in the loft, something they did a lot more of since she had moved her jewelry supplies into his studio. Relaxing with his paintbrush while Tracy sat in the corner next to the front window making jewelry was how they wound down after a long day's work. Sharing leisure time together, inspiring each other, and stealing a kiss here and there, he could think of no better way to spend the evening.

So there he was painting the most beautiful sunset of his life, inspired by the light that shown through the window, casting Tracy's hair in a brilliant, blazing orange. Through the glare, he spotted Officer Riley, or more accurately, he spotted his white SUV. Randy didn't mention it to Tracy. Why ruin an otherwise perfect afternoon? Instead, he watched through squinted eyes as the truck slowly rolled along the highway, slowing down and almost stopping at times. He couldn't tell what Riley was doing, but after the third trip past the house, he was damn sure he'd find out.

"You want some ice cream?" Randy waited to ask until Tracy was busy with a necklace; otherwise, she would have offered to get it for him.

"No, I'm good." She looked up and smiled but continued twisting a thin silver wire around a bead.

Randy glanced back toward the window before placing his paintbrush in a can of water. "I'll be right back then." He moved out from behind the easel. If he hurried outside, he might actually catch Riley making another trip past the house. Tracy was brow deep, examining the piece of jewelry she was working on, and hadn't noticed Officer Riley driving by. He stepped around her chair, pausing briefly, but she picked up a pair of pliers, the ice cream instantly forgotten.

He casually sauntered out of the room and took the stairs down, three at a time, jumping the last five. Glancing up at the loft, he quietly slipped out the backdoor so Tracy wouldn't see him leaving the house. Skirting the pond to the back of the barn, he ducked behind the old wagon. When he was certain Tracy couldn't see him, he darted into the tree line that ran the length of the driveway. He knew what he was about to do wouldn't gain him any favors with the law, but enough was enough.

Stooping down beside a birch tree while waiting on that damn white vehicle to drive past again, was like watching paint dry. It seemed to take forever and just as Randy was about to give up, the SUV came into sight. He stood and leaned against the tree, peeking out from beneath the low-hanging branches while waiting to see what Riley would do. He narrowed his eyes when the SUV slowed practically to a stop, and seized the opportunity to jump out in front of the vehicle.

"What the hell?" Randy yelled, glaring through the windshield, prompting Officer Riley to slam on the brakes. Stopping mere inches from disaster, it was unusual to catch Riley off guard, and for once, Randy felt like he had the upper hand. He marched around to the driver's door, his frown firmly in place.

"That's a good way to get you hurt," Riley growled. Tension set his jaw and pressed his lips into a straight line.

"It's also a good way for you to get shot," Randy countered, adding, "we have stalking laws in Kentucky, and right now you're pushing the limits." Randy didn't miss the way Officer Riley fidgeted with his radio, or the way his jaw ticked.

"No, I'm working on a case and you are interfering. Now, if you would kindly mind your own business, I'll get back to mine." His scowl wasn't threatening but Randy noticed the aggravation in his eyes.

"Then take your business down the road and quit staking out my house. There's nothing to see here." Riley's face turned an angry shade of red but Randy didn't give two shits. He flipped his hand, dismissing the officer as he turned and headed back across the road. It was a warning to the officer, and not to be taken lightly. He cut a glance over his shoulder when Officer Riley sped off, heading out of town.

Satisfied to get his point across, he hurried up the drive, feeling positive he was busted as soon as he went upstairs. Being gone longer than he expected, he was surprised Tracy didn't come looking for him. As he quietly entered the backdoor, he tiptoed into the kitchen where he closed the cabinet doors loudly, so she would hear him moving around. Then he scooped two bowls of chocolate ice cream and hurried up to the loft.

Tracy chewed her lip as he walked into the room. Twisting the wire tight, she placed the pliers on the table and didn't look up until he placed the bowl of ice cream in front of her. "Thought you might need a break." Taking the spoon he offered, she picked up the bowl and took a bite. He was thankful she hadn't notice how long he was gone and quickly moved back behind the easel. But when he glanced out the window at the tree line, heat moved up his neck. "He's made four passes down the road." That was his only defense, whether she believed it or not.

"Five, actually, and that would make six." Her eyes

flicked toward the window, and he scowled.

"I don't know what he's looking for, but he needs to do it down the road. There's nothing for him here."

"Oh, he's just doing his job. Since the break-in at the store, he's been running extra patrols." She waved her spoon in the air and he grunted.

"Yeah, but we're not at the store so there's no reason for him to patrol the highway." He scowled, suddenly feeling like he was in the wrong.

"Tell you what. How about you stripping down and I'll give you a massage? Maybe we can relieve some of that pent-up tension," she said as he peeked out from behind the easel and grinned. *Hell yes!* Anytime he could get her hands on his body, he was there.

Randy temporarily forgot about Officer Riley as Tracy's fingers worked over his sore muscles. Now relaxed, he could see things clearer, and he wondered if Riley was trying to frame him for the break-in at the store. He'd had his share of run-ins with the law, but none of them included breaking and entering. Then he glanced down as Tracy snuggled against his side. *He's watching her.* He couldn't explain the gut feeling, but deep down, he knew it was true. "How often does Officer Riley stop in at the store?"

"Just that first morning when he met with Jesse, as far as I know. He usually sits across the park, or drives past, but he doesn't actually stop and come in. Why?" She stifled a yawn.

"When I stopped him in front of the house, he said he was working on a case and I was interfering. What else is there besides the break-in?"

"I doubt you were interfering with a case, more like interfering with him driving down the road. Just ignore him."

"No, it's more than that. Just promise me you'll stay away from him. He's up to something." With his chin resting on the top of her head, his fingers worked circles over her belly and she quivered beneath his touch. "It's a good thing morning comes early on the farm or I might be tempted to have my way," he murmured as he pulled her over on top of him. She was perfect, the way her body fit with his, and suddenly, the pajama pants he wore were way too thin. He moved against her and moaned when she wiggled. He was in heaven.

"Yeah, I'm ready to hit the sack," she said again, stifling a yawn.

"But you're already in the sack," he countered and wrapped his legs around hers, holding her in place. She couldn't escape, he didn't want her to. "Can I stay with you tonight? I promise to sleep on my side of the bed." She had him so worked up, he wasn't sure he could walk across the room without tripping. And going down the stairs, he would probably break his neck. Plus, he damn sure didn't want to sleep on the couch again, knowing she was wearing those tiny, little, silk shorts that barely covered her ass. Yeah, he noticed. Any guy would.

"Fine, but you have to shut off the light." She glanced across the room.

"But you're closer," he argued as he dropped his legs, releasing her.

"That's a cop-out." She flashed a sleepy grin and rolled off the bed, giving him an eyeful as she sashayed across the room. Her sweetness had him licking his lips, and by the time she crawled back into bed, he was on his side, staring at the wall.

Keeping true to his word, he closed his eyes as she pushed open the curtains and settled down beside him. Not wanting to spoil their bonding night, he considered taking a cold shower, but instead, whispered, "Good night," unwilling to give her more. She was so tempting, but who knows? Maybe he would get lucky in his dreams. When the bed moved, his eyes shot open as her body pressed against his backside. Her soft curves had him biting his jaw in order to distract his mind. It was pure torture, and he sucked in a sharp breath when her hand moved over his side and slid up to his chest. His heart strummed as her breathing leveled out. Not only was she teasing him, but now she was asleep.

Needless to say, he lay awake half the night, relishing the heat that radiated around her. It was like being on that damn bike with her body wrapped around his, only ten times better. That was until she placed her leg over his hip and he grabbed onto her thigh to hold it there. Now he was being a perv. Finally, when his heart stopped racing, he drifted into a deep sleep.

Eighteen

Jesse

What were the odds of Lori's vision having something to do with the store being broken into? *Pretty darn good*, Jesse surmised. Officer Riley had yet to nail down a suspect, and it just seemed peculiar. He was there the morning of the break-in and the reason dispatch contacted her—which was why she and Tucker were at the store before the sun was above the horizon. But why not contact Megan? She was the alpha female for the Cloverly pack; shouldn't she have been notified first?

Without answers, Jesse's mind tried to piece together what little evidence Officer Riley gathered after the break-in at the store. There weren't any fingerprints, and because so many people visited the store daily, a scent trail was useless. The cameras being wiped clean still boggled her mind and thinking about it ticked her off. After all their hard work to make the store a nice place to shop, how dare someone have the audacity to just bust in and snoop through things that didn't belong to them?

Thankfully, Tucker took matters into his own hands and installed an alarm system. If any of them were ever caught there alone, an alarm would sound if the side door opened. And although irritated, Jesse had to give props to Officer Riley. He kept his word, and not only did he make extra patrols in the area, he also took it upon himself to watch the store from across the park. That was reassuring, and towards the end of the work week, nearly everyone had forgotten about the break-in, except her.

"So, who's up for a run?" Jesse asked, cleaning up her work area while waiting for Tucker that afternoon. "I know it's last minute, but I phase on the new moon." That was the difference between her and the rest of the pack. Being a new-blood, her wolf preferred running beneath the new moon, or as Dr. Stevens called it, the dark moon.

"Count me in. We'll meet up at your cabin and leave from there. Maybe we can get Whitney to go and if Tracy wants to..." Megan glanced over at Tracy's grin. "We can make it an all-girls run. No need for chaperones."

"That sounds great, but I have a lot of sucking up to do. I probably won't be able to make it." Tracy walked over and stood at the counter, staring out the window and across the park. "Is it me, or does Officer Riley have a reserved parking space in front of the library? I mean, I think it's great he's keeping an eye on the place, but it looks like he's staking out the store."

"No, I think he's just looking out for us," Jesse said, walking to the front of the store to join her. "He doesn't have family here, other than the pack. I think he's lonely."

"I understand that," Tracy said with a sad smile. "But maybe he'll get lucky and find a mate. He's getting up in years, though."

Jesse winced, wanting to bite her tongue once the words left her mouth. Tracy didn't hold her responsible for what happened to Travis or Vivian, but they were her only family and now they too were gone. She couldn't imagine what it was like for Tracy, not having a single blood relative attending her bonding ceremony. Her eyes misted and she looked away. At least she had the opportunity to do something nice for her, which was why she took Randy up on the offer to make her dress. It wouldn't replace what Tracy had lost, but if it put a smile on her face, and made her feel special for just one day, it would be well worth it.

The roar of a motorcycle drew her attention to the street as Randy pulled over in front of the boutique. He was a hottie; *sizzling*, Lori would say, and she grinned, remembering. It seemed like ages ago when in reality, it was just last year. "Have a good night," Jesse said as Tracy rushed out the door, knowing no matter what happened, Tracy would have a secure future with Randy. Jesse waved from the window as the sun lit Tracy's hair, casting a soft orange glow about her head. Tracy was the most stunning girl Jesse had ever seen, and beneath all that feminine charm, she could cut a person down with mere words. That also came from being raised by a madman, but the more time Tracy spent with Randy, the less often the old Tracy made an appearance.

"See you in the morning," Tracy yelled, pushing the visor down over her face.

"I'm out too," Megan said when Jack walked up to the door.

Jesse followed her out to the sidewalk as Randy pulled out onto Main Street. Her thoughts went back to the night Randy gave her a ride home, and she grinned. It was a wild ride that lasted a total of three minutes, but recalling the appeal of hugging against him, maybe she could talk Tucker into buying a motorcycle. Her grin widened, imagining her huddled up behind Tucker, and then she waved as Randy circled the park before heading out to the highway.

"You don't have to wait, Tucker will be here shortly," Jesse said, turning back to Megan and Jack. She took a seat on the wrought-iron bench that Jack had bought for the store. Casually glancing across the park, she tucked a strand of hair behind her ear, her attention drawn to Officer Riley.

"Are you sure?"

"Yeah. I told Tucker I would meet him at the café," she said and quickly opened her purse as if that would sell the story. "Plus, Officer Riley is right across the street."

Megan was hesitant at first, but seeing the SUV parked in front of the library, she said, "I'll see you in the morning."

Jesse waved as she started towards the café when Jack pulled away from the curb. It was the only thing she knew to do, since Officer Riley had just taken off with his lights on heading out the highway. She pulled open the café door but once Megan and Jack were out of sight, she rushed back to the boutique. Ducking into the building, she quickly locked the door and placed her purse on the counter so when Tucker arrived, he would know she was there and let himself in.

The boutique didn't have a full alarm system until a few days ago, and not until after remodeling the building did Tucker install the security cameras. Except for the camera Sonya had, which was hidden beneath the metal staircase when she lived in the upstairs apartment. No one knew about that camera, other than she and Jesse, and at the time, it sounded silly to have it. But who would dare to break-in on a wolf? *Another wolf?* That was the theory, and although she didn't like where her thoughts were going, or whom they were implicating, she grabbed the key from behind the counter and hurried to the warehouse door.

After unlocking the door between the store and the warehouse, another security measure Tucker added since the break-in, she wrung her hands. "Here goes nothing." She swung open the door and kicked down the doorstop, waiting for the lights to click on. In the seconds that followed, she noticed two things. One, the security lights did not come on as expected; and two, the area beneath the steps looked awfully dark. That was about the same time she realized her plan was flawed, but it was too late to turn back.

With only minutes before she lost her nerve, she dashed over to the panel box and switched on the overhead lights. She didn't want to jump to conclusions, but someone had intentionally flipped the switch off and she would have bet money that someone wore a badge. Why he became her main suspect had nothing to do with evidence, and everything to do with Lori's vision. *He watches from a distance.* Okay, so maybe she requested extra patrols in the area, but she didn't ask him to stake out the place. That was his choice, and in her mind, it would also be the perfect cover if he truly was the person watching Tracy. To prove her theory, she hurried over and ducked beneath the staircase, where an old box camera hung above the heating unit. It looked similar to the ones Brian set up in the woods last year, and as she moved closer, she realized the camera was off. Her lips curved downward. "So much for that theory," she nearly growled, thinking she would suck as a private investigator.

Deciding it best to meet Tucker at the front door, she spun to leave, but her foot landed on a hard object— sliding out from beneath her. Reaching for the stair railing to stop her fall, she glanced down to see what caused her to slip. Her heart pounded in her chest, and her eyes glazed over. The urge to grab the knife off the floor dared her to come nearer until she noticed the small red R, circled, and centered in a triangle. She'd never seen the knife before, but based on the description Lori gave of her dream, she would have recognized it anywhere. Then her eyes widened with fear and she suddenly wished she were anywhere except there, in the warehouse. In a full-blown panic, she didn't hear Tucker entering the store, and when he caged her against his chest, she screamed.

"It's me," he said, tightening his grip. "You're safe." Her body trembled as she turned in his arms, burying her face against his chest. Knowing someone had a knife inside the building, she mentally freaked out. "Jesse, snap out of it!"

She pointed to the ground, refusing to leave his side as he leaned and grabbed the knife off the floor. If there were blood on the blade, she didn't want to see, so she looked away.

"Is this what frightened you?" Tucker asked, holding the knife to the light. She nodded and narrowed her eyes at the slight smile that turned his lips. Now was not the time to tease.

Once her pulse finally slowed, she found her voice and asked, "Who do you think it belongs to?"

"It's Officer Riley's. He dropped it the morning he was securing the building. I'll let him know you found it."

"But what was it doing back here? There's nothing back here."

"The lock on the apartment door was broken, so he used the knife to shimmy the door open. He dropped it and forgot to get it before he left the store. I told him I would look for it as soon as I had the time."

"Well, that just blew my theory clear out of the water." Jesse stepped back as Tucker placed the knife on top of the heating unit, below the camera.

"Can we discuss your theory over dinner? I'm starving." Insinuating one thing with the bounce of his brows, Tucker rubbed his stomach, and she rolled her eyes.

"I don't think you're starving, but yeah, let's get out of here." She took his hand and followed him across the warehouse.

Feeling better since Tucker was there, she forgot about Officer Riley until Tucker asked, "What were you doing under the steps?"

"I had a hunch and wanted to check the camera, and also to turn off the heater." She bumped into him when he stopped and looked back.

"That's not a security camera. I didn't install that." He

continued into the store and closed the door, but not before looking back one last time.

"No, it's a hunting camera that Sonya installed when she lived here. It's the only camera we didn't check because I forgot it was there. But the camera was off so I assume the batteries need replacing," she said as he locked the door.

"How do you know what kind of camera it is? You don't hunt."

"True, but Brian installed hunting cameras in the woods after we found the pack's prints at Sallee's Rock. I got the picture of your wolf from the camera card." Her smile beamed when his brow furrowed. Clearly, he wasn't expecting that.

"But, I didn't think Brian knew about us," he said, gathering her things off the counter.

"He doesn't. He only checked one card. I checked the other two."

"But you didn't tell him."

"Of course not! Had he not stood me up, I wouldn't have been in the backyard the night Travis attacked me. And the following day when I told him about the attack, he acted like a pompous, little twit and basically called me crazy. So when I came across the pictures, I decided he didn't need to know."

"Why do I suddenly feel like this building is booby-trapped, and if I move the wrong way, I'll end up in a net?" Tucker laughed and glanced at the ceiling as if he thought it were possible.

"Getting paranoid, are you?"

"No, but this is an old building and if these walls could talk, what would they say?" He pulled open the front door.

"They would say that knife was the same as the knife in Lori's dream." She smirked and walked out onto the sidewalk, waiting for him to lock the front door.

"But it was just a dream. It meant nothing."

"Maybe, but that doesn't explain how she knew about the knife."

"She knew about the knife because it was the one Riley used to pinpoint the area on the map when we were searching for Megan. Remember? It was sticking through the paper, into the table. Everyone that walked up saw it. And if I recall correctly, Lori was front and center leading the way."

"Yeah, but it doesn't explain the blood she saw on the blade." Her brows lifted, and he sighed.

Nineteen

Tracy

Sitting out beneath the stars, Tracy's mind drifted back to a day she had purposely banished from her memory. *Why was it vital to remember the details of her parents' death after years of hiding them away?* She wondered. Lately, her wolf seemed more on edge. Sensing something amiss, something she couldn't explain? She couldn't pinpoint when it started, but it was definitely there, niggling in the back of her mind. It had her searching the darkest corners of her memories—a place of fear, uncertainty, and death. She sighed dramatically as Randy tightened his arms around her waist. She was really too young to recall very much about her mother, and thanks to Alpha Hudson, she didn't have pictures of her parents anymore.

Leaning into Randy's embrace, her shoulders resting

against his chest, she stared up at the night sky and the stars. Longing to be millions of miles away, she often dreamed of making an escape. Now she was content with her life because she had Randy, and if it weren't for him, she would have left Kentucky and gone... where? She didn't know.

"You're awfully quiet tonight, what's bothering you?"

"I was just thinking is all." She closed her eyes, enjoying the breeze as it brushed the hair from her face.

"Maybe, but I can feel the tension in your shoulders. Are you sure you don't want to talk about it? I'm a good listener." He rested his chin on top of her head and she opened her eyes, looking up.

"I was at the alpha's house the night the pack turned against my family. Alpha Hudson, my grandfather, set an outbuilding on fire, trapping several females inside. It scared me as I watched from the upstairs window and the flames were so high, they caught the trees on fire. Travis said it was because they didn't follow orders, and that was how a real alpha dealt with rebellious females. For years after that, I had nightmares of Travis setting my room on fire. He was always reminding me of that night, but I refused to revisit it in my mind." She swallowed back her tears and adjusted herself on his lap.

"Once the fire spread, no one paid much attention to the alpha house as it burned to the ground. Mom and I were inside, and Dad was furious when he came into the room. She was trying to get me to come out from beneath the bed. She was afraid of him and it terrified me. I think because of all the fighting. Mom refused to leave, and held onto the bedpost, struggling against him, screaming for him to let her go. He didn't seem to care and eventually strong-armed her out of the room, leaving me behind." Tracy's tears flowed freely as Randy crushed her in his arms, his way of protecting her. "I don't know why I suddenly remembered that. My dad took my mother and left me to burn."

"Your dad was an asshole to leave you behind. You were how old, barely five?" he asked and she nodded. "Do you remember how you got out of the house?"

"Yeah, when I realized they weren't coming back, I panicked and tried to follow them. I saw my dad push my mom into the family room, but before I could get to the door, the whole ceiling fell in flames. I instantly ran in the opposite direction and ended up in the kitchen. The door was open, so I ran out into the backyard. There was so much smoke and the heat was unbearable. I couldn't catch my breath. I was coughing hard and my lungs hurt. Then the house just collapsed, and my parents were still inside."

"I'm sorry you had to go through that," Randy said, kissing the top of her head.

"It's weird. Suddenly, I remember it like it was yesterday. I guess I've been thinking a lot about Mom since our bonding ceremony is only two weeks away. I wish she were here."

Randy nodded, struggling to hold back tears.

Tracy never spoke to him about her parents, terrified he might consider her the reject her family apparently thought she was. She closed her eyes and made a wish on a star, something she often did as a child. Then she looked up at Randy. "My parents died obeying an alpha for the wrong reasons. My grandfather wasn't a very nice man and Travis was just like him. He wanted power, no matter the price, and it cost him not only his life but his whole pack." She looked back at the sky.

"Was that the night the pack split? I've heard the story. Mom was telling me the other day. She remembered all the rumors." He rubbed her arms, and she sighed sadly.

"Yeah. Our family lost everything; we were lucky Alpha Cooper didn't force us out of the pack. And even though he allowed us to stay, Travis never changed. He was the only family I had after that night; and soon afterward, he and Vivian got together. I was too young to know what was going on but Travis told Alpha Cooper it was only right that he should raise me because I was his only surviving relative. That's how I got stuck with him and Viv, but no one suspected he was grooming me to help him steal back the pack. He wanted me to eventually bond with Jack, thinking if Jack had a mate, his dad would step aside and let him have the pack. He also thought it would be easier to challenge Jack than Alpha Cooper. I should have said something back then, but Travis chased off anyone who dared be my friend. Most of the pack didn't trust Travis, and because of him, they didn't trust me." She shrugged.

"Then what changed?"

"Tucker. He moved to Kinsley, and that's when I met him at a pack meeting. He didn't know Travis like the others did so he had no qualms in telling him exactly what he thought. I liked watching him stand up to Travis, which was how he became my best friend. He's the reason I moved to Cloverly. Travis didn't like it, but there wasn't anything he could do because of my age."

"Well, I'm glad Tucker was there for you."

"Me too. He did a lot for me, and kept me out of trouble. Poor Jack had his hands full." She chuckled sadly.

"But it was you that saved me that day in the woods. I was looking for Jack to apologize for something I'd done. I hoped to make him think I would be a worthy mate. Travis threatened me to bond with Jack, and I honestly thought Jack was my chosen mate. Then you just happened to be on the path that day. You're the reason I'm here now." She kissed his knuckles and held his hand to her heart. "I knew as soon as I looked into your eyes that everything Travis had told me was a lie."

"Maybe so, but I'm still sorry about what you had to endure. If I could go back and magically change things, I would. You deserved better."

Tracy nodded, blinking the tears from her eyes. "The past is something I can't change, and to dwell on it only disrupts the future. I don't want to be what Travis tried to make me. Life is too short to live without happiness, and right now I'm the happiest I've ever been."

Tracy remained in Randy's arms until well after midnight, mulling over the fresh memories. Even when she was little, no one wanted her! Why else would her dad leave her behind? *Stop dwelling!* She screamed in her head. She had a wonderful mate and he was all she needed—him and his family. "You ready for bed?"

"Guess we should, morning comes early on the farm," he joked, but that was for her benefit.

"A lot earlier if you're a new-blood. I suspect Jesse and the others will head out soon. It's a girls-only run."

"Is that really a smart thing to do?" He didn't think it was safe, but that didn't matter because she quickly dropped the subject. She was still trying to make amends for her behavior at Iretta's, even if it meant kissing up to him. She followed him across the yard to the house.

Tracy had just finished dressing for bed when Randy walked over and stood in the bathroom doorway. His brows pinched together and his tongue was working his cheek until he finally said, "I don't think it's safe for a bunch of girls to be running through the woods at night; but I also have a human brain, so I clearly don't understand the dynamics of being a shifter. I know you can take care of yourself as a wolf, so who am I to keep you from your pack?"

She nearly grabbed him and kissed the breath out of him, but instead, she squealed. "It is safe, I promise, but you're my mate and if you don't want me to go, I won't."

"You're an adult, Tracy. You don't need me or anyone else telling you when and where you can come and go. It's your life to live; I only ask that you let me share it."

That was what started the ball rolling, and after changing into suitable clothes and promising to be careful, Tracy was out the door, in the truck, and heading down the highway. With the window cranked down, she inhaled the crisp morning air as she clicked between radio stations.

Jesse and Megan weren't expecting her, but they had talked about going up to Hunter's Ridge so she'd try to meet up with them there first.

Being trained by the best scout in the pack, she and Tucker knew every square inch of Cloverly. And unlike most females, she had no worries about being in the woods at night, alone. She was more at home there than anywhere else, which was why Jack offered her a scout position, and she so eagerly accepted.

Turning off the highway, she followed the gravel road around to the stretch of blacktop that ran in front of the cemetery. It was early morning, about four, she guessed, and if she knew her friends at all, they were already on the ridge. She turned onto the service road, following it to the furthest corner of the cemetery, and parked next to the tree line. As she got out of the truck, she scanned the area.

Beyond view of the neighboring houses, she kicked off her shoes and froze when a black vehicle turned into the drive. The hair on her nape bristled with suspicion. She quickly undressed and tossed her clothes into the truck before darting up the hill to duck behind a tree. She kneeled down to watch the SUV slowly make its way to the back lot and turn in her direction. To avoid the headlights that lit the hill, she leaned back against the tree as the lights illuminated the ground, only slowing briefly when it turned and passed the truck. After she felt certain the vehicle wouldn't stop, she peeked out from her hiding spot and watched it make another turn. The headlights swept across the cemetery and finally, the SUV headed out of the parking lot, going up the road, back in the direction it had come.

Tracy chuckled nervously and got to her feet. As a wolf, she could protect herself, so why be afraid? She chalked it up to her foolish imagination, but her wolf wasn't convinced. She phased and headed up the hill, praying the others would already be there.

Twenty

Jesse

Things weren't adding up and although Jesse couldn't explain what troubled her most, she knew it had to involve Officer Riley. That conclusion came after she checked the small camera beneath the staircase and found it turned off. Sure, she made an excuse and said the batteries were dead, but she had replaced them every three months like clockwork, so that wasn't the case. To make matters worse, Tucker didn't think it was a big deal that Officer Riley dropped his knife while (he claimed) he was trying to secure the building. Jesse, however, believed he dropped it when he was snooping in an area where he didn't belong.

Jesse squeezed her eyes shut, hoping to ward off the stress-induced headache that throbbed behind her lids.

She was exhausted and only wanted a few hours' sleep before her run, but that wasn't likely to happen. Tucker lay sleeping beside her, and her mind drifted back to the day Lori told her about the dream. *The handle was camo with a small red R circled and centered inside a triangle. I've never seen that brand before.* Her eyes shot open, and she stared at the ceiling as a thin sheen of sweat soaked her skin.

Preparing for her run, Jesse tiptoed out of the cabin, careful not to wake Tucker. Phasing on the porch once Megan and Whitney showed up, they took off across the road and jumped the ditch. It was a short run to the lake and Sallee's Rock, and then to Hunter's Ridge where they phased and dressed in the clothes that were hidden beneath a tree. It wasn't their usual resting place since Tucker didn't like her going there, but deer season was over, and despite what he thought, there weren't many hunters hunting coyotes.

Jesse sat down and stared out over the farmland, glad to be there until Tracy came barreling through the trees in a panicked rush. Her guard went up as Tracy phased and joined them on the cliff's edge, taking the clothes Whitney held out. Making an excuse for why she was running late, Jesse caught the quiver in her voice, and it wasn't because she was in a hurry. Something had spooked Tracy, but she was tight-lipped, and would never admit to being afraid. She had alpha tendencies and seldom showed her emotions, but Jesse's gut instinct told her to keep her eyes open.

"So, you waited until Randy was asleep before sneaking out of the house?" Megan asked, making Tracy laugh.

"I didn't have to. I just mentioned it was a girls-only run and I think Randy was afraid I'd miss out." She winked.

"Guilt works every time," Whitney said, fist-bumping Tracy.

"Yeah, I'm just glad you all were here," Tracy said, stretching her shoulders.

"Well, I'm glad you could make it. We should do this every month. Make it a girl's night out." Jesse nodded to Whitney and she grinned.

"I'm all for that. I can't remember the last time we hung out together without the guys. I like talking smack," Whitney said as she looked over at Tracy. "So, tell me about the fresh-rolled cat turd."

The conversation grew lively after that, and once the sun topped the horizon, Whitney and Megan headed back to their cabin.

"Remember, same time next month." Jesse waved and then turned to Tracy. "Can I get a ride to the café?"

"Sure, if you don't mind riding in an old farm truck." Tracy chuckled as they headed down the hill to the cemetery.

Standing next to the truck, wearing black sweats, something Jesse absolutely hated, she waited for Tracy to unlock the passenger door. As she got into the truck, she noticed the discarded clothes tossed on the seat and moved them out of the way so Tracy could slide in behind the wheel.

"Sorry I missed the run, but thanks for inviting me. It was a blast just hanging out with you all," Tracy said as she backed out of the parking space—heading toward Walnut Street.

"You're welcome and we expect you'll be back next month, so mark the date," Jesse said, noticing Tracy had relaxed so much she was actually smiling. And after a conversation about Tracy's wolf wearing earrings, it was hard not to laugh.

"Most females wear stud earrings, but I like the clinking kind." Tracy flicked the dangling earring that nearly touched her shoulder. "It makes it harder to sneak up on someone, but with enough speed, even that's doable." She pulled over in front of the café, behind Officer Riley's white SUV.

"Aren't you coming in?" Jesse pushed open the truck door, looking back at Tracy.

"I think I'll pass. Randy's probably pacing a hole in the rug, wanting to know how the run went."

Jesse grinned when Tracy wrinkled her nose, but it was her chance to confront Riley, so she thanked Tracy for the ride, and made a show of waving while holding open the café door. She wanted to see if Riley noticed Tracy, and if so, would he follow? She casually scanned the room as she made her way to the counter, but Officer Riley was nowhere to be seen. Taking a seat, she sighed, flustered. "Coffee, please."

"One of those days?" Mallory asked and she nodded.

"And it's just starting." Wrapping her fingers around the styrofoam cup, she inhaled the rich aroma before taking a sip.

Mallory was a good friend after standing up with her at the town council meeting. But Jesse wasn't in the mood for small talk, and it wasn't until Mallory said, "Hey, Brett, the usual," that she turned to see who Brett was.

Her face heated when she looked up at the officer

now standing beside her. He was tall and slender with short blond spikes and the prettiest sky-blue eyes. Most definitely good looking and a wolf, but she couldn't place him.

"Morning," he said when he noticed her staring.

"Good morning," Jesse blushed and added, "I've never seen you around here before."

"Probably not. I'm Brett, the new hire. Only been here a few days. And you are?"

"Oh, I'm Jesse. I own the boutique next door." She offered her hand while scolding herself for acting like a giddy schoolgirl.

He took hold of her hand and looked toward the wall as if he could see through to the building. "The Lucky Leaf. Officer Riley informed me of the break-in and advised me to stay extra alert in the area." He released her hand and smiled.

"Yeah, I was hoping I'd get to talk with him this morning. Isn't that his truck parked out front?" She turned and looked out the window, Brett doing the same.

"No, that's mine. There're actually four that look exactly alike," Brett said and she wanted to roll her eyes. "The only difference is the plates."

"Duh, I knew that." *Good grief. Could you be any cornier?* Now she was starting to act like Mallory, but playing dumb didn't look good on her. Wiping her sweaty hands on her pants, she couldn't stop her knee from bouncing. "I think I need another shot of caffeine."

Brett grinned and lifted his brows as if disagreeing. "Is there something I can help you with?"

"No. I was just hoping to see Riley. It's not anything work-related; it's personal, actually. I guess I got my days mixed up."

"Well, I'm sure he'll be sorry he missed you." Brett turned and took the bag Mallory held out and a small coffee. "Have a good day."

"You too," Jesse said and turned back to the counter where Mallory stood grinning. "What?"

"He's a doll." She waggled her brows and Jesse groaned, remembering the way Mallory drooled over Seth. That wasn't a road Jesse was willing to travel, especially after making a fool of herself in front of Brett.

She finished her coffee and placed an order for her and Sonya before moving over to a booth and staring out the window. Her dad was working the weekend shift so it would give her time to hang out with her step-mom while also picking her brain. She waved Sonya over when she entered the café.

"How was your run?" Sonya asked taking the cup of coffee Mallory placed in front of her. She blew across the liquid before taking a sip.

"Great! You should have joined us."

"How about I just join you for breakfast afterward? I'm an early bird, but not that early." She laughed and took another sip of coffee as Mallory set a plate of eggs and toast in front of her.

Catching up on everything from Moose, to when her grandmother wanted to plant the garden, it was nice just to talk. Sonya was honest to a fault no matter the question. "Have you met the new officer?"

Sonya looked up and out the window. "Where?"

"He was in here earlier. His name is Brett."

"Oh, yeah. I know Brett. He's a good guy, moved here from Danbury. He's replacing Officer Riley."

Shocked by the news, Jesse looked out the window. "Brett didn't mention anything about replacing Riley."

"Probably at Officer Riley's request since he is a very private person, who rarely shares personal details. I think he's leaving because of his family. You know, he's not originally from here." Sonya picked up her knife to spread a pat of butter over her toast. "I guess he finally decided to go home."

"But I thought... Wow." She shook her head. Officer Riley's departure meant he couldn't be the one watching Tracy, and now she was back to square one. "Did he say when he was leaving?"

"No, but since Seth took over Nigel's position at the station temporarily, and now Brett, I'd say it could be any day."

Jesse should've been glad of the news, but now she felt guilty. Tucker had told her not to jump to conclusions, but did she listen? Oh, no. Not her. "Well, I hope I get the chance to talk to him before he leaves. I'd like to thank him for the extra patrols."

"I'm sure there's still time. He'll have to finalize everything in the office before he goes. I really do hate to see him go though. He's such a nice man."

"Yeah, Tucker liked him well enough."

"Alpha Cooper did too. It'll be hard to find someone as dedicated as Riley, but I think once Brett gets a routine going, he'll do just fine."

"I hope you're right."

After breakfast, Jesse rushed home to shower and change, but still wasn't ready to start the day. Stuck in a crappy mood, although Tucker tried to ease her mind, she felt embarrassed for thinking the worst about Officer Riley. So arriving at the boutique thirty minutes early, she was pleased to see Officer Riley pulling up in front of the store. "I'm so glad you stopped by. I heard you were leaving us," she said, holding open the door.

"Apparently, I've worn out my welcome." Riley smiled a genuine smile that lit up his eyes. "But Brett is taking over so you shouldn't have any problems." He handed her a printed copy of the police report, but instead of his number, he listed Brett's number at the bottom. "If you need anything, you can reach him with either of those numbers," he said, glancing at the paper.

Jesse nodded, noticing how he didn't go into detail about why he was leaving, or if he intended to go home, wherever home was, but she wasn't curious enough to ask either. *You've done enough.* Great! She would be scolding herself for the next month. "Oh, before you leave, I have something for you. I'll be right back." She rushed into the warehouse and grabbed the knife off the heating unit— thankful the security lights clicked on—and a small Lucky Leaf bag. Stuffing the bag with samples of Megan's beauty supplies, she hurried back into the store to find him standing in the same place beside the front counter. "I found this the other day and Tucker said it belonged to you." She handed him the knife as a small smile spread on his face. "What's the R stand for?" She couldn't help but ask.

"It's my pack's emblem," he said as he shoved the knife into the side of his boot. "It was a gift from my father."

"Oh, well, I'm glad I found it then," she said when he cleared his throat. "This is a little something for... I assume there's a Mrs.?" His position shifted, and he nodded as she handed him the bag. He was most definitely a private person!

"Good morning, Officer Riley. How are you today?" Megan greeted him cheerfully as she entered the store. "Are you on duty or just shopping?" Megan glanced down at the bag in his hand and he chuckled. It was strange to see him so relaxed, and now Jesse felt even more like a dimwit.

"Neither, I stopped by to drop off a copy of the police report before I head out." He turned when the door opened again and Tracy walked into the store. Smiling, he turned back to Jesse. "As I said, if you need anything at all, Brett is up to date on the case and the one you'll want to speak with."

"Thank you," Jesse said when he turned for the door. "If you're ever back this way, stop in and visit." He tipped his hat and without looking back, exited the building.

"What was that about?" Tracy asked, removing her sweater as she walked back to the lounge area.

"Officer Riley is leaving Cloverly." Jesse watched him get into the SUV and fasten his seatbelt before pulling out onto the road. "He didn't say where he was going, but apparently he has a mate, so I assume he's going home."

"Well, I say good riddance!" Tracy stifled a yawn. "It will thrill Randy to know he won't be watching the house anymore."

"Why would he do that?" Jesse asked as she and Megan joined Tracy for their morning coffee.

"I think because we asked for extra patrols," Megan chimed in. "I've seen him over by the cabins. He takes his job pretty seriously."

"Oh, well, it looks like we'll be dealing with Brett from now on. I hope he takes his job seriously, too." Jesse sat down on the sofa.

"You'll like Brett. He's super sweet. I met him at Alpha Cooper's," Megan said, filling the coffeepot.

"I wouldn't repeat that in front of Mallory or she'll want you to fix her up on a date." Jesse chuckled and rested her head back on the sofa. "I think I need a vacation." She yawned.

"I know what you mean." Tracy covered a yawn, making Jesse chuckle.

"So, was Randy waiting for you when you got home this morning?" Megan asked, starting their early morning chat session.

"No, he was still asleep." Tracy waggled her brows as mischief danced in her eyes. "I unplugged the alarm clock before I left and told him it was a power surge."

"Oh, my gosh, that's brilliant! I'll have to pull that on Tucker one day." Jesse laughed.

Twenty-One

Tracy

By noon, Tracy was bursting with energy, her fourth cup of coffee only added to her pep. Busily buzzing about the store, she popped out from behind the dividing wall to toss her styrofoam cup in the trash. "What are you all doing for lunch?"

"I'm skipping. I really need to get this dress finished ASAP," Jesse said.

"I'm waiting for Jack to bring something from home. Do you want him to bring you something?" Megan offered.

"No, actually, I was hoping to finish tagging the new inventory before leaving early for the day. Unless you all need me to stay," Tracy said over her shoulder, getting both of their attention.

"We're good," Jesse said as she stuck her pencil behind her ear and picked up a pair of scissors. "Megan and I can watch the store."

"Thanks, I appreciate it! I've been experimenting with wire-wrapping and I need some river rock," Tracy said as she rushed into the warehouse. Pulling three large boxes off the shelf, she pushed up the sleeves of her sweater, knowing if she worked fast enough she could easily finish by two.

An hour-and-a-half later, she dusted off her navy slacks and slipped on a pair of running shoes before darting back into the store with a small boutique bag in her hand. "I'm leaving my purse here; so if Randy stops by, just tell him I'll be down by the bridge." She waved as she headed out the door.

It was a pleasant day for a walk and the warmer than normal temperature reminded Tracy summer was just around the corner. Since moving to the farm, she rarely walked anywhere, so it was a treat to get a little exercise and be alone with her thoughts. Strolling past the Flower Pot, she noticed the line of customers at the counter and Brid waving through the open front door. *He watches from a distance.* Tracy looked back over her shoulder as a couple entered the flower shop and dismissed what she thought was a voice in her head. With her superb hearing, it was easy to eavesdrop on other people's conversations when she wasn't paying attention.

Continuing down the road, she passed the theater as memories of Randy standing against the building brought tears to her eyes. That was one of the worst nights of her life, thinking he wanted nothing to do with her. She inhaled a deep breath; the memory leaving with her exhale. It seemed like yesterday, and another memory she would push to the back of her mind.

Tracy looked both ways before crossing the street and then followed a narrow dirt road, picking up random pebbles until she eventually made her way to the river. Her nose wrinkled, catching a whiff of the murky water, but then she smiled when she noticed the large painting beneath the bridge. Despite what Officer Riley thought, it definitely wasn't graffiti, and nothing about it was tacky. Gazing into the landscaped mural that blended with the riverbank, it was the most amazing thing she'd ever seen and the reason she wasn't paying attention to the black SUV that pulled up behind her—until the driver's door slammed shut.

"Checking out Boyfriend's handiwork?"

Tracy spun around, surprised to see Officer Riley there. She looked past him to the truck as images of the headlights in the trees flashed in her mind.

"No, actually, I'm gathering rocks. Do you mind? Or is it just a bad habit of yours to stick your nose into other people's business?" She leveled him with a glare.

"Oh, pardon me. I didn't intend to pry into your business. Just curious is all." He looked at the mural. "Pretty nice for graffiti."

Of course he would label it that. "I think it looks great, but then again, I'm partial to anything *Boyfriend* paints." She smirked, using the name Riley used for Randy and he grinned.

"As you should be. I was wondering how long it would take before you admitted he was your boyfriend." He rubbed the back of his neck and she scowled, doubting he honestly thought that way.

"Did you need something, or are you stalking me? Don't think for one minute that I don't recognize your truck." She glanced over at the black SUV and planted her hands on her hips while smirking at the sudden awareness in his eyes.

"I wasn't stalking you. I saw the truck turn into the lot from a block away and I was curious." He held her gaze, the corners of his mouth twitching, almost into a smile.

"I doubt that very much," she groused, rolling her eyes when he tilted his head, his brows drawn down in confusion. "And how is it you managed to see me from a block away, but I didn't see you?"

He chuckled, but it sounded more like a grunt. "Because I wasn't actually driving. I was parked on the side of the road."

Blah, blah, blah, I was parked on the side of the road; she mimicked in her head. "And you instantly knew it would be me driving the truck?"

"Hey, I might be older but my eyesight is fairly good. So yeah, I knew it was you unless Boyfriend was up to no good." He arched a brow.

Okay, he had a point. Randy told her about all the things he did when he was younger. Granted, it wasn't anything *too* bad, but enough to warrant the intervention of a law officer from time to time.

"I was just curious why you were out so early. And alone."

"Well, for curiosity's sake, because we don't want to kill a cat, allow me to clarify a few things for you. I'm looking for rocks." She held up the boutique bag, adding, "and that is why I'm here today. And since you're so fascinated with my life, then you should know that Boyfriend grew up, so you don't have to worry about him coming out here and breaking the law. Also," she cleared her throat, "I don't need you worrying over me. I'm a big girl and I go into the woods alone all the time." He grinned and she wanted to smack it off his face.

"Good. That's what I like to hear." He glanced around as he stepped closer and whispered, "But do you really think going into the woods alone is a good idea?" He pulled back. "I mean, you never know who could be out there and Hunter's Ridge is a notorious area for hunters, if you get my drift."

She ran the woods plenty of times alone; it was required training to be a scout. So what was his deal? "I do it all the time, you know that. The woods are my second home."

"So I've been told, but that doesn't make it any safer," he said, causing her lips to draw down even more. Since when did he worry about her safety?

"You driving past Randy's house six times in one afternoon don't make me safer either. What the hell were you looking for?" Now she was pissed and was ready to give him a piece of her mind.

"I was looking for you. I wanted to talk to you before I left town."

"And you couldn't just stop and come up to the door like a normal person?"

"You know as well as I that Boyfriend wouldn't allow me to get within fifty feet of you. I have some information I wanted to share with you, something that doesn't pertain to him." Riley turned and walked back to his truck, leaning against the hood. "I'm not saying you can't tell him, I just need to tell you first."

"What could you possibly need to tell me? Did Travis somehow come back from the dead?" She rolled her eyes but didn't think he noticed until he chuckled. "Or does this have to do with the break-in at the store?" She stooped to add a few more rocks to her bag while wishing he would just get into his damn truck and leave. She didn't want anyone to see her talking to him much less, have to explain why. Randy didn't trust Riley, but Tracy never had a problem with the officer until now. *He nearly arrested you.* She stood and glanced over as he shifted on his feet.

"I have something to show you, and then you can decide if you want any others to know or not. It's private, and probably not something you'll brag about, but something you need to see."

Tracy didn't like what he was insinuating and a low growl rose in her chest. "If you think for one minute I had something to do with the break-in, you're crazy. Or maybe you're a chauvinistic pig that hates knowing a female such as me could own my own business. Heaven forbid if I do something for myself without satisfying a male's every whim. Only like-minded males such as Travis think that way."

"I see you've painted a nice picture of me in your mind, but you shouldn't assume you can read my thoughts. I'm nothing like Travis, and you, of all people, should know that by now." He flashed a smirk that made her uneasy.

"Well, if you know anything at all about the Hudson pack, then you'd know that was what they expected. I bet right now every Hudson male is rolling in his grave." She spun on her toes, done with the conversation and with listening to Officer Riley. But before she could take that first step, he shoved her up against the truck and cuffed her hands behind her back. "What the hell are you doing?" She jerked, shoving her shoulder into his chest.

"Calm down. I'm not going to hurt you. I want you to go somewhere with me. We need to talk," he hissed in her ear and spun her around to face him.

"We can talk here," she huffed and looked down at the collection of rocks scattered at her feet. "Look what you made me do!" He ignored her outburst and walked her to the back of the vehicle as she struggled against his unrelenting grasp.

"Keep it down or I'll gag you too," he said as he opened the back hatch. She tried head-butting him, but he was too tall and hitting his chest didn't have the same effect. "I'm not going to hurt you. So stop fighting me."

"You expect me to believe that? And I'm handcuffed? You must really think I'm stupid." She glared, and when the corner of his lips twitched, she spat in his face. She expected him to smack the crap out of her because that's what Travis would have done. Instead, he turned away and pulled a handkerchief from his pocket to wipe his face. When he looked back, she held her breath but there was nothing threatening about his demeanor.

"The cuffs are to keep you from phasing. I need you to remain in human form. So, if you continue to cause trouble, I'll hogtie you and I really don't want to do that." His pleading eyes spoke to her wolf, but Tracy wasn't any pushover.

"Fine, can I at least call Randy and tell him you're arresting me? I assume that's why I'm in cuffs." She had to try even though she knew it wouldn't work. "You know he'll come looking for me if I don't check in with him," she said smugly.

"I expect as much, but that won't be until what, quitting time?"

Damn! He knew her game. She scowled when he pulled her phone from her back pocket and pushed her into the back of the SUV, slamming the door. The windows were tinted black and she could barely see outside. She was certain that alone was against the law. Not that it mattered. He was the law. She listened as he climbed into the driver's seat and started the truck. Unable to see out the windows, he might as well have blindfolded her.

"At least, tell me why you're arresting me."

"I'm not; I'm taking you to the lake."

"Why the hell would I want to go with you to the lake? You know kidnapping is against the law."

"So is breaking and entering," he said over his shoulder.

"I did not break into the store. That's a lie!" she hissed and kicked the window—and a sharp pain shot through her ankle.

"I didn't say you did."

Tracy's teeth hurt from the constant clenching of her jaw as she tried to figure out how she would get out of the truck without killing herself. Then she thought about Randy not trusting Officer Riley—she shouldn't have either. Randy was right, Riley was an ass. She wondered how long it would be before Jesse and Megan raised the red flag and reported her missing? She told them she was taking the afternoon off to gather rocks, so it could be hours before anyone questioned her whereabouts. A sinking feeling settled in her stomach. Even Randy wouldn't know to look for her until five that afternoon.

Tracy braced herself as Riley turned the first corner and rolled slightly to the right. He was heading back to Main Street. Frustrated, she lay flat on her back and closed her eyes, using her body to determine their direction. Another lean right meant they weren't heading to the lake, and it wasn't until they crossed the bridge that she opened her eyes. "You said we were going to the lake." Her voice held a bit of anger and luckily for him, she was handcuffed, or she would have ripped him a new one.

Twenty-Two

Jesse

Jesse stood up from her worktable when flashing lights lit the front window and Officer Brett parked in front of the boutique. But instead of coming into the store, he walked up to the vehicle that was pulled over at the corner. "They sure are cracking down on speeders," she said when Megan walked out of the warehouse.

"Yeah, it would seem so, but with summer coming on, there will be a lot of kids playing in the park so it's better to crack the whip now." Megan walked with Jesse to the front of the store and watched Brett as a smile stretched on her face. "But If I were being pulled over, he'd be the one I'd want writing my ticket."

"Megan!" Jesse couldn't help but giggle. "I know. He can pull me over any day." She rolled her eyes when a low growl sounded in her head. Sending a dirty thought back to Tucker, she suggested he buy handcuffs.

"Tracy, come in here and check out the badge on this guy," Megan yelled over her shoulder, causing Jesse to laugh.

You best be looking at a badge. Jesse laughed again, hearing Tucker's voice in her head. Boy, how she loved her wolf-sight.

"Isn't she back?" Megan looked up at the clock, as did Jesse.

"I don't think she was coming back until later."

"Yeah, but how many rocks could that little bag hold?" Megan questioned as Brett walked back to his truck before driving away.

"Maybe she met up with Randy," Jesse said, knowing that wasn't the case. More than a little concerned, she pulled her phone from her pocket and dialed Tracy's number.

"What is it?" Megan asked, noticing the frown on Jesse's face.

"Tracy's not answering." Jesse held up her phone. "I wasn't supposed to say anything, but someone is watching Tracy."

"What do you mean?" Megan asked.

"Lori had a vision."

"No." Megan held up her hand. "Don't tell me anything more. I know what the visions are, and the less people who know, the better."

"Can you cover here while I walk down to the river? I won't be gone long."

"You have to ask? Go! I'll send Jack that way..." Megan grabbed her purse from behind the counter as Jesse rushed out the door.

The more Jesse thought about how long Tracy had been gone, the more anxious she became. *He watches from a distance.* Her breath caught and she couldn't shake the unease that caused her stomach to twist. She pressed redial, but still no answer.

Standing at the corner, waiting on traffic, Jesse glanced over her shoulder when she heard Randy's motorcycle slide to a stop. He was frantic as he lay down the bike and ran to the door, hollering for Tracy.

"Randy!" Jesse yelled and rushed back to the store. But by the look in his eyes when she approached, she immediately knew Tracy was in trouble.

"Where's Tracy?" He glanced over his shoulder as if expecting Tracy to walk out the door, but instead it was Megan.

"She went looking for rocks at the river. I was on my way there to find her." Jesse's eyes glazed and Randy's voice sounded miles away.

"How long has she been gone?"

"A couple hours or so. Why, what happened?" Megan asked, coming to stand beside them.

"I don't know, she's not answering my calls." He shoved his fingers through his hair.

"She didn't answer mine either," Jesse said, now in full panic mode.

"She's in trouble. I can feel it through the bond." His eyes were wild when he looked between them. "I have to find her."

"Go, I've already called Jack. He'll meet you at the river." Megan turned back to the store as Jesse bolted across the sidewalk.

"Wait, I'm going with you." Jesse jumped on the motorcycle behind Randy, but he didn't seem to care. "The bridge." She pointed straight ahead as if he didn't know where the bridge was located.

"Why would she be at the bridge?" he yelled over the engine noise.

"Because that's where she said to tell you to go." She held onto Randy as he sped down Main Street, her hair whipping in the wind. His panic scared the crap out of her, and considering he wasn't wearing a helmet, he must have been teetering on the edge. Randy was reckless in a lot of ways, but only once had she seen him ride without a helmet. She ducked her head to block the wind and prayed they would get to the bridge in one piece.

Within minutes, they were turning onto a narrow dirt road that followed the riverbank to the underside of the bridge. She pointed again, as if he couldn't see the massive concrete structure when in reality, she was giving Tucker directions through her wolf-sight. She hoped she was mistaken, but she had a feeling they wouldn't like what they found. She could hear a truck blazing up the road and knew it was Tucker.

Jesse's chest ached as Randy pulled beneath the bridge and stopped the bike. She hopped off the back, instantly captivated by the large scenic mural. At first, she thought it was an open field, it seemed so realistic, and then Randy stepped to her side.

"Where is she?" he asked, his eyes searching the overgrown hill leading up to Main Street. His words filled her with dread and she clenched her jaw to keep from throwing up.

"She said she was coming down here. There has to be

something..." Jesse scanned the rocky ground, looking for any sign that Tracy had in fact been there. As she slowly moved further beneath the bridge, dread lodged in her throat when she noticed a small bag that could have only come from the Lucky Leaf Boutique. "She's been here." She pointed and for some strange reason, dropped to her knees to gather the rocks that spilled out of the bag.

"Tracy!" Randy yelled as he took off up the hill where he stopped to scan the area below. "I don't see anything," he shouted down to Jesse. She watched him pace, searching, like a caged animal looking for an escape. He was angry and pissed, but beneath all that, he was terrified.

"Jesse, what the hell is going on?" Tucker's voice surrounded her as he pulled her off the ground. "I'm here. Tell me what happened." He rubbed her eyes, making her blink until she was staring into his.

"Tracy came down here to gather rocks, and now she's missing," Jesse said before collapsing into his arms.

"Start at the beginning and tell me everything." Tucker led her over to the truck to sit down, but she couldn't. She shook her head, still unconvinced Tracy could just disappear in the middle of the day without anyone noticing.

"Tracy took the afternoon off to come down here to look for rocks. Randy showed up at the boutique a few minutes ago saying Tracy was in trouble, something he picked up through the bond. We found the bag and the rocks that Tracy gathered, but she's not here." Jesse glanced down at the bag she was holding in her hand. "He has her, doesn't he?"

"Who is she talking about?" Randy growled, and for a

minute, Jesse forgot he wasn't a wolf. She glanced up at Jack who had followed Randy down the hill.

"Officer Riley." She held her breath when a slew of swear words aimed at the officer, blasted in her ears. "He was at the store this morning and said he was leaving Cloverly."

"Jesse, you can't accuse anyone without proof." The tone of Tucker's voice made her cringe and she scowled. If he didn't like that, he definitely wouldn't like what she said next, but what choice did she have? It was her responsibility to expose Riley, and she would.

"It just seems suspicious that he was here this morning and now he's gone and so is Tracy." She glanced between him and Jack, seeing neither liked her assumption.

"Stop! You don't have evidence to back up what you say. And Randy is in no condition to hear it. You see how he's acting. He's about to lose it." Tucker ran his hand over his jaw as Randy continued to grumble and search for some kind of proof, other than the rocks.

"I know you think the only reason Riley's been watching the store is because of the break-in, and there's probably some truth to that. But at the end of the day, it's not me or Megan he follows home. Now, if that doesn't look suspicious, nothing could. Tracy even admitted Riley was driving past Randy's house, and because she knows nothing about the vision, she assumed he was watching Randy."

"What vision?" Randy asked, coming up behind Jesse, and her face paled.

"Someone is watching Tracy, and Jesse will be the one to expose him. We couldn't tell you or Tracy, though, because doing so would alter the vision," Tucker explained.

"So you would rather she was kidnapped than to watch out for some sick asshole? That's fucking messed up!"

"No. what's messed up is if she found out about the vision and then altered it. She could have ended up like Lori on the side of the highway, only dead." The growl that resonated from Tucker had Jack stepping between him and Randy.

"Back off! He didn't mean it that way. Both of you." It was a direct order from Jack, and being the alpha in Cloverly, they had no choice but to obey.

Tucker turned and walked back over to the bridge, staring out across the water. Tracy was like a sister to him, and Jesse could feel his desperation seeping through their bond.

"Can you feel the bond?" Jack asked, and Randy nodded, pacing a small circle. "Can you sense her emotions and tell what's going on?"

"She's upset, nervous, maybe frustrated," he said, watching Tucker as he bent to pick up something off the ground.

Jesse walked over to Jack and placed her hand on his shoulder while Randy gazed out over the water, his lip trembling. "In the vision, I'm the one that will expose the watcher. Find Officer Riley, and you will find Tracy. Don't ask me how I know, but we're wasting time."

"It's true. We found his knife at the store. He's the one that broke in," Tucker said and Jesse looked back, knowing it was hard for Tucker to admit since he and Riley had become good friends back when Megan was missing. Standing at her side, he felt betrayed and she could see it on his face, but what he handed her was all the proof they needed.

Tears filled Jesse's eyes as she stared down at the circled R, stitched on the corner of the handkerchief. There was no doubt in her mind now and wherever Tracy was, Officer Riley was also there. "This belongs to Officer Riley. It's his pack's emblem."

"Are you sure?" Jack asked, as if suddenly aware that Officer Riley wasn't part of the Cloverly Pack.

Jesse looked up and nodded. "Yeah, he lost his knife at the store and I gave it back to him this morning. I asked him what the R stood for and he said it was his pack's emblem." What Lori assumed was a dream was actually a vision, and that had Jesse worried. Not only was Lori right about the description of the knife, but the smell of river water as well. She swallowed hard, but didn't say anything about that vision, deciding it was best to send it to Tucker through their bond. But apparently, Jack picked up on their communication when he noticed the horrified look on Tucker's face, prompting him into action.

"I'll call Dad and tell him what's going on since he's the one that allowed Riley to stay with the pack. Randy, you call Seth and have him meet us here. Tucker, take Jesse back to the boutique and then swing by and pick up Mason." Jack was quick to bark off orders, sounding like a true alpha.

"It is my vision to reveal, so I'm going with you," Jesse hissed as Tucker hurried her to the truck.

"No, you're not. You've done your part, and we'll take it from here. We don't know what we'll find and I don't want you there if things turn bad." He jumped into the driver's seat and started the truck as she fastened her belt. Squealing tires when he pulled onto Main Street, he caught the attention of Brett, who followed them to the boutique. "Just stay with Megan and let Brett know what's going on."

"Tracy will need someone," Jesse pleaded, but Tucker wasn't budging.

"She'll have Randy, and I'm sure right now he's the only person she wants."

He was right, and Jesse would go crazy waiting. "Fine, but you have to promise to keep me updated. Use the bond," Jesse said, and when Tucker pulled to the side of the road, she quickly jumped out of the truck.

Twenty-Three

Tracy

When the phone rang, Tracy teared up and her thoughts instantly went to Randy. She should have listened to him but she told herself he wasn't a shifter and he didn't understand their world. *That sounds like something Travis would say.* Tears rolled down the side of her face, she was so unwilling to believe she could be like him. *He's human, he's beneath you.* She shook her head, fighting an internal battle. Then another thought entered her mind when the phone rang a second time. *What if Randy assumed she left him again? Would he come looking for her? Or give up on them altogether?* Regardless, the consequences of her past actions were now staring her in the face and she didn't like what she saw.

Tracy peeked out the back window, barely able to see

the sun through the dark tint. It was clear they weren't going to the lake, and the longer they were on the road, the more worried she became. *You deserve everything you get.* That she could agree with. Randy had only ever looked out for her, and she mistakenly presumed she was untouchable.

As her eyes closed, her thoughts went back to the night when Officer Riley responded to the call of a car in a cornfield. *Seeing the blue lights, flashing, she wanted to run but didn't know the area. Her heart thumped madly, wondering how Travis would punish her for tarnishing the family's name. He will kill you! She trembled, expecting a beating once she returned home, and then to be chained in the cellar, something Travis often did when he was in a foul mood.*

With her head resting in her hands, she stared down at her mud-caked shoes as Officer Riley draped a blanket around her shoulders. He never raised his voice, and instead, assured her everything would be okay. "Are you taking me to jail?" she asked, and he said, "No, sweetie, I'm taking you home." She would've preferred jail to the prison she escaped from, but Officer Riley picked up on her uncertainty and again promised her she would be okay.

She could hear Travis ranting as he stomped into the house, once Officer Riley drove away. It seemed odd to her fourteen-year-old mind that a stranger could be concerned about her wellbeing, but apparently, he set Travis straight. "You got lucky. The next time, even he won't be able to save your ass," Travis said, his jaw tight and his fists balled at his sides. Tracy stiffened when he kicked open her bedroom door and shoved her inside.

"Just because he has a badge, doesn't give him the authority to tell us how to discipline the ungrateful brat," Vivian sneered, helping Travis secure the bedroom door with a padlock.

"She'll get hers in due time, for now though, just lay low. He's trouble, and too damn nosy for his own good." So instead of being chained in the cellar, as she expected, she was locked in her bedroom for an entire month.

Jolted from her thoughts as the truck sped up, Tracy knew then they were on the highway, but heading where? She pretended to doze until Riley took a sharp turn, causing her to roll to the opposite side of the vehicle. Hitting her head against the side wall, she winced. Any injury that wasn't too severe would heal quickly, but that didn't prevent it from hurting like hell.

"Would you stop moving around before you hurt yourself?" Irritation laced his words, and she could almost hear his scowl.

"That is the point, isn't it? You hurting me?" He didn't answer, which was frightening in itself. Did that mean he would hurt her? She yanked against the cuffs until her wrist ached—another reminder she needed to think of something quick. She could kick the window out, but with her flimsy running shoes, she would probably injure her ankle again. *If you can't run, you can't escape.* Then the roar of a car sounded behind them and she popped up, hoping to get the attention of the driver, but the car flew past at an ungodly speed.

"It's no use, so settle down. We're almost there."

She twisted around to look out the windshield, not recognizing the area. "Almost where?"

"The lake."

Her eyes widened as panic stole her breath and she thought she would pass out. Maybe that would be best in her situation. If he were going to kill her, or worse, did she want to be awake to see? "Are you going to kill me?" she asked in a whisper, although she knew he would hear.

"No! I'm not going to hurt you. Why would you think that?"

"Why would I not?" She dropped over on her side and figured her best bet was to conserve her energy. As soon as the cuffs came off, the fight would be on. She was tired of always being pushed around by any damn male, and it would stop today. She closed her eyes and allowed her body to relax while talking to Randy through the bond. *I'm so sorry for everything I put you through.*

She had dozed off at least once, maybe twice, by the time the truck slowed to a stop. Completely disoriented, her heart pounded so hard she thought it would crack a rib. Dead from a heart attack would be her luck. But when the driver's door slammed, her panic returned, forcing her mind to clear.

Tracy didn't know where they were once Riley helped her out of the SUV, or what lake the small cabin sat beside. There were no distinguishing signs or smells that her wolf could pick up on. It was still daylight, and she looked at the sky but couldn't see the sun through the thick canopy of overhead branches. "Where are we?" she asked, not expecting an answer.

"Being a scout, I'm surprised you don't recognize the area. We're across the lake from Camp Semiway." He gripped her arm and motioned her forward.

"I've never scouted this side of the river and I've never been to the camp," she sneered.

"I thought all shifters were required to attend summer camp before their first change."

"Yeah, well, I wasn't as privileged as the others, I guess. What time is it?" she asked, hearing her phone ring again as he led her to the cabin and pushed open the door.

She glanced up at the wall clock when he said, "Three-thirty."

Calculating the time factor, she looked around the room, knowing if she could escape and cross the lake before nightfall, she could get home. *But how wide is the lake?*

"So, are you going to remove the bracelets, or are you into bondage?" Angering him probably wouldn't help her cause, but if he had ill intentions, she wanted him to know he would have one hell of a fight on his hands.

"Where do you come up with this stuff? I've already told you, I'm not going to kill you or hurt you, and I'm definitely not going to take advantage of you. That's not why I brought you here. Now, please, sit down at the table. I have something to show you."

Again, the charade of wanting to show her something, but reluctantly she did as he asked and took a seat, resting her forehead on the table. Her arms ached from being bound behind her back and her frickin' hands were numb. *I need help!* She sent through the bond, praying it was Randy that kept calling her and knew she was missing. *Help me!* She screamed in her head. It was probably useless, but she had to try.

Her bond with Randy was the one thing she had that Officer Riley knew nothing about. Tears welled in her eyes and her body quivered. Could she trust that he wouldn't kill her? Did he hate Randy so much that he would take it out on her? She exhaled a hiccupped breath and pleaded once more through the bond as her phone rang for the umpteenth time.

Exhausted and annoyed, thinking Officer Riley had it out for her, Tracy couldn't think of anything she'd done to warrant any trouble from him. He was part of the Kinsley Pack, a newcomer to the area about five years ago. She wasn't sure where he came from originally, but having law enforcement training, Alpha Cooper was quick to station him in Cloverly. With her eyes closed, she listened as Riley moved about the room, wondering how long he planned to keep her there as his prisoner.

"My name is Trace Riley," he said, and she lifted her head off the table and blinked to clear her eyes. "I never intended to stay in Cloverly as long as I have but without proof, I had no choice."

She scowled and turned to look out the small window atop the sink. The kitchen was the bare minimum with an apartment-sized stove and a small refrigerator. The stainless steel sink looked out of place, as did the dishwasher tucked away in the corner of the room. The upper cabinets were nothing more than shelves, holding everything from glassware to pots and pans. It was definitely a cabin for campers and offered very little in the way of creature comforts. "You always have choices," she finally said.

"Not always," he countered and continued. "When Travis died, no one wanted to dispose of his things, so I told Alpha Cooper I would take care of it. It was the break I'd been waiting for; it just took nineteen years to get it." He placed a manila folder on the table in front of her and she frowned. "I've already overstayed my welcome." He ignored her grunt. "My father is getting up in years, and I've delayed my duties to the pack long enough."

"And that's supposed to matter to me?" It came out a bit rude, but she was still wearing the cuffs and her wrists were starting to swell. She cocked her head to the side and bit back the curse word that came to mind.

"Yes. I'm the alpha of the Red River Pack in Montana and you are my daughter."

Her eyes narrowed as she shook her head. He couldn't be her father because her father was dead. "No." She wouldn't believe the lie. "I don't believe you! My father died trying to save my mother. The house was on fire and it collapsed on them. I saw it with my own eyes."

Officer Riley glowered and his jaw clenched. "Where were you when the house caught fire?"

"I was hiding. My mother was trying to get me out from beneath the bed, but I was too scared." She lowered her eyes to conceal her shame. Had she not hidden, her parents might still be alive.

"And your dad?"

"It's really none of your business," she hissed, thinking maybe she was wrong and he targeted her because he didn't like her dad, a Hudson male, who was known to have plenty of enemies.

"And your dad?" he repeated, his glare making her uneasy.

"He took off with my mother, okay? I tried to follow them, but I was afraid to go into the living room." She looked away, fighting back tears. "I ran into the kitchen and out the back door before the fire consumed the house and took it down."

"So your father left you behind in a burning house,

but tried to rescue your mother?" The low rumble that filled the room made her quiver. "He was there to save your mother, not you. He was willing to let you die because he knew you belonged to me." His fist slammed down on the table, startling Tracy. "I knew I should have killed him when I had the chance." He glanced across the table and his eyes softened. "I'm sorry for what you went through with the Hudson Pack, and I know this is a shock, but just look at the evidence and then decide for yourself. I'm not here to pressure you, but even your name suggests your mother knew I was your father."

She mulled that over while he opened the folder and pulled out a picture of her mother and him from their teenage years. He was smiling for the camera and her mother was kissing his cheek. They looked happy, but it couldn't be. Her mother had a bond with her father.

"I'm not sure how much you know about your mother, but she was born in Montana. We dated in high school, and although we didn't share a bond, we were in love. It was a remote area and rarely did anyone in the pack find their true mates. So with the pack dwindling, the alpha opened the bonding ceremony to couples that wanted to be together, knowing if a wolf's true bond mate showed up, the relationship would end immediately."

"So what you're saying is you and my mom shacked up and then she met my dad," Tracy sneered, but she wasn't expecting to see the hurt in his eyes.

"Not exactly the words I would use, but yes, we had a bonding ceremony and we planned to raise a family together."

"Then what happened?" She wasn't sure she bought his story, but she couldn't take her eyes from the picture, or her mother's smiling face. She was radiant, and her face glowed when she looked up at Trace. His dark hair touched his collar and the scruff on his jaw—she realized he reminded her of Randy. She studied the picture—his green eyes matched hers. He was a looker back then, and if she were being honest, he was a looker now. Her eyes scanned over the photos he laid out in front of her. All were pictures of him and her mom with a pack she didn't recognize. She never knew where her mother was born, but he had a copy of her birth certificate as well. "So, my grandparents, my mother's family, are they still..." She couldn't bring herself to finish the question but she desperately wanted the answer. If what he was saying was true, she had a family that was still alive.

"Yes. Both of her parents are alive, as are her three sisters, and a brother. I know you thought you lost your family, but that's not true. Owen and a few of the Hudson Pack were passing through our area. They weren't any threat to us, so my father allowed them to stay for a few days until the weather cleared and they could move on. Your mom was sick with what she thought was a stomach bug and had missed work that day. It wasn't until the second day when Owen stopped in at the diner that he ran into your mother. Their bond was instant, but when he found out about me, he blew up. He swore I would never see Rebecca again and they left that afternoon for Kentucky. He didn't care if she were sick; he only wanted to get her as far away from me as possible. I was devastated, but knew your mother only went with him out of fear. She didn't want me to fight for her because the law wouldn't be on my side. She was his true mate, and I had no choice but to step aside."

"She could have denied the bond." Tracy lifted a brow, waiting for him to explain that away.

"She could have, and maybe she did, but I never saw her after that day and I assume Owen threatened my life to keep her with him."

"But you really didn't step aside. You followed her."

"When I found out where they were, yes. I wanted to beg her to come back, to break the bond, but once word got out that I was in the territory, Owen and five of his friends came after me. They caught up with me in Wyoming, and after a vicious battle, they tied me up and Owen buried my knife deep in my chest."

"But your wolf could have healed the wound."

"True, but only after the knife was removed. They bound my feet and I couldn't phase. So leaving me beside the river, they expected no one would find me until the buzzards circled. But they also didn't know the area, or the Indian Reservation on the opposite side of the river. It was a medicine man that found my wolf. I kept the knife and hoped one day I'd cross paths with Owen again. It wasn't until after the pack split that I got word there was a new alpha. I came down here as soon as I could, but it was too late."

"So why did you stay? If you knew Mom was gone?" Tracy shifted on the chair and arched her back to relieve the pressure between her shoulder blades.

"I didn't at first. I went back home with my tail between my legs. It destroyed me. I was angry and depressed and didn't care if I lived or died. Your mother was my world. Then about three years later, I found my mate. I met her in a roadside diner, the same way Owen met your mother. I realized then what it meant to have a bond. I still loved your mother, though, and would have spent the rest of my life with her, but it just wasn't meant to be.

"It was my Julie that suggested I come back to Cloverly after our son was born. She mysteriously came down with the same stomach bug your mother had, only it happened days later after the doctor told her she was pregnant. I didn't want to believe I fathered a child with Rebecca after all the years that passed. But as time went on, the need to know nearly drove me mad. My wolf should have been content with the family I'd started with my bond mate, but it was always on edge, and the only way to appease it was to be in Cloverly. It was searching for you."

"So you just walked away from your family? What kind of father would do that?" She had him there and noticed the tears well up in his eyes.

"The kind that was desperately searching for his daughter. And despite what you think about me, my family visited me here. Why do you think I live so far away from the rest of the pack? It was to keep them safe and away from prying eyes."

"Maybe so, but I find it hard to believe Alpha Cooper didn't know." She pursed her lips but held back the eye roll.

"He knew, but he thought I was going through a tough time with my pack, so he allowed my immediate family to visit, hoping someday I would eventually go back and take my place where I belonged."

That bit of information wasn't surprising to Tracy. Of course Alpha Cooper knew, just like he knew about Iretta. She wanted to snarl but thought better of it. "So how did you figure out who I was?"

"When I came across your birth certificate. I always thought you looked like your mother, but Travis and Vivian claimed to be your parents. I couldn't argue the point and since he had your hair color and I had no proof..."

"And the birth certificate?"

"Travis hid it under a rug in his closet. Had I not volunteered to clean out his cabin, I never would've found it. There's no way Owen could be your father. He hadn't known your mother long enough. She was three months pregnant when she left Montana. Either Rebecca didn't know, or she didn't want me to know. I would've fought to keep her with me had I known."

Tracy dropped her head back to the table and squeezed her eyes tight. "The pictures are convincing, even the birth certificate, but... I don't know. It's just too much."

"I broke into the store. I've been watching you," he said and she lifted her head, shocked by his confession. "I needed proof, and I made it look like a break-in to avoid suspicion."

"So you dumped the trashcan? That was brilliant." She actually rolled her eyes when he chuckled.

"No, I was looking in the trashcan for a sample of your DNA."

"And you found that in the trash?"

"Yeah, but first I had to figure out which cup was yours."

"Right. It was that simple to know which cup was mine. Did it have lipstick on the rim?" She simpered sweetly, her smart-ass attitude peaking.

"I took all the cups I could find and sent them to the lab back home. There were only three that belonged to wolves. One was a new-blood, one a half-blood and one a pureblood."

Her pulse raced and her vision blurred as she shook off the dizziness and tried to calm her now restless wolf. It was true. She was the only pureblood at the store.

"Here's a copy of the DNA report. You are my daughter." Trace walked around the table and stooped down to unfasten the cuffs. "I didn't mean to scare you. I just had to let you know." He shoved his hands through his hair as he stood and moved back to the opposite side of the table. "You're free to go whenever you like. I can give you a ride back or you can call someone." He pulled Tracy's phone from his back pocket and placed it on the table.

Tracy stared at the phone and sat back in the chair. She wanted to snatch it up and call anyone that could help, but deep down, she wanted to believe Trace more. She swallowed hard and looked back at the photos while rubbing her wrist. "Did he beat her?" Her voice cracked as he pulled out a chair and set down across from her.

"I hate to think that, but I don't know for sure," Trace said, taking a seat. He picked up a picture of him and Rebecca, and judging from the way his eyes misted, he still cared for her.

"I think he did. I've been having dreams."

"That would explain why Rebecca attempted to escape, but apparently Owen caught her and moved her into the alpha house. She basically became his prisoner. Her sister tried to talk them into letting her visit, but your mother was afraid and ended all contact with Jessica."

"She went through hell because of me." Tears filled Tracy's eyes and she lowered her head. "I've seen it in my dreams."

"No! She endured whatever she had to in order to keep you safe. She loved you more than life." Trace pulled out a hand-written letter addressed to Jessica. "She wrote Jessica once a month until she was moved to the alpha's house."

"So, you really are my dad."

It wasn't a question, but he still answered with a "Yes."

She lay against the table, unable to blink away the tears in her eyes. "I think I'm going to pass out."

"You're in shock. You should probably lie down and I'll fix you something warm to drink." Trace helped her into the living room onto the sofa. He covered her with a thick quilt, but even then, Tracy couldn't keep the shivers from assaulting her body—although she wasn't cold. Her mind tried to work through the details of her mother's life, but all she could hear was Trace saying, "You're my daughter."

"Trace?" Tracy said as he walked back toward the kitchen. He stopped and glanced down to where she was curled beneath the blanket. "You said you had to find me because your wolf was on edge. Is it still?" Another tear slipped from her eye and she wiped it away.

"No. My wolf is overjoyed."

"Mine is too." She closed her eyes as more hot tears rolled down her cheeks.

Twenty-Four

Tracy

Tracy wasn't sure how long she slept, but when she awoke, Trace had supper waiting on the stove. The open floor plan allowed her to watch him moving about the small kitchen, the sweet smell of savory chicken filling the air. She sniffed, causing her stomach to rumble. She hadn't eaten since breakfast and now she was starved.

Focusing back on Trace... he was tall, probably where she got her height, and broad, reminding her of Tucker and Hayden. She could see why her mom was attracted to him but was she really named after him? That was probably a question she'd never know the true answer to. She smiled sadly, thinking *what if?* It would mean she had a grandmother and grandfather. Aunts and uncles, and possibly, cousins. Then her heart stalled and she choked on a breath. *I have a brother.*

"Are you okay? I hope I didn't wake you," Trace said, removing a pan from the oven. "You were upset. I thought it would do you good to sleep it off and then if you wanted..." He placed the pan on the table and walked over to where she was still lying on the sofa and stooped down, pushing the hair out of her face. "I guess I handled this badly, but I was running out of time. I should have told Alpha Cooper and let him tell you. Then if you wanted to meet me... I know you don't know me that well, and I understand why you wouldn't trust me. I just... I needed for you to know you have a family that loves you." He rubbed her hair and suddenly, Tracy became that five-year-old little girl again.

She closed her eyes, imagining what it would have been like to have him tuck her in at night. His kind gesture and understanding eyes; could she believe he was telling the truth? She tried to think back when she was smaller, when her mother and Owen were alive. She had very few memories she could recall, but none of them suggested Owen wasn't her dad. *He abandoned you when you needed him the most.* Flames filled her memory, and she opened her eyes, her heart racing at the thought.

"You look like your mother, but you have my eyes." Trace cocked his head as if he were seeing her for the first time. He took hold of her hands, rubbing her wrist, the red ring still visible from the cuffs. "I'm sorry for cuffing you, but you have to know I've been trying to prove you were mine for the past five years. I would have cuffed the alpha if necessary." He stood and offered a small smile before leaning down and kissing the side of her head.

The love she felt when he was near almost stole her

breath. It was too much, and yet not enough. Her heart ached and she wanted to run away and hide from her crazy, screwed-up life. But at the same time, she wanted to hear him call her his daughter again. She always dreamed of what it was like to have a family, and he was offering her one. "What time is it?" Randy would be pissed if she didn't call him. She glanced up at the wall clock to see it was just past five.

"I silenced your phone so it wouldn't wake you. I wanted to spend a little more time with you before I have to give you up. I don't want to lose you, but I have a pack that depends on me." He looked away but not before she noticed his glassy eyes.

"Can I come with you?" She sat up as he turned and dropped to one knee, his hand gently cupping her face. "To meet my family." That would be the best proof she could think of, to actually meet and see for herself if he spoke the truth. But before he could answer, the front door bounced off the wall and Trace jumped to his feet and backed away, his hands held high in the air.

Fear flashed in her eyes and she turned as the busted door settled against the wall, hanging from one hinge. Randy stormed the room, followed by Tucker and Jack before Alpha Cooper's frame filled the doorway. "No!" she screamed as chaos erupted and a bone-crunching sound echoed in the room. Her entire body trembled, knowing Randy just punched Trace in the face. Blood gushed from his nose and Trace stumbled back against the wall, but he never lifted a hand to defend himself. Instead, he looked over at Tracy and winked, then smiled as another well-aimed punch doubled him over.

"Randy, stop!" Tracy screamed, again, tripping over

the blanket as she rushed across the room to wedge her body between them. "It's not what you think." Why was that always the first thing people said, which usually meant it was exactly what they thought?

"Get out of the way, Tracy." It was a direct order and one she would normally obey, but instead, her wolf growled a low warning. Tracy trusted her wolf's judgment as much as she didn't want to defy Randy. But he didn't understand the situation, and her wolf recognized Trace for who he was.

"Stop! Let me go!" Kicking when Tucker lifted her out of the line of fire, she grabbed hold of Randy's shirt and yelled, "He's my dad!" She pushed away from Tucker when he placed her on her feet and threw out her hands defensively as Jack caught Randy's fist in the air. Randy fell back against Tucker, who landed on Jack, who scowled when Alpha Cooper stepped to the side and grinned.

"I see you finally found what you were searching for." Everyone turned to Alpha Cooper like he had lost his mind and stared down at Tracy, their collective shock etched on their faces.

But what troubled Tracy most was the utter devastation she saw on Randy's face as he ran his fingers through his hair. She glanced back at Trace, instantly feeling a connection to him. He was home. He was family. He was her dad. She laid her hand on his shoulder and he wrapped his fingers around hers—she never wanted him to leave her again.

"You don't honestly believe him, do you?" Randy cursed below his breath when she nodded, causing everyone to grin when Trace flinched. Randy was pissed, actually more like frightened, and when he got that way, his mouth knew no bounds. "How long have you known?" The question came out harsh, demanding, and she wasn't sure if he were angry at her or Trace. She wasn't even sure to whom the question was addressed, but they both answered.

"I found out today," Tracy said.

"Confirmed yesterday," Trace said.

"So you find out she's your daughter and then you kidnap her?" Tracy could see the rage building in Randy's eyes when he added, "I thought you were going to kill her!"

"I had no choice. You weren't about to let me get close to her." Trace pushed to a sitting position and Tracy scooted to his side, protectively. "I have proof if that's what you need."

Randy grabbed Tracy's arm and pulled her off the floor and across the room, again, cussing below his breath. Confused and pissed, he led her out the door, not bothering to see the proof Trace offered. He buried his face in her hair as his arms wrapped around her waist, crushing her against his chest. His hold was tight, and she thought he would crack her ribs, but when his body jerked with silent sobs, her heart broke. He clung to her no matter what she put him through, and it was time she put him first in her life. "I honestly thought he would kill you."

Tracy wrapped her arms around his waist, tears now streaming down her face. "I know. I feared I would never see you again when he first took me. I tried to connect with you through our bond."

"I felt your fear, which is what frightened me the

most. My whole world was gone in a flash and I didn't know what to do." He took a seat on the edge of the porch and pulled Tracy down in his lap. "It was Jesse who told us you were with Officer Riley." His body quivered and again, he buried his face in her hair. "Lori had a vision about you and Jesse. That's why Jesse went to Tennessee."

"I'm sorry. I didn't know, but it's over now. I'm here and we're together." She peppered kisses along his jaw, hoping he would kiss her in return. She didn't have to wait long. Just feeling his lips on hers, her body relaxed and her wolf rumbled contentedly. "I don't condone what Trace did, but I understand *why* he did it. You said so yourself, he couldn't be trusted, and you didn't like him."

"It's not that I don't like him, he just has a shitty way of doing things." Randy looked back at the door where Mason and Seth were standing. "Is he really your dad?"

"He is." She nodded.

"Are you happy about it?"

She nodded again.

"Then I'm glad he found you." Randy ran his hand over the scruff of his jaw and she fought the urge to do the same. "Talk about a good first impression."

"Yeah, that will be a story to tell our little ones someday." Tracy grinned when he kissed the tip of her nose.

"I like the sound of that."

She snuggled closer, breathing in his scent. He was the best thing that ever happened to her, and now he was there sharing one of the best days of her life.

"Come on, guys. I think this is a family issue that needs to be worked out in private," Alpha Cooper said, leading the others out to the yard. "Randy, here's the key to my truck when you're ready to leave."

It shocked Tracy to see Alpha Cooper handing over the keys to his truck, and even more so when Trace invited Randy to stay for supper. Randy was hesitant at first but finally got up and followed Tracy inside. "Do you trust him?"

"Yeah, I think I do."

Twenty-Five

Tracy

Spending the evening with two males that despised each other was awkward. Sitting at the small kitchen table, Trace kept eyeing Randy, and Randy kept glowering at everything that caught his eye. Even the poor coffeepot couldn't escape his death glare. Tracy tried not to laugh because Randy was trying not to be an ass, but it was obvious he was extremely uncomfortable.

"So, Trace, since we're getting acquainted, did you know Randy was my bond mate?" Tracy asked and Randy glanced up.

"Yeah, I've known for years," Trace said matter-of-factly and Randy grunted, refusing to look his way.

"That's not possible. We just met last year," Tracy said and Randy smirked.

"No, you crossed paths five years ago when Travis flagged me down at the station. I was taking knucklehead here home after he TP'd the mayor's house." Trace chuckled at Randy's scowl.

"But I was only ever at the station..." Her words trailed off and she glanced over at Randy. "You were in the patrol car. I remember you peering out the back window."

"That was you?" Randy tilted his head while studying her face. "It was your eyes. I've always loved green eyes."

"Yeah, well, those green eyes almost got you killed," Trace said, and Randy shot a glare across the table. "Travis also noticed her eyes, and I promise, he wasn't happy. He never experienced a bond himself so it was easy to convince him what he saw was nothing more than a trick of the light. The Hudson males were ruthless and would take out anyone they deemed a threat. And he damn sure considered you a threat."

"But he had a bond with Vivian," Tracy said and for the first time, she realized just how close she came to losing Randy.

"No, Vivian wasn't his bond mate. They were only together out of necessity. I found that out one night when she approached me down by the river. Apparently, Travis was so enthused about training his daughter, Vivian wasn't given the attention she craved. Hearing that, I knew she wasn't your mother, and that got me to thinking maybe you weren't Travis's daughter, either. After talking to a few of the pack males, they warned me to stay as far away from her as possible. I heard all about her and the Hudson males. She wasn't a picky female."

"So you and Viv?" Tracy wrinkled her nose and made

a gagging sound.

"No. Definitely not. I kept my distance but from time to time she would approach me with some sob story. I learned a lot about Travis from her, which was why I was constantly watching Randy. Travis already had his suspicions and Randy was notorious for finding trouble."

"It was harmless fun. It was only trouble when you came into the picture," Randy argued.

"And I only came into the picture when I felt there was a direct threat to you. Putting you in the back of my car kept you safe because no one questioned my authority. And that stunt of putting sugar in that boy's gas tank almost did you in, but my eyesight was better than his. When he dropped his keys in the console of his Jeep, it was the break you needed. I gave him a choice that night, to keep his mouth shut or I'd have his ass for keying your bike."

"How did you know? I never told anyone other than Tracy." Randy looked over at Tracy and she shrugged.

"His console was full of paint chips."

"So the night you followed me home and didn't tell my parents about me spiking the gas tank..." Randy looked over at Trace as everything fell into place. "All these years, I thought you were being a dick, but you really weren't."

"No, I was trying to keep you out of trouble because you wouldn't be much good to Tracy in jail."

"Then you've been looking out for me since you came to Cloverly?" Tracy asked, surprised.

"That's what families are for. We look out for each other as best we can." Trace shrugged and looked over at Randy. "And just between us, you went easy on that boy for keying your bike."

Randy grinned, an honest to goodness full-faced grin and reached his hand across the table to Trace. Seeing them shake hands, Tracy leaned back in her chair, silently clapping as tears filled her eyes. At that moment, two things happened. Randy and Trace's relationship moved to a more mature level, which unfolded before her eyes, and love bloomed in her heart for the two most important males in her life.

As the evening wound down, Tracy dreaded leaving Trace. After finding out he was her father, she wasn't ready to let him go. There were so many questions and things she wanted to know, especially about her little brother, but she was running out of time. She glanced over at Trace who smiled back at her. He was thinking the same thing she was if his glassy eyes were any indication. She looked back at Randy and squeezed his hand. What she was about to say would not only shock him but maybe even piss him off. They shared a bond, and she wanted to keep it that way, but she also had a family that she needed to know as well. She quickly blinked her eyes, fighting back a new batch of tears. It was the hardest thing she would ever do, but she had to do it.

"Randy, can I talk to you in private?" Tracy got up from the table and led Randy out the front door and around the cabin to the lake. Taking a seat on the dock, she glanced up at the stars, sending a prayer to the heavens.

"What's bothering you?" Randy asked as he sat down beside her. She turned and although it was pitch-black outside, she could still see the concern in his eyes. He was so handsome, and everything about him drew her in.

Remembering the day he accepted her bond, she hoped now he wouldn't walk away.

"I've decided to go with Trace to Montana." She held her breath, expecting to see the hurt in his eyes.

"For good? What about our bond? What about me?" His voice cracked as he pulled her chin up to see her eyes.

"No, I love you! I just want to meet my family. I won't be there long." Her pleading eyes couldn't remove the frown on his face. "Please understand. I have to do this for me. I have a family and yet, I can't imagine what they're like. I need to meet them to know they're real."

"Do you? I mean, you just found out today and now you want to go cross-country to meet people you don't know? What if he's lying?" Randy tightened his grip on her hand and then pulled her into his lap.

"You saw the proof. He's not. He's my father. That's why my wolf defended him. He's pack. Family."

"And I'm not? We share a bond!" His voice rose and Tracy scowled.

"You are my world, and without you, I wouldn't be here today. Our bond will always be there but my family may not. I love you more than life itself, but you know how I feel about family. I've always wanted what you had." She turned away so he wouldn't see the tears in her eyes. It seemed like she was doing a lot of that lately, and she wasn't a weak female.

"You're my family and my family is yours. You were fine with that until now. How can you forget everything we've been through?" He moved her off his lap and stood, staring out at the water. "What about our ceremony? It's only a week away."

"I know." She looked down at the water, thinking she

should have just kept her mouth shut. *No,* she shouldn't have and if it were him, he wouldn't either. She got to her feet and took hold of his arm. "If you were in my situation, you would go to Montana. You know you would. Family is the most important thing to you. Can't you at least give me that?" She closed her eyes as her head dropped down, the tension growing thick between them. If the situation were reversed, he would damn sure go to Montana and not think twice about it.

"That's a full day's trip, driving nonstop, one way. Can't you at least postpone it until after our bonding ceremony? We've waited such a long time." It frustrated him, based on the way his brow creased.

"I know, but it's nowhere near as long as I've dreamed of having a family and it won't kill us to wait another month. We originally planned an April ceremony, so why can't we go back to that date? I have to do this. My family is there. I want to meet the pack that I belong to. If you were a wolf, you would understand." She knew it was a cheap shot, but dammit, he had to see it from her point of view. "It wasn't right that they took me away from a pack that would have fully accepted me from the moment I was born, instead of being raised by a pack that despised everything about me. I need to know I have a place in this world. That I have roots."

"Your place is with me," he growled, holding her gaze.

"And I will be with you as soon as I get back, but this is something I have to do for me. I'm sorry if you don't understand, and I hope you can see I'm not trying to hurt us, but I have to do this."

Randy huffed out a breath, his shoulders dropping in defeat. "So your need to talk wasn't actually you wanting to talk, but to tell me you were postponing our ceremony. Just like that, you've made a decision that involves us both, and I'm supposed to be okay with it? I didn't realize that was how the bond works. You have the right to do as you please while I sit home being the perfect bond mate. Hell, if I even look at someone the wrong way, you question my motives." He held up his hand to stop her from speaking. "I'm not okay with this. You and our bond have become the center of my life. Everything I've done this past year has all been for nothing. I don't even know who you are anymore."

Tracy winced at hearing his harsh words as a stabbing pain burned in her chest. How had she gone from being happy to experiencing the worst day of her life? She shouldn't have to choose between her mate and her family, but isn't that what Randy was forcing her to do? "You can come with me. I'm sure they would love to meet you." It was all the argument she had and she hoped he would agree.

"You know I can't. I have responsibilities." With the shake of his head, he turned and headed to the cabin without looking back.

"Randy, wait." She ran to catch up, trailing behind him. "Please don't do this. You can go with me; we can have a bonding ceremony there. I'm the daughter of an alpha. That's huge."

"No!" He spun around, catching her before she slammed into him. "I've already told you where I stand. If you go, you go without me." He stared into her eyes as a tear slipped free. "You're going, aren't you?"

She nodded as another tear rolled down her cheek. "I have to do this for me. For my wolf." She squeezed her eyes shut when he pulled her into his arms—despair slipping through the bond. She wanted to say something to ease his mind, but as her heart shattered into a million pieces, he released her and walked away.

Twenty-Six

Randy

It was devastating to think Tracy could up and leave without a second thought, especially with their bonding ceremony planned for the following weekend. But seeing the hurt in her eyes when he stormed off, leaving her at the cabin, Randy couldn't blame her if she was reconsidering their bond.

It was a simple request, to meet her family, and he all but blew up. He was an inconsiderate asshole, but she had to know he would sacrifice his entire world to give her the family she wanted. Now, with Trace in the picture, she didn't need him or his family. He hopped on his bike and headed into Cloverly, hoping to clear his mind before facing off with Jesse and Megan. He had explained the situation to Alpha Cooper when he returned his truck last night, but he didn't think the girls would be as forgiving of his actions. He dreaded that more than anything, and pulling up in front of the boutique that morning, he could see they were already inside, waiting.

Randy parked his bike in front of the store and walked up to the door where Jesse met him with a frown on her face. "I heard and I'm sorry," she said as he entered the building. She reached back to lock the door as he glanced up at the clock; it was eight-forty.

"I don't know when she'll be back." He glanced over at Lori's Lingerie, remembering the day he handed Tracy the key. *She was happy.*

"But what about the ceremony?" Megan asked, walking over to join them. She handed Randy a cup of coffee and gestured for him to sit on the sofa.

"She suggested having it next month." He sat down and placed the coffee on the table. His nerves were shot and the last thing he needed was caffeine.

"Why? That makes little sense." Jesse's narrowed brow said she was onboard with his thoughts. He appreciated that.

"Because our initial date was in April, and right now, she wants to meet her pack. The pack that would have accepted her from the moment she was born. I understand why she wanted to go. I just wish she had waited until after the ceremony."

"I agree. I think she should have waited, but..." Jesse shook her head and briefly squeezed her eyes shut. "No, I don't agree. I would love to see things your way, but I'm guilty of doing the same thing as she. I left here for Tennessee because I wanted to meet Tucker's family. I wanted what he had, a large family. I wasn't there ten minutes before asking Alpha Wilson to perform our bonding ceremony that night. It wasn't anything against the Cloverly Pack. By default, I was a member here, but I had to know they would accept me there. I think that's what Tracy is going through. She's a member here, but she also needs to belong to her family's pack too." Jesse flopped down on the sofa next to Megan. "I know you can't see it right now, but once you consummate your bond, you'll understand her need. They cheated her out of her family, something she had no control over. And if her mother had only told Officer Riley the truth, she wouldn't have had to endure all the hell Travis dished out. She needs this to make her whole and to be the mate you deserve."

Randy dropped his head in his hands, unwilling to hear about her damn pack or what he deserved.

"Randy," Megan said as she slid off the sofa to sit on the floor in front of him. "Give her this. If you want to strengthen your bond, you need to support her." She gripped onto his hands, pulling them from his face. "I know it's hard thinking she walked away from you, but she didn't. I know she didn't. I went through the same thing she's going through. The pack that destroyed her life also destroyed mine. I lost my parents in the cruelest way. I watched the Hudson males kill my father. And I don't even want to think about what they did to my mother. They were a savage bunch, and if Owen Hudson knew Tracy wasn't his, I can only imagine the life she would have been subjected to had he not died. She doesn't realize it yet, and she won't until she's with a family that loves her, but she really dodged a bullet on that one. Unlike me, she still has a father that loves her. All I have are the awful memories of my father's tortured death."

For the first time in his life, Randy saw Megan differently. He always liked her, even dated her a time or two, but there was never anything between them that went beyond good friends. He trusted her, and would often visit her late at night when she was sitting out by the pool. He liked talking to her. It felt like one of those talks right then, minus the pool.

He looked up and glimpsed the sincere concern in her green eyes. He always loved her green eyes, and now he knew it was because of seeing Tracy's at the station. He shuddered as warmth traveled through his body. "What would you do?" He didn't know how many times he sought her advice, but not once over the years did she ever steer him wrong.

"Wait for her. She needs her family to make her whole, and when she returns, she'll need you to complete her. It's not about loving you or her family more or less. It's about being accepted for just being the person you are, a family member. She's trying to find her place in the world, to prove to herself she can and will overcome any hardship that was inflicted upon her years ago. She has to feel whole before she can see that she's fully capable of standing on her own two feet and proudly stand at your side. Please, just give her more time." Megan rose to her knees and kissed his cheek before pulling him into a hug. "You know, all I've ever wanted was to see you happy."

Randy draped his arms around the voice of reason, and as hard as he fought it, he finally cried against her shoulder. Megan was his friend, even more than Iretta. He loved her like a sister and he believed she only wanted the best for him. Needless to say, his sissy boy crying started her tears flowing and by nine o'clock, the three of them were a blubbering mess.

To salvage the morning, Randy offered to help at the store and ended up staying all day. He wanted to know what it felt like to walk in Tracy's shoes, and boy, did he learn a few things! Greeting the ladies as they strolled about the boutique, he expected the bike parked outside to bring in extra customers, and he was so right. He dressed that morning to reflect his attitude, wearing frayed jeans, a black tee, and a black leather jacket. His earring in place and the scruff on his face proof he hadn't shaved in several days gave him a sexy vibe, according to Jesse. He had to believe her, considering pretty much every girl that entered the building flocked to Lori's Lingerie. Yeah, it was crazy to think he could sell women's underwear, but there he was, doing just that.

"If I hadn't seen it with my own eyes, I'd never have believed it," Seth said as he walked into the boutique. "Mallory told me the talk around town, and boy, have you stirred up the ladies!" He glanced over at Jesse and winked. "Have you ever thought about being a male escort? I hear they bring in the cash, especially with older women." Seth waggled his brows, and Randy rolled his eyes.

"You're just jealous because I'm getting all the attention, and you're not man enough to stand here in the middle of women's sexy underwear."

The smirk on Randy's face made Seth laugh right before he hit below the belt. "So this is what happens when your bond mate stands you up? You instantly fall into her shoes?"

Randy knew Seth was teasing, but some things should never be ragged on, and his relationship with Tracy was one of those things. "You know, I like you Seth, but you really should learn to mind your own business and leave the bonding issues to those of us that actually have bonds."

The look that crossed Seth's face said he didn't like Randy calling him out, but if they were his pack, he had just as much right as Seth did. What came next, to Randy's surprise, was a deep chuckle from Seth as he replied, "I bet I can sell more underwear than you."

The boutique did significantly more business that day. Enough to extend the hours to accommodate all the women who came in after work. That was owing to the gossip mill, aka, Mallory at the café. She successfully spread the word that sexy-ass men were selling lingerie at the boutique. Not only did Randy turn a huge profit for Tracy, but he also received a few marriage proposals, which he quickly directed Seth's way. Seth was in seventh heaven, of course, but hey, it was Randy's way of helping out a fellow pack member.

"Well, I think that was the last customer," Randy said and quickly shut off the front lights before anyone else could enter the store. It was seven-thirty and his feet were killing him. He couldn't imagine what it felt like to stand on three-inch heels all day and would make a point of massaging Tracy's feet more often if she came back and gave him the chance. His mind drifted and he sighed.

The drive to Montana would be exhausting, but he prayed when Tracy got there, she would finally have the family she truly deserved. He should have gone with her, but hindsight was brutally honest and crystal clear. He was stupid to assume his refusal to go meant she wouldn't go either. He wanted her to know her family, but feared she would choose them over him. Only time would tell.

"Since you did so well today, are you coming back tomorrow?" Megan asked, gathering her things out from beneath the counter.

"No, I think my underwear selling days are over." He laughed and pulled Megan to his side, her arm wrapping his waist as they walked out the door.

"Thanks for spending the day with us. It's been too long." She looked up, and he nodded.

"Need a ride home?"

"You have to ask?" She poked his side and took the helmet from his hand.

"Considering who your old man is, yeah, we should probably ask," he teased as he mounted the bike and turned the key.

"Whatever. I've already called and told him I had a ride. He said to take the gravel road slowly," she yelled over the engine noise as she settled in behind Randy, holding tight to his jacket.

With plans to drop Megan off and then head home to an empty house, the last thing Randy expected was for Jack and Mason to be waiting for them on the porch.

"Whitney just put supper on the table. There's plenty if you want to join us," Jack offered, walking out to meet them.

"And Whitney's a great cook." Megan removed her helmet, and stepped back for Randy to get off the bike.

"Guess it couldn't hurt." He wasn't really hungry, more depressed, but if he intended to become part of the pack, he needed to spend more time with them. So, doing what he knew Tracy would want him to do, he stayed.

The pack was a close-knit group, more like extended

family, and would be there for him no matter his ego. And admitting his pride was the reason he'd walked away from Tracy when she needed him most, was one of the hardest things he'd ever done.

"As protective as you are of Tracy, I'm beginning to think you might be part wolf," Jack said and added, "It's not a bad thing."

"Not at all," Megan agreed and took hold of Randy's hand. "We've all said and done things we're not proud of, but in the end, the bond holds true."

Twenty-Seven

Tracy

"We're here." The voice in her head sounded vaguely familiar, but Tracy was too tired to care. "Tracy, wake up." Trace reached over the seat to nudge her awake.

"Ugh. What time is it?" Tracy muttered, her arm resting over her eyes. Her first flight on an airplane and she could feel every bump and every sway. Squeezing her eyes shut as the plane took off, even her knuckles ached from the death grip she had on the armrest. Once the plane had landed, though, Trace rented a car to drive the last forty miles, giving her time to relax and finally drift off to sleep.

Mentally fatigued, she yawned and pried open her eyes as a blast of cold air raised goosebumps all over her body. Unfastening her seatbelt while Trace held open the passenger door, she grabbed her phone off the seat before climbing out of the vehicle. It was frickin' cold, and the thin slacks and sweater she wore were no match for the harsh Montana winter. "Brrr. Does it ever get warm here?" She shivered, making Trace laugh as he reached into the backseat before closing the door.

"Yeah, but this is typical for spring."

Growing up in Kinsley, Tracy was definitely spoiled by the mild Kentucky winters. One day hot, the next day cold, you had a better chance of accurately predicting the weather by walking out the door to see it, rather than relying on any forecast. It wasn't unusual for the temperature to change rapidly from day to day, and not nearly as cold as the Northern states. She cut a glance towards Trace who was holding out a camo coat, and eagerly snatched it from his hands. She pulled the coat around her shoulders, inhaling the frigid air.

"So this is what Montana looks like." She glanced around and although it was dark, every building and every house stood out against the mountains.

"It looks better in the morning light," Trace teased, glancing over his shoulder at the large two-story house. It was definitely the house of an alpha, based on the size alone.

"Wow, this is super nice," she whispered. One, because it was late, and she didn't want to wake anyone; and two, because she didn't know what else to say.

"My family lives here, including my parents." She shifted nervously but Trace was quick to put his arm around her and add, "It's okay, they're expecting us and can't wait to meet you."

Great! That did nothing to ease her mind. She wanted

to roll her eyes but as cold as it was, she thought better of it. She shivered again and pulled the coat tighter, holding it together.

"Watch your step," Trace said, holding her elbow as they walked up on the large front porch. The wood and stone cabin was beyond anything she could imagine, and the massive front windows reflected the moonlight. Lantern-style lamps, spaced evenly along the front of the house, gave it a rustic look, like something she expected to see in Cowboy Country. She turned and looked out across the yard.

It was probably an old saloon town, updated throughout the years. So peaceful and quiet, if she listened hard enough, she could almost hear cowboys from days gone by bringing in the herd. She turned as Trace pushed open the large, wooden door, and the heat from inside beckoned her forward.

Walking into the capacious family room, Tracy could tell the pack had done well and wasn't surprised to learn there were 424 wolves that made up the pack. All of which lived in the small town.

Tracy followed Trace across the room and up the wide staircase that led to the second story. It felt surreal to think she was in the house where her dad grew up and lived all his life. She might have also been born in that house, had her mother not met Owen. She could picture herself as a little girl, playing on the staircase, and the Christmas tree that probably stood beside it, lighting up the holiday with twinkling cheer.

The Hudson family never celebrated Christmas or any holiday that Tracy could remember. It was considered a human tradition, putting it well beneath their superior status. It wasn't until Alpha Cooper took over the pack that things changed, but even then, Travis frowned on the sentimentalism.

She recalled her first Christmas with Randy, back in December, and remembered sitting for what seemed like hours just watching the tree lights blinking. And the eggnog! Who knew that stuff was so good? She absolutely loved it. Her favorite thing about the holiday, other than opening gifts with Randy, was the meal his mother prepared. To sit down at a table full of smiling faces and enjoy good food and pleasant conversation was heavenly... She was humbled to be part of something so significant, and she longed for more.

"You can have this room. It has a nice view of the mountains, and it's far enough away that TJ won't disturb you. He's pretty eager to meet his big sister," Trace said, rousing her from her thoughts.

Tracy smiled, thinking if she were small in a house that big, they could never find her. Then the memory of her hiding beneath the bed flashed in her mind, and she cast it away. She didn't want to revisit that day. She had a family here in Montana and would never think of the Hudson Pack as such again.

"Thanks," Tracy said as he flipped on the light. The room was large with a spacious bed and a wall of windows. She could imagine a princess living there. The fancy wood trim and heavy burgundy drapes that touched the floor were gorgeous, but nothing compared to the stone fireplace where a small fire burned. Instantly, she wanted to curl up on the beige sofa and stretch her toes. She could already feel the heat. "All this for me?" She didn't mean to ask it, but there it was.

"Anytime you want to visit, or if you decide you want to stay, this is your room," Trace said as he moved to the opposite side of the bed. "You have a private bath and there's a linen closet with everything you need. My room is on the first floor, the hallway to the left of the steps; the hallway to the right leads to my parents' room. Your grandparents."

Feeling a bit overwhelmed, she nodded, a nervous smile on her face. What was she thinking by coming there alone? She needed Randy. He was her safety net, her buffer, the only one to keep her from slipping back into the shadows of what she used to be. He kept her sane.

Once Trace left the room, Tracy walked over to the window and stared out at the night sky. She was tired, but now she couldn't sleep from worrying about Randy. *I miss you terribly,* she sent through the bond, picturing him in her mind. If only he were there to read to her, something he did when she was stressed and couldn't sleep. He usually read fiction; aliens were a big hit with him. On occasion, it would be a romance novel because he knew she was a sucker for love stories. But unlike her, he was probably sleeping. Just thinking that made her feel somewhat better. "This is your family. You were meant to be here," she whispered, but until she met them, she wouldn't know that for sure. She moved across the room and slipped off her shoes, standing in front of the fireplace until her feet thawed. The warm tile felt like Sallee's Rock after soaking up the noonday sun.

The closet was beside the bathroom, and she hadn't noticed it before, so that was where she ventured next. It was not only a large, walk-in closet but it was filled with clothes, things she would actually love to wear. Sorting through the hangers, she would ask to borrow a change of clothes in the morning to get out of the wrinkled pants and shirt she currently wore. At the far end of the closet hung an assortment of nightgowns, mostly flannel, and she instantly knew why. She took a pink one off the hanger and quickly changed right there in the closet. She wanted a shower, but didn't dare risk waking anyone so it too would have to wait until morning. She quietly closed the closet door and went into the bathroom, happy to see the new toothbrush and toothpaste waiting for her there. After doing her business and cleaning her teeth, she turned in for the night.

Tracy never slept in a king-sized bed before but she had to admit she loved all the extra space. Maybe Randy could get them a large bed once she returned to Cloverly. *If he's still waiting.* She didn't mean to hurt him by insisting on leaving with Trace, but she knew she did. She only wanted to meet her family to see where she came from. He didn't understand what it was like not to have a family to call his own. She punched the pillow and pulled the comforter up to her chin. The bed was soft and warm and within minutes, she was dozing until she heard a light tap on the door.

Soundlessly, Tracy climbed out of the massive bed and quickly made her way to the door, glad she had forgotten to shut off the light. With eager anticipation, she turned the knob and stepped back as a small, dark-haired male walked into the room. Unable to hide her smile, she instantly knew she was staring down at her little brother. He was a small version of Trace with green eyes that matched hers.

"Are you my sister?" he whispered as he rubbed the

sleep from his eyes.

"Well, if you're TJ then yes, I am. I'm Tracy."

"Mama said I can't bother you, but I couldn't sleep and your light was on. Am I bothering you?"

Tracy chuckled and shook her head. "Not at all. I'm very glad you stopped by."

"You are!?" His eyes widened with delight, making her giggle.

"Yeah. I am. This is a very big room, and I couldn't sleep."

"Mama said you live far away. Do you miss your home?" He walked over and sat on the edge of the bed, so Tracy joined him.

"Yeah, I think I do. But I wanted to come here and meet you, because it was more important."

"You're pretty."

"And you're a sweetheart." To that, he wrinkled his nose and she chuckled. "I didn't wake you up, did I?"

His feet dangled over the edge of the bed and he kicked off his dark-blue slippers. "Nah, Dad came into my room to tell me good night. He always does that when he gets home from his trips. I miss him not being here."

So precious.

Tracy could feel her heart breaking for the little guy and she hated being the reason Trace was gone for so long. "Well, what if I told you your dad will be spending a lot more time at home now? Would that make you feel better?"

He nodded. "He's your dad too."

"Yeah, he is, but I have a mate in Kentucky. So I think Dad needs to be here with you." Tears welled in her eyes and she quickly blinked them away. It was so easy to call

Trace *Dad* and saying it out loud only verified it was true.

"You have a mate? Is he here too?" He looked around the room and Tracy so wished Randy had come. She knew he would be a hit with TJ, the same way he was with Oliver. One day, Randy would make a great dad. She smiled, imagining that as TJ moved further back on the bed.

"No, he couldn't make it because he has to work, but you'll get to meet him soon." Even as she said it, she wasn't sure it was true. It would all depend on how Randy felt when she returned home. Tracy lay over on the bed and propped up on a pillow while TJ stretched out across the foot of the bed.

"I'm glad you came home," he said and her heart melted. *Home.* It was often a word she thought about but not something she ever had, except with Randy. She wished she were at home with him right then, although she was glad to be there with TJ. She would have to figure out a way to balance both because she doubted she could ever walk away from the little guy since meeting him.

"I'm glad I did too." Tracy smiled when he grinned. "So what do you do when your dad's not home?"

"After my studies, I play video games, mostly. Sometimes, I go to the movies with Nana because she likes the scary ones. My favorite thing is scouting the mountainside with Papaw. Mama don't think I should go because I don't have my wolf yet. But she's not a scout, so she doesn't know how much fun it is."

"I'm a scout so I know how much fun it is." Tracy nodded as his eyes rounded.

"You are? Maybe you can go with me and Papaw. We don't have any female scouts in our pack." His excitement filled the room and she laughed.

"Maybe I could. I would like to see the mountains." Tracy could see he was thinking about the possibility and the little smile on his face as he closed his eyes warmed her soul. If the rest of the family were anything like him, she would be ecstatic.

The morning sun shining through the window brought Tracy out of her slumber and she glanced down at the end of the bed where TJ was sleeping soundly. A light tap landed on the door and she looked over as Trace cracked it open and said, "I'm missing a little guy about yay high." He put his hand out to show the size, and she pointed to the end of the bed. "I hope he didn't keep you up all night. His mother told him not to bother you."

"No, he didn't bother me at all. I'm really glad he came to my room," she whispered as Trace walked over to the bed and lifted little TJ in his arms.

"Missing home already?" Funny how she just found out he was her father, and yet he read her like a book.

"Yeah, I was until TJ stopped by. He's a sweetie." She picked up his slippers and handed them to Trace.

"Julie said he's been talking non-stop about you since he found out you were coming home with me."

"Yeah, he seemed pretty excited and even invited me to go scouting with him and Papaw." Tracy grinned when Trace rolled his eyes.

"He loves to scout. I have a feeling when he gets older we'll never see him."

"If he's anything like me, you're probably right." That made Trace chuckle. "Oh, I borrowed someone's gown, I hope you don't mind."

"No, those are all for you. Julie wasn't sure what you would like. I tried to tell her the style of clothes you wore, and she picked out a few things so you would have something comfortable to wear besides the jogging suits. She hates them as much as you do."

"Thanks, I was dreading having to wear them the whole time I was here. Doesn't make a very good first impression." She chuckled, remembering Randy saying that exact same thing.

"You don't have to worry about that. If TJ likes you, you're a shoo-in for the others," Trace said as he walked to the door. "He'll probably sleep for another couple hours, but if you're hungry, Mom has already started breakfast. Just come down whenever you're ready. You can't miss the kitchen, because that's where all the noise will be."

Tracy waited until Trace left the room with TJ before heading to the shower. She felt better now that the sun was up, and the loneliness of missing Randy was more bearable since meeting her little brother. Just seeing his bright smile, she knew she made the right decision to come to Montana and she couldn't wait to meet the rest of her family.

Twenty-Eight

Tracy

After a quick shower, Tracy slipped on a pair of jeans that fit her perfectly and a wine-colored sweater that reminded her of the boutique back home. She smiled at her reflection in the mirror and decided to leave her hair down as she walked back into the bedroom. Taking a seat on the edge of the bed, she put on a pair of heavy socks and the sturdy hiking boots she found in the closet. She didn't know how Julie could have known her size, but she was more than content to wear something nice.

She made the bed and strolled out of the room, taking in the paintings that hung on the hallway walls. Various wolf prints and mountain landscapes made it obvious that wolves were in the house. She grinned and pictured Randy groaning. He would have preferred the open fields and bright sunrises, rather than the snowcapped peaks. She had to agree with him on that.

Tracy followed the soft chatter and laughter as she quietly descended the stairs and paused just outside the kitchen door. Unable to remove the grin on her face, she was amazed by how quickly her wolf accepted the pack without her ever meeting them. *Home.* It's what her heart longed for and she knew it was true the moment she walked through the front door. She sighed, suddenly understanding what Trace went through to unite her with the pack. She would never in a million years be able to repay him for not giving up on her; and she hoped someday Randy would be as accepting as she. She rolled her tongue the way Randy did to stop the ache in her jaws. Her pack was eager to meet her after all the years of her absence, and she could feel the excitement in the air.

The kitchen was open and airy with a huge window that framed a large mountain in the distance and she assumed that was where TJ and Papaw liked to scout. She peeked at a large, wooden table where an older male sat sipping coffee while reading the daily paper. Judging by the hint of gray in his dark hair, she guessed it was Papaw. The dark-haired woman sitting beside him must be his mate, although Tracy wasn't sure how to address her.

As she continued to scan the room, she noticed a pretty female standing at the stove, and Trace as he walked over and put his hand on her hip. It had to be Julie. She was about Tracy's height, with long, coffee-hued hair that tumbled down her back. As Trace leaned in to kiss her cheek, he paused and grinned in Tracy's direction.

"Come on in, we don't bite," he said, leaving Julie and

sauntering over to where Tracy stood. Tracy felt awkward at first, like an intruder, but Trace was quick to point out they were her family. "This is our alpha, your Papaw and Nana. Or if you prefer, you can call them Nina and Jon." She smiled and nodded.

"Oh, my! You are the living vision of your mother! I always adored her lovely red hair," Nina said as she stepped around the table to pull Tracy into a hug.

"Nana, stop, you're making her blush," Jon said, but joined in the hug as Trace laughed and brought Julie to his side.

"And this is my mate, Julie," Trace said and Tracy was happily surprised when Julie walked over and pulled her right into a hug.

"You are so beautiful. I wasn't sure about your taste in clothes but after the description Trace gave me, I thought we might wear the same size."

"Thank you so much for the clothes. I didn't have time to pack anything," Tracy replied.

"I was afraid she would change her mind about coming home with me." Trace leaned in and kissed the top of Tracy's head as he pulled out two chairs for her and Julie before grabbing the coffee pot and placing it on the table.

Sitting there while Trace poured the coffee, Tracy couldn't stop smiling. She wasn't into the politics of pack life so while Jon caught Trace up on the daily schedule, she politely turned when Julie mentioned shopping. That was a subject she could always relate to.

"So, Tracy, would you like to go shopping with me tomorrow? There's a little store on the main strip I think you'll love. Trace told me you work in a boutique. What do you sell?"

Her face colored every shade of red imaginable as she glanced over at the males now listening to their conversation. "Mostly lingerie and I also make jewelry." She held her breath when Julie's eyes widened. She probably thought Tracy was a harlot or worse.

"I love silk lingerie! It doesn't matter what it is as long as it's silk." Her hand rested on her chest as she gushed. "That's one thing we have to buy in the neighboring town. You would think a town this size would have at least one store where a female could buy silk panties, but no, not here, like we need another store selling hiking boots and wool coats!"

"Hey, those boots and coats keep you warm," Trace objected.

"Yeah, but if I were wearing silk lingerie, you would keep me warm." Julie smiled cunningly and Tracy snickered. That was something she could imagine saying to Randy. She instantly knew Julie and she would get along just fine.

Nana shook her head, saying, "Jon wouldn't know a pair of silk panties if they slapped him upside his head." That caused Trace to groan and Papaw to chuckle, hiding behind his newspaper. Tracy covered her mouth, nearly spewing her coffee.

"I'd love to go shopping," Tracy finally said once she stopped coughing.

The morning ended way too soon as Trace and Tracy got into the pickup and began driving across town to meet her mother's parents. The small mountain town was like stepping back into the Wild West. Old buildings, stained in every shade of wood, lined the business strip and she could hardly wait to hit the shops with Julie. At the edge of town, they turned onto a narrow dirt road that led to a cabin nestled behind rows of cedar trees and she tried to picture her mother living there.

"They know you're coming and they're so excited to meet you. I think you'll like them," Trace said, pulling up beside a rustic, split-rail fence.

"I need to catch my breath for a minute." Tracy gulped, trying to stop from literally shaking in her boots as Trace studied her and concern shone in his eyes.

"You don't have to do this now, not if it's too much. We can come back another time."

"No. I need to do this for me." She glanced out the passenger window as the front door swung open and a red-haired female walked out onto the porch. Sucking in a breath when Trace placed his hand on her arm, she panted, "I shouldn't have come. I need to go."

"Tracy, look at me." Tracy turned to meet his troubled eyes. "She's not your mother. She's her twin." Tracy felt like someone had kicked her in the stomach as his words tumbled around in her head. Confused and lightheaded, she feared she would pass out on the spot. Then he repeated, "She's Jessica, Rebecca's twin sister."

Tracy blinked a few more times until her mind cleared. "Her twin," she said, needing to say and hear the words herself. She glanced out of the corner of her eye, noticing Jessica was now standing on the sidewalk with an uneasy look on her face. "I didn't know my mother had a twin." She drew in a deep breath and forced her body to calm down.

"I'm sorry. I should have told you. We can leave. I'll just tell them we'll come back another time."

"If I leave now, I don't think I'll ever come back," she whispered, and he squeezed her hand.

"I'll be with you the entire time. I won't leave your side," Trace promised, but Tracy had already slid her hand free of his and pushed open the passenger door by the time he rounded the truck.

Tracy felt alone without Randy and his warm embrace, assuring her everything would be all right. Sending that thought through the bond, for no other reason than to soothe her nerves, now she wished their connection gave them a direct link to each other's thoughts, like most other bonded wolves had. She assumed it was because Randy was human, but at least they could pick up on each other's emotions, which was better than nothing. *You got this. They're your family.* She briefly closed her eyes, hoping the warmth filling her body was Randy trying to quiet her nerves.

"Are you sure you want to do this?" Trace asked, and she opened her eyes and nodded. She was an adult. She could see this through. She slipped out of the seat and Trace latched onto her arm, pulling her to his side. It was nerve-wracking, but she loved knowing she had a father that was so willing to protect her.

As they continued along the sidewalk, Tracy looked up and smiled. Jessica was standing there with her hands covering her mouth and tears streaming down her face. Her tears were of joy and happiness, not the sadness Tracy expected to find. Jessica pulled her into an embrace without bothering to introduce herself.

"Oh, Tracy, you look so much like your mother. I can't believe you're here," Jessica said as she pushed her back to arm's length to stare into her eyes. "You have your father's eyes, but everything else is pure Rebecca."

Tracy blushed beneath Jessica's gaze, her soft blue eyes scanning every inch of Tracy's face. Jessica was her mother's clone, even down to the beauty mark below her right eye. And if it hadn't been for her dad, Tracy would have sworn it was her mother standing there. *Oh, to pretend.* She so badly wanted to, but that would only bring heartache, and she couldn't go back now. She already crossed that bridge, and as painful as it once seemed, she had survived.

"How did you know her name?" Trace asked. "I wasn't even sure she was my daughter until three days ago."

"We were twins," Jessica said as if that explained everything. "We spent countless nights planning our futures. Even down to what we would name our firstborn child."

"So, my mom named me..."

"Apparently, after your dad," Jessica said. "Becca used to drive me crazy with talk of raising a family with Trace. She wanted to name her firstborn Trace if he was a boy or Tracy if she was a girl." Jessica glanced over at Trace and rolled her eyes. "Becca never mentioned you by name in her letters, but she always bragged about how precious you were to her."

Tracy looked over at her dad who was thrilled with the confirmation. "Of course, she's precious. She takes after her old man."

"Oh, Lord, we best get inside before his head swells so huge, he can't squeeze through the front door," Jessica teased as she took hold of Tracy's hand and Trace followed them into the house.

The cabin was comfy and it reminded Tracy of the cabins on Cabin Run Road, only three times as big. The vaulted ceilings and wood floors matched the cabins in Cloverly, and the only difference was the large front window that welcomed the afternoon sun.

"Tracy, these are your grandparents, my mom, Gloria, and my dad, Devin."

Her grandmother stared at her for the longest time and Tracy was about to make a beeline to the door when Gloria finally said, "I see my Rebecca when I look at you." Tracy took that as a compliment and smiled, which only brought her grandmother to tears. She gracefully moved across the room to where Tracy stood and lifted her chin and kissed her on the cheek. "Welcome home, my dear."

Gloria latched onto Tracy's arm, moving them further into the family room, and sat down on a sectional before patting the seat next to her. Her grandmother was as lovely as Tracy remembered her mother, and she could have easily passed for an older sister. Her hair was auburn brown, and Tracy instantly realized her mother got her red hair from Devin. "Kurt, Annette, and Sheryl will be here later, and they can't wait to meet you. Can you stay for dinner?" Gloria asked when Tracy sat down beside her.

Tracy looked up at Trace, who kept his promise of not leaving her side. "If you would like to, of course we can," Trace said, and she nodded, unable to keep from smiling as Devin sat down across from them and winked. She glanced between her grandparents, trying to decide which one her mother most favored. She was thinking Devin until Gloria grinned and then she was certain it was she.

Tracy enjoyed spending time with her grandparents

while Jessica threw together a quick lunch. Gloria showed her pictures of her mother as a little girl and offered Tracy a few to keep for when she returned home. There were no pictures of Owen, thankfully, but plenty of Trace and the family. That alone convinced Tracy that Trace told the truth about Owen, and it was clear her grandparents preferred Trace to him.

After lunch and meeting Kurt, Annette, and Sheryl, her mother's other siblings, Tracy promised to stop by in a few days to spend more time with them before heading home. It was CRAZY, with all capitals, and strange to be around so many people wanting to spend time with her. And as much as she loved their unconditional attention and love, the one person she preferred to spend most of her time with was her little brother. She wanted to hug him up and make him laugh until his eyes lit up with wonder. He was her dad made over with her eyes, and she didn't want him to grow up thinking she didn't care about him. So after spending the afternoon with her mother's family and eating supper at the alpha house, Tracy was ready to settle down with TJ and play video games. It was a taxing day, and although she thoroughly enjoyed being with her family, as nightfall fell over the mountains, it was Randy her heart longed for.

Twenty-Nine

Tracy

"Are you awake?" Tracy peeked out from beneath the blanket to find Julie entering her room. With a cup of coffee in one hand and a sale ad in the other, she was eager to get the shopping day started. Tracy chuckled seeing the red markings on the paper. Apparently, Julie had already scoped out the ads and had several items circled. "Meet me downstairs in an hour, and be sure to wear comfortable shoes." Julie dropped the paper on the nightstand, next to the mug of hot coffee, before hurrying out of the room.

It was nine-thirty by the time Tracy made it downstairs to the kitchen where the others were eating, and Julie was standing with her purse. "No time for breakfast, the store will be packed with bargain shoppers, and now is when we'll find the best deals. We'll grab something when we get to town."

Tracy threw her hand up and waved as Julie took hold of her arm, steering her toward the front door.

"Don't wait up," Julie said, closing the door and cutting off any replies. Tracy couldn't hold back any longer and laughed.

The drive through town was pleasant and Tracy loved listening to Julie talk about the family. Julie was a breath of fresh air and made her feel at home, like she'd been there her entire life. Plus, her step-mom was funny and feisty, two traits she appreciated and adored in a person. Actually, she reminded Tracy of Lori, minus the foul mouth.

Their first stop was at the Eagle King Coat store where Julie said, and with a straight face, "We need to get you a decent coat. No one will notice you wearing your father's camo."

Yeah, she was hilarious, but after trying on a sage green, knee-length, wool coat, Tracy agreed. She loved the look and feel; and not surprisingly, people noticed her. She smiled as they continued down the street to the next store. *Breakfast!*

The Sleeping Crow café was packed, and the only available seats were three barstools at the counter and one small table near the door. Julie opted for the table and Tracy pulled off her coat and draped it over the back of a chair before taking a seat. Wearing a charcoal-colored blouse and washed out jeans, Tracy felt stylish and sexy with the V-neck offering a peek at her cleavage.

"This is nice," Tracy said, peering around the room. The café was cozy with ivory painted wood beams on the

ceiling and matching painted walls. It was rustic, yet
updated, and even the small wooden tables with
mismatched chairs only added to the rustic charm. The
large, stone fireplace was her favorite, and the heat from
the flames warmed her cheeks. "I see why you like this."

"Yeah, I stop in every chance I get. I love their daily
specials, and the hazelnut coffee is to die for," Julie said
while pulling her coat off and draping it over her chair. "I
need to run to the ladies' room. I'll be right back." Julie
waved to a waitress as she rounded the counter, and
disappeared down a narrow hallway.

Tracy picked up the breakfast menu and debated what
to order as a shadow fell across the table. She looked up to
meet blue-eyes and a dimpled grin.

"I'm Jarrod and you must be my mate," he said in a
deep rumbly voice. He was tall, lean, and not bulky like
most of the pack males, but muscled nonetheless. She
arched a skeptical brow regarding the truth to his
statement, and he winked.

"Pretty sure you have me confused with someone
else." Tracy chuckled, her face turning a brilliant rosy red
when his grin widened.

"No, darlin', you're it for me."

She smirked at the jokester, expecting him to walk
away, but instead, he pulled out a chair and took a seat.
Goosebumps rose on her skin when he lifted her hand and
kissed her wrist. It was way too personal. So doing what
she thought Randy would do in her situation, she pulled
her hand from Jarrod's and wiped off any trace of his kiss
on her jeans. "I'm happily bonded," Tracy said with a
slight scowl.

"Funny, I was under the impression you were new in

town, and alone." He tried to scoot closer, but her foot pushed against his chair and he chuckled. Jarrod was definitely good looking, and his golden-blond hair, roughly tousled, was appealing, but he was too forward in her opinion. His eyes swept over her and heat filled her cheeks. He was honestly checking her out.

"I hope I'm not interrupting anything," Julie said, to Tracy's relief.

"Not at all," Jarrod smirked. "Just thought I'd stop by and introduce myself."

"Well, then, let me help you out here," Julie said readily as Jarrod finally glanced over his shoulder, looking unamused. "Jarrod, this is Trace's daughter, Tracy."

Confusion clouded his features and he pushed back in the chair. "I didn't know Trace had a daughter."

"Now you do." Julie smiled as Jarrod slowly stood and pushed the chair back under the table.

"Pardon me. I must have mistaken you for someone else." With a quick nod in Tracy's direction, Jarrod turned and walked away.

"Sorry about that. Sometimes the single males can be a bit daunting. Just tell them who you are and they'll leave you alone," Julie said and picked up the menu. "So, do you want breakfast or lunch?"

Tracy and Julie settled into a light conversation over an old-fashioned breakfast of biscuits, gravy, sausage and fluffy scrambled eggs. "This is delicious," Tracy said, adding a slice of tomato to her plate. She glanced up at a smiling brunette and equally pretty blonde, walking their way.

"Welcome to the pack! I'm Kathleen, and you look nothing like your daddy."

"That's not true. You have his eyes. I'm Evelyn and you must be Trace's daughter…"

"Tracy," Tracy said amused by the two females. "It's nice to meet you both."

Kathleen tilted her head, her grin matching her sisters. "Do I detect a slight accent? Southern?"

"Kentucky," Julie offered, motioning for Kathleen and Evelyn to have a seat.

"I wish we could but Mom is holding us a place in line at Walter's. You know how crazy that place gets on sale day," Evelyn reminded.

"Which is why you need to hurry and finish eating or next week you'll be crying to borrow my new shoes," Kathleen added.

"You know me too well." Julie stood and pulled Kathleen into a hug. "If I'm not there in fifteen, you best grab me a pair of red pumps."

"That I can do." Kathleen turned to Tracy. "It was nice meeting you."

"Likewise."

The pack seemed visibly excited that Tracy was there, especially when they found out she was Trace's daughter. She smiled when a rowdy group of males walked up to the table and spoke to Julie before turning their attention to her.

"Trace's daughter, you say," said the male named Adam while shaking her hand. "You must take after your mother." His soft laughter filled the room, and Tracy grinned.

"What's this rumor I'm hearing about you leaving us this summer?" Julie narrowed her brows, and Adam chuckled.

"Not a rumor. Actually, I plan to meet up with Trace tomorrow to finalize everything."

"Well, just don't forget your way home," Julie scolded.

"Don't worry. I know where I belong." Adam tipped his hat and added, "It was nice meeting you, Tracy. Julie."

Tracy waited until Adam had joined his friends at the counter before leaning closer to Julie to whisper, "He seems really nice."

"Oh, he's a doll. They don't make males like that anymore." Julie smiled warmly. "His family owns the lumberyard on the far side of town. He just turned twenty-four and is ready to find his mate and settle down."

"So his leaving is not really a bad thing. I mean, isn't that how you met Trace?"

"Yeah. It's just a shame to see him go." Tracy could tell by the soft smile on Julie's face she was thinking back to the day she met Trace.

"You know, it's been a long time since I've seen a movie, and I was thinking I could wrangle TJ for the evening if you don't already have something planned. It would give you and Trace some alone time."

"I'm sure that could be arranged. If you're absolutely positive you don't mind." Julie bit her lip to hide her grin.

"Anything for love." Tracy laughed. "And at the rate we're going, we'll probably be shopping till dark. So when you're ready, I'll wait at the theater for Trace to bring TJ. That will give you enough time to rush home and change into those new red pumps."

"Oh, I like the way you think. I can use you and TJ as a reason to send Jon and Nina on a dinner date and afterward, they can swing by and give you all a ride home." Julie's eyes lit with excitement and she pulled her phone from her purse to set their plan into motion.

While waiting on Julie to make the call, Tracy glanced over at the counter where Adam was joshing with the waitress, but it was Jarrod that caught her attention. He winked, and she rolled her eyes, grinning when he chuckled.

"So, is it a go?" Tracy asked when Julie shoved her phone back in her purse.

"Yeah, but we still have several stores to hit before we head home." Julie pushed out of her chair and pulled on her coat while walking over to the counter to pay for breakfast.

Tracy stood, and was surprised when Jarrod hurried across the room and held her coat. She wanted to roll her eyes again but resisted the urge.

"Like I said, you're it for me," he whispered and moved over to hold the door when Julie joined them. "You ladies have a nice day."

"You too, Jarrod," Julie said without looking back.

The warmth from the pack appealed to Tracy as they strolled down the sidewalk, and the cold Montana weather no longer seemed unbearable. "So, what's next on the agenda?"

"Shoes!" Julie said enthusiastically, leading her across the street.

After a day of shopping, Tracy was exhausted and more than ready for movie time with TJ. Shoving the last of their bags into the trunk, she turned to Julie. "Don't worry about TJ. I'll keep him out of your hair for the rest of the night."

"Thank you. I can't remember the last time Trace and I spent an evening alone. I really miss his company."

"Don't thank me. I'm looking forward to spending time with TJ. You just hurry home and get ready."

"Are you sure you don't want me to wait here until Trace arrives? I don't mind, and I can always…"

"No." Tracy cut her off, lifting her hand. "I'll stall Trace when he gets here to buy you more time. You just go do what you need to," Tracy insisted as she stepped back from the car. "Just make it memorable." She waggled her brows and swore she saw Julie blush as she ducked into the car and drove away. Turning toward the large movie posters taped to the window, she scanned each of them to pass the time. Action. Horror. Romantic comedy. Dinosaur. She smiled and shoved her hands into her pockets, expecting TJ would choose the T-Rex. She walked over to stand against the building, glad to be wearing the wool coat as the sun dropped behind the mountain.

"So we meet again." Tracy turned and smiled at the cocky grin on Jarrod's face. "Are you waiting for someone, or will anyone do?"

"I'm actually waiting for someone. Why? Are you following me?"

Ignoring her question, he cut to the chase. "Too bad. A female as pretty as you…" His voice trailed off as he leaned in, his breath brushing over her lips. "Just a taste, that's all." His mouth crashed down on hers and she struggled to pull her hands out of her pockets.

"Get off me!" she tried to yell against his lips, but he wasn't backing down. She jerked her head to the side, lifting her knee and nailing him directly in the crotch.

Jarrod bowed over and dropped to his knees, holding himself. "It was just a kiss," he grunted, unbearable pain lacing his words.

"I told you I was bonded, so touch me again and you'll be carrying your balls home in your pocket." She looked past Jarrod when Trace pulled over to the curb.

"What's going on here?" Trace asked as he jumped out of the truck, his eyes moving down to Jarrod's hands.

"Nothing, I was just passing my time by giving Jarrod here, a lesson in self-preservation." Tracy smiled sweetly, causing Trace to grin.

"By all means, don't let me stop you," Trace said, holding up his hands.

"What! She just..." Jarrod staggered to his feet, his eyes moving from Trace to Tracy, and then back to Trace. "It's not what it looks like."

"I'm willing to bet it's exactly what it looks like, so the way I see it, you have three options." Trace motioned for TJ to get out of the truck. "You can deal with me. Or you can deal with her. Or you can turn and walk away while everything is still intact. It's your call, but be forewarned, she's not a female you want to cross."

"Apparently," Jarrod mumbled as he turned and limped away but not before Trace slapped him across the back of the head.

"You might need to put ice on that when you get home." Trace shook his head and turned back to Tracy. "Are you really okay?"

"I'm fine, but you should probably check on him in a few days. I nailed him pretty hard." She grinned when Trace laughed.

Thirty

Randy

Normally, Randy stayed busy with plowing, planting and harvesting crops, depending on the season. It was hard work, but rewarding, and it kept him in great physical shape. But lately, the long hours and lack of sleep were slowly breaking him down. His lack of clarity and mental fatigue were a recipe for disaster when working with heavy machinery, especially when his mind couldn't stay focused. His thoughts revolved around Tracy no matter how hard he tried to push her out of his head. He was finally seeing things from her perspective by hanging out with the pack in the evenings—and it crushed him to admit he wasn't the most important person in her life. He understood the security her new family offered, but what about the security he provided for her on the farm?

"You're thinking too much into it," Jesse argued, but

the silver lining on an otherwise shitty week was when Seth disagreed.

"Pack is pack and family is family, and no matter what, family always comes first."

The frustration that chipped away at Randy's heart as the week wound down, without a single call from Tracy, was devastating. *You're not her family,* his weary mind rationalized, *but I am her bond mate,* his heart reasoned. He tried to give Tracy time as Megan and Jesse suggested but how hard was it to pick up a phone?

"The phone rings both ways," his mother warned, disapproving of his new attitude. But his male pride held out and he kept telling himself, *she has to make the first move.*

By the end of the week, there was still no word from Tracy and even his mother worried that she might not be coming home. "You need to eat something," his mom said, placing the evening meal on the table. Pining over Tracy was how she put it, and with each passing day, he knew it was true. But as the hours ticked down to their bond night, Cloverly was the last place he wanted to be so he jumped in the truck and headed out the highway.

It was late evening when Randy pulled into the drive that led to Iretta's house. He rarely visited her after hours, but dammit, he needed someone to talk to outside of the pack. He pulled up in front of the large garage and the security light clicked on. He beeped and waited, but who was he kidding? It was a full moon and Iretta was a shifter. *Did you honestly think she would be home?* Apparently, he didn't think, and that was the problem. Then he heard her motorcycle coming down the road and felt relieved that she didn't creep out from the shadows.

Seeing her in shifter form would have probably really freaked him out. He was buds with Tracy's wolf, but Iretta? He never claimed to be a cat person.

Iretta pulled up to the garage and opened the door, waving as she drove inside. Randy waited, watching her, still amazed that she was under Alpha Cooper's protection. She placed her helmet on the bike before walking out of the building towards the truck.

"What are you doing here?" She was suspicious and with good reason. Even he didn't know why he was there. Was he desperate? Maybe. He wanted to escape his life and get away from everything that reminded him of Tracy. And to talk to someone that wasn't in Cloverly.

"I need a friendly face." It was a lame answer, utterly vapid, and ambiguous. Perhaps she would take it to mean more than it was, and maybe he wanted her to. He never felt as empty as he did in that moment and the bond he shared with Tracy seemed completely nonexistent. The thought of Tracy breaking their bond made his hands fist around the steering wheel. He had tried numerous times to reach out to her, but apparently, bonds didn't span the miles. And if she stayed in Montana long enough, their bond would probably fade away altogether. His jaw tightened.

"Well, I'm glad you stopped by. I'm sorry for the way things ended the other day. I never meant to offend your mate." Iretta hopped into the seat and closed the passenger door. "I'm sure she's a sweet female."

"Don't sweat it. I'm not even sure I have a mate these days." He loosened his grip and exhaled loudly, his breath lifting the hair off his face.

"Why, what happened?" She reached over and

gripped his hand as he glanced down at her slender fingers, tipped with black nail polish.

"She went to Montana." Okay, he should have told the complete story, but he wasn't there to talk about Tracy.

"And..."

"And, honestly, I'm not sure she's ever coming back. Turns out her family is there. She has no one here, and no reason to come back." Randy pulled his hand from Iretta's and ran it over the scruff on his jaw. "It's like I don't matter to her anymore." *So much for not talking about Tracy.*

"Well, since we're being honest, I never thought she was a good match for you." He looked over to meet Iretta's golden eyes and for a split second, caught the flash, proving she was indeed a shifter. "And unlike her, I'll always be here for you. You know that."

Randy nodded, but said nothing for fear of leading her on. He stared out the side window to hide his scowl as Megan's voice resonated in his head. *Give her this. If you want your bond to be strong, you need to support her.* Was that where he failed Tracy? Did he not support her enough? He did practically everything he could to prove he loved her, but obviously, love wasn't enough to keep her from leaving. "Can a bond just fade away?" He turned back to Iretta as the seriousness of his question settled on her brows.

"I'm probably not the best person to ask since I never actually bonded with my intended mate. I guess anything's possible. Why?" Iretta slid over in the seat and pushed the hair out of his eyes.

"Tonight was when we planned to have our ceremony and it's like the bond is no longer there." He swallowed hard, his emotions threatening to burst forward.

"I've never heard of anyone breaking a bond, but then again, I've never known of a shifter bonding with a human." Iretta lifted his hand and kissed his knuckles, her eyes now darker. "You have to stop this. I can't stand to see you so downhearted. Did you ever think all this happened *because* of her, and she didn't really deserve you?" A soft purr filled the cab.

"No, and apparently, I'm not in the habit of thinking, at least not with my brain." With his head resting against the back window, he closed his eyes to keep from rolling them when Iretta licked her lips. Surely it couldn't be that easy to break a bond, and he doubted Tracy would unless she found someone better in Montana.

"A male that's not afraid to tell the truth. And to think I let you get away." Her flirty words and sudden turning in the seat made him open his eyes and he hissed, his still tender chest taking the brunt of her weight when she hopped into his lap. She was heavier than she looked as her chest pressed against his and her eyes flared. *Oh shit!*

He gripped her waist when her hands latched onto his shoulders, but before he could object, her lips mashed down onto his. Mortified by her boldness, he nearly gagged when she shoved her tongue deep into his mouth. Jerking his head to the side to catch his breath and end the kiss, even that didn't dislodge her lips. It felt wrong on so many levels, like sucking on an emery board or licking tree bark. He heaved with the thought and quickly shoved her out of his lap, uncaring that she nearly toppled head first onto the floorboard. His stomach reeled and he fought the urge to spit. "What the hell? You trying to get us both killed?" He turned and glared at the catty grin on her face.

"You're welcome, and you most definitely still have a bond," she said, righting herself in the passenger seat with a satisfied smirk on her face.

"And you know this because?" He clamped his jaws shut, again, fighting the urge to spit.

"Because you're the first male I've ever met that didn't like a little tongue action." She waggled her eyebrows, and he scowled.

"Not from you! That's just wrong." His body quivered down to his toes at the thought of... He shook off one last shiver and she narrowed her eyes.

"Oh, get over yourself! I merely gave you the proof you lacked. Personally, I prefer the older males that stay a little rough around the edges," she said and he rolled his eyes. He feared what would come out of his mouth if he spoke.

Randy never considered Iretta as anything more than a friend. That was all he wanted from her, and after that little act of aggression, he planned to definitely brush his tongue with a scouring pad as soon as he got home.

"Look, you can't expect your mate's world to revolve around you every minute of every day. What is it with males thinking they can control us, anyway? Save your chest beating for the bedroom where it will do you the most good." She flashed a sneering grin. "No female wants to be controlled!" Her words were tinged with anger and he realized all at once why Iretta wasn't bonded.

I wasn't beating my chest... was I? She could see the question in his eyes and she nodded, making him chuckle. "Thanks."

"No thanks needed. But you have a lot of sucking up to do, and the sooner you start, the better. Let me know when you get things worked out and don't forget to stop by and visit sometime." Iretta got out of the truck and looked back before closing the door. "I would love to stay and chat, but I have a date. He's also a chest beater... if you know what I mean." Randy's jaw dropped, making her laugh. "Good luck with Tracy."

Randy waited until Iretta was inside the garage and the door lowered before backing out of the driveway. As he turned onto the highway, his thoughts drifted. *Bad things happened to good people; Tracy was proof of that. And hiding her from Travis was the start of his problems. He wasn't the possessive type, and yet he felt he had to save her from the world. Unlike Iretta, who enjoyed her solitude, Tracy needed her pack. They were a tight-knit group, and she was an integral part of that. He wanted to be a part of it too, and would be if she ever came back.*

He turned into the drive, glad to be home, until he caught sight of Seth pulling in behind him and following him to the barn. He quickly parked, thinking something bad had happened to Tracy. Why else would Seth be there? He jumped out of the truck and slammed the door. "What's wrong?" His feet had him running in Seth's direction before his mind realized what he was doing.

Seth wrinkled his nose as Randy came to a sudden stop next to the driver's door. "What is that funk?" Seth fanned his hand as if to push the stink away and got out of the car.

"Cat piss," Randy chuckled.

"Hey, I'm not judging, and I don't want to know, but you might want to hit the shower, like twice, before you join us at the alpha house because I can smell female all over you."

"I'm not going to the alpha house. There's no reason for me to be there." Randy glanced up at the night sky, dreading what was to come once the moon reached its highpoint.

"Look, what you do is your own business, but Tracy is a pack sister and I won't stand by and let you humiliate her in front of everyone. If you don't want to be with her, then say so, but don't take away what little self-worth she has left. She's been through enough." The low rumble made him scowl as he glanced over, and Seth's anger flashed in his silvery eyes.

"Shut up! I wasn't with anyone, and you know as well as I do that Tracy's in Montana."

Seth threw his hands in the air, frustrated. "No, dammit, she's on her way home! And had you not been hanging out with some slinky feline, you might have sensed that on your own." His finger jabbed Randy's chest and Randy clenched his jaw, wanting to smack that smug smirk off Seth's face.

"Damn, that hurt!" Randy carefully pulled his shirt away from his chest and glared at Seth, knowing he did it on purpose. "So when did they leave?" he ground out, still feeling the sting from Seth's poke.

"They're on their way to Cloverly. Apparently, she wanted to surprise you and called Jesse to have her meet them at the alpha house. And you, in addition to being my best friend, are the best thing that ever happened to Tracy. I didn't want to ruin her surprise by you not showing up. So get your ass in gear and soak in a tub with some super strong soap. Then, when you're finished, take a hot shower for good measure. I don't know what you've been rolling in, but it's not very appealing."

"Oh, piss! If Tracy's here before noon tomorrow, she'll be lucky," Randy said as Seth pulled open the car door.

"She'll be here by eleven; she's on a plane, not a tour bus." Seth rolled his eyes. "So be waiting. I'll be back to get you at ten-thirty."

Randy did the calculations in his head. He still had at least two hours before Seth would return, so what was the hurry? Then he remembered the dress, the bike, and the... *Shit!* He was running out of time!

Racing to the house, he shoved open the door and grabbed his phone off the kitchen table. Sure enough, he had not one, but three missed messages. That was when he realized the pack was just as much a part of him as Tracy, and he pushed redial on the first call.

"Jesse, take the gown with you and I'll meet you there." He hung up and dialed Megan. "I know! Do you have the necklace?" He cut her off because she was rambling. "Take it to the alpha house." He hung up and dialed Seth just to hear him laugh, rolling his eyes when Seth informed him that Jack was coming back with him and would take the bike. His hands trembled as the thought of having their bonding ceremony settled in his mind, and he quickly ended the call. If he made it out of the shower before he blacked out from lack of oxygen, it would be a miracle. He sucked in a much-needed breath as he raced up the stairs, four steps at a time.

Thirty-One

Jesse

As the moon ascended higher in the sky, Jesse plopped down into a chair, her anxiety teetering on the edge of a mega-meltdown. Her insides were twisting, making her nauseous, and she expected before the night was over, the buttery crab legs she ate for supper would resurface. She was being overly dramatic, as usual, but anytime she was stressed, she had to prepare herself for the drama that was sure to ensue. Restless and nearly in a frenzy, she checked off her to-do-list, not once, but three more times.

"There you are. I thought you were coming down to the kitchen," Whitney said from the doorway.

"I just wanted to double check something first." Jesse's daily intake of caffeine only added to her edginess; yet the thought of another super-strong cup to kick her rear in gear seemed like heaven.

"Would you stop nitpicking? You got this." Whitney kept warning her to slow down all day, but the last-minute details, ordered at the last minute, were a disaster in the making.

"I'm not trying to nitpick, but how tragic would it be if I'm the one who ruins Tracy's special night?" Jesse pushed herself out of the leather chair and handed Tracy's bonding gown to Whitney. "Take this to the alpha's bedroom. Please." The other dress, the one only she and Randy knew about, would remain in the guest bedroom until they were ready to bring it out. She grabbed her to-do list and followed Whitney out of the room.

The night would be monumental not only for Tracy but Tucker as well. Tracy would officially proclaim Randy a member of the pack, an act that would garner a few dropped jaws, especially after being raised to despise humans, and Randy was about as human as they came. Tucker, on the other hand, had finished his alpha training and would soon take possession of the Berkley cabin, making Jesse an alpha female. It sounded wonderful in the beginning. Although, she wondered whom the elders had chosen to place in their pack—which only added to her anxiety. In order to distract her mind, she focused on Tracy and how best to make her night unforgettable.

So yeah, Jesse definitely needed that extra cup of coffee and it was just after ten when she walked into the kitchen, seeking the much-needed energy boost. That was about the time Whitney yelled, "They're here!" to Jesse's surprise.

Tracy always enjoyed making an entrance, and arriving an hour early definitely did that. Jesse chuckled.

Only Tracy could speed up a plane.

Tucking the to-do list into her pocket, Jesse quickly scanned the kitchen and family room to make sure everything was stashed out of sight. She wrung her hands as she turned toward the window, hearing numerous car doors slam.

"Welcome home," Alpha Cooper greeted when Tracy stepped out of the vehicle, smiling. She seemed happy, but Jesse noticed the way she looked past everyone, probably searching for Randy.

Randy was upset when Tracy left for Montana, but after spending the day with her and Megan, he seemed more at ease with the situation. However, absence doesn't always make the heart grow fonder, especially when insecurity is a factor. So calling Jesse back at the late evening hour was better than not calling at all. *And yet he still isn't here.* She rushed into the foyer as the front door swung open.

The wide smile on Trace's face when he walked into the cabin behind Tracy was amazing to witness. Jesse would blame her ill thoughts of him on her interpretation of the vision. *Not all visions are bad.* Apparently, that lesson had to be learned the hard way. She grinned when Trace waved and moved further into the room.

"We have food and drinks in the kitchen," Alpha Cooper announced, motioning the group across the foyer.

"You go with Whitney and I'll be there in a minute." Tracy ruffled TJ's hair and added, "Save me some cake." She winked, and he grinned. Once everyone was gathered in the kitchen, she turned and pulled Jesse into the family room. "Have you talked to Randy?" she whispered. "I tried to call him when we arrived at the airport but he's not

answering."

"He's probably spit-shining his shoes," Jesse joked, but the unease in Tracy's eyes said she wasn't buying it.

"I don't know. He was so hurt and angry when I told him I was leaving. But when I found out I had a little brother, I had to meet him. Do you think he'll understand?"

"He was afraid you wouldn't come back is all. He understands now, he'll be here," Jesse said optimistically when all she really wanted to do was slowly and tortuously wring Randy's neck. She grinned with the laughter coming from the kitchen. "Oh, crap! I forgot about Megan. I'll be back and we'll talk then."

Jesse hated to lie but needed an excuse to leave because Mr. Sizzle Factor was about to get a piece of her mind. She hurried out the door and around to the back of the cabin to where she knew Tucker had parked the truck—the keys hanging in the ignition. Starting the truck, she took off without a second thought; certain she could find Randy's house at the late hour. It was the first driveway past the Welcome to Cloverly sign—how much easier could it get?

Fifteen minutes later Jesse turned into the driveway, following the tree line to the back of the house and parked next to the farm truck. There were lights on at both houses, so she assumed Randy was still at home.

Standing on the small slab porch, she lifted her hand to knock when the door swung open and Randy motioned her inside. "I need help with my tie," he said, apparently thinking she came there precisely for that.

"Fine, but first we have to talk." Jesse wasn't asking, although she wasn't exactly comfortable when she noticed his jeans were unfastened, his tee was only partially tucked in and his feet were bare.

"Don't tell me, Tracy's changed her mind." He turned, standing next to the kitchen counter.

Oh, she wanted to slap that smirk off his face, and probably would have had she not seen the devastation in his eyes. "Why didn't you answer her calls? She's sweating bullets that you won't show up for the ceremony. Are you still pissed that she went to Montana?"

He ran his fingers through his damp hair and took a seat at the small kitchen table. She could see how mentally fatigued he was by the dark circles ringed beneath his eyes. "I wasn't sure she would come back."

"We told you at the boutique to give her time. You were okay with it. What happened?" She moved over to stand across from him.

"I guess I figured she would get to Montana and decide she didn't want to be with me any longer and break the bond. Hell, I'm not sure I can even feel the bond anymore."

Jesse huffed and rolled her bottom lip, capturing it between her teeth. After a minute, she finally said, "Did you or did you not accept the bond when Tracy offered it?"

"Well, yeah, I did, but who's saying she didn't change her mind?"

Again, Jesse huffed. "It doesn't work like that. Once you accept the bond, it's a done deal. The ceremony is more about you joining the pack than anything else. The only thing left for you all is to... well..." She swallowed the lump of embarrassment that lodged in her throat.

"Consummate our bond by having sex," Randy said,

and she nodded, her face heating with his grin.

"Once you... you know, the bond will strengthen even more and you'll fully sense it with every cell in your body. It's indescribable."

Randy's head dropped as his elbows landed on his knees. "How do I face her? I mean, I knew she wasn't trying to hurt me, yet I got so angry at how easily she could walk away." He looked up.

"From what I understand, nothing ever comes easy for her. And if you were in her situation, you'd have done the same thing. We all would have."

"She asked me to go and I should have, but I wasn't ready to trust Officer Riley." Rubbing his face, he got up and grabbed his shirt off the sofa. "I'm sorry." He looked away to hide the glassy sheen in his eyes. "I honestly didn't think she would come back."

"But she did and she's waiting for you at the alpha house." Jesse frowned when he fumbled with the buttons on his shirt. He was oddly nervous, nothing like his normally confident self. "She asked about you." That got his attention and he glanced up. "She's worried you won't be there because you didn't answer her call."

"I've missed her so much that I'm afraid if I talk to her on the phone, I'll choke up. When you see her, would you tell her I'll be the one wearing purple?" He held up the tie and Jesse grinned.

"So, only the tie?"

That made him smile. "No, I also have a tux."

Not only did Jesse's eyes bug out, but her jaw dropped so far, she thought she'd have to pick it up off the floor. Normally, the guys wore dress slacks, but a tux? They would surely be the talk of the pack for months to come. "She doesn't know, does she?"

"No. Just like she doesn't know we're leaving on our bikes tonight." He opened the door and waved Jack and Seth in while hiding his insecurity behind a superficial grin.

"Wait, you can't drive the bike to the alpha house. Tracy's already there. She'll hear you," Jesse warned.

"Not if she stays inside and Brayden's been working on a dirt bike so she'll probably just assume it's him," Jack said.

"Well, then, I guess my work here is done. I'll relay the message to Tracy and see you all when you get there." Jesse turned to Randy and mouthed, "She loves you," before walking to the door. He didn't understand the magnitude of the bond they shared. And where did he come up with the idea that she could break it? It was absurd. With a subtle nod, he closed the door behind her.

Thirty-Two

Tracy

"This is insane. I feel like every nerve in my body is clawing to escape." Tracy's fingers spread out like talons next to her head. "I've never been so wired, and I haven't even had a single cup of coffee today." Her hands trembled and she tucked them beneath her chin.

"Nervous jitters. It's normal," Reva assured her while holding out the bonding dress. "Just focus on Randy and let everything and everyone else fade away. It's your night and you deserve to enjoy it." Tracy nodded, feeling a bit better now that Jack's mother was there to help her prepare for the ceremony.

"I know, I've... so many things have happened in the past week and I can't keep track of it all." Tracy paced while wringing her hands, a habit she'd picked up from

Jesse.

"You're just a little overwhelmed is all," Reva said, bringing her to a halt before pulling her into a hug. "You've handled everything better than most, and your mother would be so proud. She was a good person and she only wanted the best for you."

Tracy looked up with tears in her eyes. "Did you know her?"

"I did. We became friends when she first joined the pack. We used to sit for hours at the lake and talk. I miss the stories she would tell about her home. I always envied her. She was beautiful and smart, and so caring. She never failed to make me smile," Reva said as Tracy stepped into the dress.

"Did you know Trace was my dad?"

"No, but I was with her the night you were born. Usually, a male wants to be with his mate—especially when his firstborn is ready to meet the world, but Owen had to go out of town on business, which seemed odd at the time. I was prepared, and expected Rebecca to be upset, but she wasn't. She was happy, smiling, and she kept whispering, "Oh, Trace she's beautiful." I just assumed she meant, "Oh, Tracy's beautiful." Now, I know that wasn't the case."

Tracy smiled and turned so Reva could tie the ribbon at her back—the soft material brushing over her bare bottom. "I miss her."

"Me too," Reva said as she hugged Tracy's shoulders and stared at Tracy's image in the mirror.

The bonding dress wasn't the gown of Tracy's dreams, but she didn't need a fancy gown to make the night perfect. All she needed was Randy at her side, and after being gone for a week, her heart longed for his touch... *to see his smile, to hear his laugh.* Lost in thought, she jumped when the bedroom door flew open. "What are you doing here? You can't see me!"

It was a silly custom for human females, forbidding their mates from seeing them in their wedding dress before the ceremony. One could argue that Tracy wasn't wearing a wedding gown and it wasn't the same type of ceremony, but she would have wholeheartedly disagreed. The similarities between the two were just frivolous, minor details. Pack females would never squander a small fortune for a dress they would only wear once. Tracy envied the humans that went to the extremes and insisted on looking like a princess in their very own fairytale. "You have to leave! It's bad luck," she moaned, but Randy's smoldering eyes said he wasn't worried about luck.

"I'll take my chances." In three bounds, Randy was across the room, wrapping her tightly in his arms. Her body trembled, but the longer he held her, the more she relaxed. "I was afraid I'd never see you again." His voice cracked and she pushed him back to kiss his chin.

"I'm sorry. I didn't mean to worry you." Tracy stared into his stormy eyes and shivered when he captured her mouth, the passionate kiss nearly lifting her onto her toes. In that brief instant, she wanted to skip the ceremony and go straight to the consummation phase. "I missed you so much," she whispered against his lips.

Randy nipped her bottom lip before pulling back and staring into her eyes. "Never leave me like that again." His voice was gruff, but he smiled it away and kissed the tip of her nose as Reva cleared her throat. Tracy blushed as mischief danced in his eyes and he reached down and pinched her on the rear. She squeaked, his playfulness in front of Jack's mother only added to the heat traveling to her ears. He turned her to the mirror, taking in the view of them standing together. His stark-white shirt and faded jeans weren't any match for the dress she was wearing, and when the door opened, he glanced back over his shoulder and said, "Jesse, this dress is all wrong."

Tracy's eyes widened with his words, and waves of panic crushed her chest. If he didn't like the dress, he should have said something beforehand, instead of waiting until the very night of their ceremony. Her heart thumped hard against her ribs as her former excitement faltered with his scrutinizing stare. She looked down, trying desperately to dam the tears that threatened to spill from her eyes. Swallowing hard, she looked up as the bedroom door opened again.

"Ignore him, you look gorgeous," Jesse said, reentering the room with a dress bag in her arms.

Tracy smiled, but what she really wanted to do was runaway and cry. He didn't like the dress! How much worse could it get? "Thank you," she muttered as she looked up to see the grin on Randy's face. *Was he paying her back for going to Montana?* She had to wonder.

"But you'll look even more gorgeous in this." Jesse hung the dress bag on the back of the bedroom door as Randy raced across the room to pull her into a hug.

Tracy frowned, unaware of his reason for being so happy with Jesse and not so much with her, but before she could ask why, he was out the door without looking back.

Reva took Tracy's hand and together they watched Jesse and Whitney unzip the bag. At the sight of the flowing, white wedding gown that Jesse had designed, Tracy's heart nearly stopped beating. Chills raced up her spine and she shivered when Reva pulled the satin ribbon from around her waist, releasing the first dress and letting it fall from her shoulders. Tracy stood shocked as tears spilled from her eyes, but she didn't wipe them away. "How did you know?"

"I wish I could take the credit for this, but it was Randy's design, not mine," Jesse said over her shoulder. "He said it was your dream dress and asked me if I could make it." She turned as Tracy collapsed to the floor. "What's wrong? Don't you like it?"

Tracy waved away her concern as she sat there crying harder than she had ever cried in her life. She took the tissue Reva offered and replied, "It's the most beautiful dress I've ever seen."

"Then what are you waiting for? Dry those tears and get up so we can get you dressed. There's a handsome groom out there waiting to make you his bride." Jesse couldn't hold back her own tears as she held out her hand and helped Tracy off the floor.

"I don't know what to say. I never imagined." With the help of Reva and Whitney, Tracy stepped into the dress and moved over to stand in front of the mirror again. Her heart melted and her bottom lip quivered. *You don't deserve him.* That was a fact, but even so, by now, she wasn't willing to ever let him go.

Smiling through teary eyes, she followed Jesse over to the small dressing table in the corner of the room. Tracy sat down and stared into the lighted mirror as Jesse twisted, rolled, and worked her magic until Tracy's hair finally rested atop her head. She had never worn her hair so elegantly, and even she thought she looked stunning. Jesse held up a silver butterfly clip and fastened it to the side of Tracy's hair. "Something old," Jesse said with a smile. "It was Gramma's."

"And these are from Whitney," Reva said, removing a shoebox from beneath the bed. The white satin heels matched the dress perfectly. "Something new." Tracy glanced over at Whitney, who also had tears in her eyes.

"I'm here!" Megan yelled as she ran down the hall and into the room. "Ohmygosh! I thought I was late." She opened a small, slender box and pulled out a beautiful necklace, the silver cross matching the one Randy wore in his ear. "Something borrowed, from Randy."

Tracy swallowed as more tears welled in her eyes. Then she looked up at Trace who was smiling from the doorway. "You are the image of your mother. Just beautiful." The dam broke and her tears flowed freely as he hurried over and stooped down in front of her, dabbing her eyes with a pale blue handkerchief. "Something blue." He pushed the smooth cloth into her palm and closed her fingers around it. "It belonged to your mother." Planting a kiss on the side of her head, he stood and exited the room. Tracy looked down at the silky cloth and rubbed it across her cheek. *I love you, Mom.* It was the only thing she had that belonged to her mother, something she would cherish forever. She closed her eyes and tried to picture her mother being there.

"We're ready," Tucker announced as Jesse helped Tracy stand. The smile on his face warmed Tracy's heart when she joined him at the door. "You couldn't be more stunning." He drew her into his arms and kissed the top of her head, something he always did.

"I'm so nervous," Tracy admitted, leaning into his chest.

"I know you are, but don't be. You have me and Trace, and as soon as you get outside, you'll have Randy."

"But... I'm overdressed, aren't I?" She looked down at the dress and he lifted her chin.

"It's beautiful and it looks beautiful on you. Who cares what others think? It's your ceremony, and you have the right to wear whatever you want. Jesse wore a long, pink gown for ours." Tucker winked at Jesse.

"You did?" Tracy asked as Jesse handed her a bouquet of tiny, purple roses.

"Yeah, and I didn't care what anyone thought. It was my ceremony, so I had it my way. Stop trying to meet other people's expectations, and just be yourself." Jesse reached up and straightened Tracy's necklace. "You truly are a beautiful bride."

"Yeah, and wait until you see what Randy's wearing." Tucker clicked his tongue, and Tracy groaned as they hurried down the hallway.

"Please tell me it's not a bathrobe or a kilt."

"Oh, don't worry; he's completely covered." Tucker grinned but gave her nothing more. She nudged him with her elbow, and he laughed. "You'll see him soon enough." Holding tightly to her arm, "Watch your step," he cautioned as they descended the stairs.

Standing in the foyer as Alpha Cooper addressed the pack, Tracy could hear snickers and laughter from time to time. Apparently, the crowd was being entertained, but by whom? She didn't know. "Wait here for your escort," Tucker said when the alpha called for him and Nigel to join him on the front deck. He opened the door and motioned for Trace. "I'll be outside if you need me."

Trace walked into the room as Tucker walked out, a large grin on his face. "I never dared believe I'd get the chance to stand beside my daughter on her bonding night." He stepped to her side and cupped her cheek. "Thank you for allowing me this special moment," he said, kissing her forehead. "Randy's a lucky man."

"I'm the lucky one, for so many reasons." She lifted the handkerchief to her nose and sniffled. "Thank you for everything." She drew in a deep breath and took her dad's arm as they waited inside the door.

This is your night. Take it all in and enjoy. She sighed and pushed her fears away. Randy went the extra mile to make their ceremony special, and she wasn't about to ruin it by worrying about what someone might think of her wearing an actual wedding gown. She would hold her head high because she knew the love that went into making the dress. It would become an heirloom she could save and pass down to her own daughter one day. She giggled softly as she watched Alpha Cooper through the crack in the open door.

Thirty-Three

Tracy

"Quiet down, we have a lot of business to conduct before our run tonight." Alpha Cooper held up his hand to silence the last of the whispers. "First, I'd like to take this opportunity to announce Tucker Wilson has completed his training and is now officially the Alpha of the Berkley Pack. Everyone joining his pack will meet here on the deck after the run." Alpha Cooper glanced over at Tucker who flashed his newly inked tattoo at the cheering crowd. "Also, I'd like to announce that Nigel Stone has accepted the alpha position in Buffer County. Anyone interested in joining Nigel's pack has until the next full moon to apply for placement by the elders." Waiting until the catcalls stopped, and for Nigel to button his shirt, Ben turned serious and nodded towards the door. "There has been a slight change of plans tonight. I have a special bonding ceremony to perform and I was supposed to give the bride away, but at the last minute, a better man stepped up to the plate." Whispers spread throughout the crowd, and once the pack silenced again, Tucker pulled open the door.

With her dad at her side, escorting her out the door, Tracy glanced down at the tiny roses. She didn't normally shy away from being the center of attention, but this time, it was different, much more personal, and she could feel everyone watching her. *It's your ceremony, your way.*

She glanced up and nearly fainted when Randy moved out from behind Nigel. Wearing a black tuxedo and a purple tie that matched the roses she was holding, she grinned at the impish gleam in his eyes. She licked her lips in appreciation of how well his tux fit him and blushed as he scanned the length of her gown. His slow smile stretched into a wicked grin, causing her heart to beat erratically as he rushed across the deck to where she was standing and pulled her into a slow, sultry kiss.

The pack went wild with howls and whistles. Tracy thought even her dad was laughing. But it wasn't until Alpha Cooper teased, "We're not there yet," that she felt the heat coloring her cheeks. Randy licked his lips and flashed a dazzling smile towards the pack as Tracy giggled nervously. Apparently, Randy didn't mind being the center of attention, and after shaking Trace's hand, he led Tracy over to where the alpha stood waiting.

Alpha Cooper gave a subtle nod and cleared his throat as he turned to the pack. "We are gathered here tonight, beneath the blue moon, to celebrate the bonding of Randy Grayson and Tracy Hudson. We come to bear witness to the promise they offer each other, and to provide our support as a pack." Alpha Cooper turned and winked as Randy cleared his throat. Now, he was nervous? "Do you Randy Grayson, promise to love, honor, and accept Tracy as your bond mate, uniting the two of you until your time on this earth is over?"

Randy lifted her hand, quickly kissing her knuckles. "Tracy, I accept you as my bond-mate. You are my heart, my soul, and everything right in my life." Taking the handkerchief from her hand, he tucked it in his pocket and then unexpectedly, slid a small gold band onto her finger causing her breath to hitch. "I promise to love you forever." Tears sprang to her eyes, and he gently wiped them away before reaching back into his pocket and placing his ring in her hand.

"And do you, Tracy Hudson, promise to love, honor, and accept Randy as your bond mate, uniting the two of you until your time on this earth is over?"

Tracy glanced up, unable to hold back her tears. "Randy, I accept you always as my bond mate. You are my heart, my soul, and the reason I look forward to each and every day." Her voice cracked and her hands trembled as she fumbled to get the ring on his finger—panic instantly setting in. Randy placed his hand over hers, sliding the ring over his knuckle and gently squeezing her hands. "I promise to love you forever." She sighed softly when he smiled.

Alpha Cooper nodded before turning toward the pack. "As the Alpha of the Green River Region, let it be known, Randy and Tracy Grayson have sealed their bond. May their union be blessed and may they bring new life to our pack." He looked over at Randy and grinned. "Now you may kiss your mate."

Randy grabbed Tracy around the waist and dipped her backwards, his whispered words tickling her ear. "I can't wait to remove this tie." Kissing her until her toes curled, she held tightly around his neck. Finally, the night they had both been waiting for had arrived, and she was eager to see what their future would bring. The pack cheered and her knees weakened as she melted in his arms. Randy gave her everything he promised that day beside the lake—a family, his love, and his name.

Then Seth yelled from somewhere out in the yard, "Come on, Randy, we won't bite."

Randy smiled and nipped her lip, teasing her, before he turned to search out Seth.

"Ignore him, he's just being silly," Tracy said, blissfully content and floating on air with the excitement of officially sealing their bond. It was a night she would never forget, and the wedding she had dreamed of since she was a little girl. But the most surprising part of their ceremony was the gold band Randy placed on her finger. That was something humans did, not wolves, another thing she would cherish for the rest of her life. She inhaled his scent, causing her wolf to stir and a low rumble settled in her chest. Standing beside Randy at the edge of the deck, Tracy tossed her bouquet in the air and peeked up at her breathtakingly handsome mate. She was fan-girling, but damn! If he wasn't the most delicious thing she'd ever laid eyes on.

Jesse rushed up the steps to help her with her dress, but Randy wasn't ready to give up the night and ushered Tracy out onto the lawn. As the pack readied for their run, he pulled her into his arms and hummed a tune that only she could hear. She shivered as the soft vibration spread goosebumps over her body. "Our first dance as a married couple," Randy said and as they swayed in the chilly night air, nothing could stop the furnace of heat that simmered between them, causing a wave of warmth to settle deep in her belly. It was hard to believe they had sealed their bond before the pack, their friends, and *her family*. Her heart overflowed with the magic of the night, and if she had to die at that moment, she would die happy.

Their spontaneous dance ended way too soon and Randy cupped her cheek, his fingers working through her hair to release the butterfly clip. "I just needed a minute away from the pack to take all this in." He shoved the clip into his coat pocket and met her eyes. "I feel it here; it's so intense." He touched his chest where his heart beat the strongest. "Our bond is alive, moving through me, reaching out to you. It's amazing, crazy, and scary as hell. The love I feel when I look at you steals my breath. How will I ever survive you?" He drew her into another earth-shattering kiss and groaned when Jesse cleared her throat behind Tracy.

"The dress?" Jesse tapped her toe on the ground and grinned when Randy stepped out of the kiss and rolled his eyes.

Tracy couldn't stop the rapid beating of her heart as Randy drew down the zipper on her gown. She couldn't restrain her giggles at his sudden gasp when he realized she wasn't wearing anything beneath the dress. Sliding it down her arms, Jesse grabbed hold of the waist, helping her to step out.

"You're even more beautiful than I remember," Randy said and Tracy glanced up at his smoldering eyes as he shrugged off his jacket and ripped the white shirt from his chest. Leaving only the tie still fastened around his neck, her breath hitched, and apparently, Jesse's did as well. Randy's newly inked tattoo wasn't an alpha's tattoo, but rather a large wolf head that took up half of his chest. When he slipped off his shoes and toed off his socks, all words escaped her. He chuckled at her reaction as he unfastened his pants, letting them fall to his feet. He kicked them to the side when Tracy's jaw dropped, and Jesse quickly bolted for the house. He grinned. "Guess we have more in common than you thought."

Tracy giggled behind her hand as Randy proudly stood stark naked for all to see. Following his tie down, her face glowed with a slight blush and she quickly blinked up to the grin on his face. "You can't run like that," she finally said as he moved closer.

"Sure I can." He glanced around at the other pack members that had yet to start their run. "I've never seen so many naked people in my life. Y'all aren't into orgies, or are you?"

"Would you stop?" She chuckled and swatted his arm as Brayden zipped up beside them on a dirt bike.

"It's all yours," Brayden said and Tracy's eyes rounded when Randy straddled the bike.

"That's how you're running?" Again, she was in shock and her jaw dropped. It was official, she had bonded with a crazy man.

"Yeah, and I'm giving you a five-second head start. Starting now." A wicked grin turned his lips and when he started the countdown, she bolted into the woods, her squeals buffered by the tree line.

Tracy phased when Randy yelled, "five," and raced up the narrow path to join the other wolves. Looking over her shoulder, it was apparent Randy's determination outweighed his common sense, but impressive nonetheless. She slowed and moved off the trail, allowing the others to continue past while listening to the bike sputter and a few choice words rang in the air. She phased back and grinned, imagining him alone in the woods, riding naked on the dirt bike. Her eyes flared and she set off in his direction as naughty thoughts flashed through her mind. Sneaking back to where the bike had stalled, she watched from behind a tree as he tried repeatedly to restart the bike. Finally, after several more failed attempts, he gave up and wiped his brow with his tie, resting his elbows on the handlebars.

Tracy stepped out from behind the tree and placed her hand on his shoulder, startling him. "Welcome to the pack," she said, unable to hold back a laugh.

"I knew you wouldn't abandon me." He pulled her into his arms, burying his face in her hair. "Come on, I'll give you a ride back." He patted the seat, and she smirked but settled in behind him.

"Unless you're going to push the bike, I don't think we're going anywhere."

"Oh, ye of little faith." Randy turned the key, and the bike roared to life. "Hang on and keep your head down." The bike shot forward and she squealed, her arms wrapping around his waist. He was irresistible to begin with and being naked on the bike only intensified the dizzying effect. She tightened her grip, her laughter muffled against his back. If there were any way she could have crawled into his lap, she most certainly would have.

Thirty-Four

Randy

The stunned look on Tracy's face was the highlight of his night. Assuming he would stand before a pack of shifters and pledge his undying love for her without running with the pack afterward was her first mistake. Riding a dirt bike was a genius idea and stripping down to nothing but his purple tie? Okay, so maybe he didn't actually run on two legs, but he most definitely participated and should have received a trophy for his effort and ingenuity. Assuming the bike had stalled, his way of catching up to her, was her second mistake.

Randy grinned, thoroughly enjoying their ride together as the bike jerked and Tracy squealed. Her hold tightened with her laughter. Taking it slowly to avoid the low-hanging branches, as soon as they cleared the trees, he glanced over at the cabin, half expecting Trace to rush out the door and arrest them for indecent exposure. Sputtering to a stop, he held the bike for Tracy to dismount as excitement rippled beneath his skin.

"That was insane!" Tracy gushed, moving to his side.

"What? You don't like riding in the woods?" he teased, although he would admit he learned a few things the hard way. First, the dirt bike was no match for the wolves; they were super-fast and capable of turning on a dime. Second, when riding in the woods, stay low. The welt on his forehead was proof of why that was good advice. And third, never trust Brayden to fill the gas tank. Apparently, Seth was behind that little derailment, but Randy was smart enough to check the gas gauge before he entered the woods. Granted, it was funny, but the joke was on them.

"I see you made it back before daylight," Seth said. Holding out a stack of clothes, he nodded to Tracy who was grinning from behind Randy.

"Yeah, no thanks to you." Randy passed a pair of jeans and a long-sleeved shirt to Tracy.

"Well, it being your first run, we wanted to make it memorable."

"And you think this ratty bike is what I'll remember? I don't think your light's clicked on in the closet." Randy tapped the side of his head. "Look around. I see a lot of naked girls here, and you being single fail to see the possibilities."

"Don't worry, my eyes are wide open," Brayden said, joining the conversation. "Oh, wait, you were talking to the uptight guy here that needs to get laid."

"Shut up." Seth punched Brayden in the arm, making

him laugh.

"He's upset because all the females are checking out this fine physique." Brayden flexed his bicep and Tracy snorted, pulling down her shirt.

"You mean your new beta title," Seth smirked.

"It's better than being an alpha. I have half the responsibility and all the benefits." Brayden winked and added, "Like that little brunette standing at the tree line. Don't wait up." He took off in a jog across the field.

"He has a point," Tracy said, moving out from behind Randy.

"Maybe so, but right now, I have all the benefits I can handle." Seth took hold of the bike. "Your dad is waiting for you all in the cabin."

After saying their goodbyes to Tracy's family, Randy mounted his bike and glanced at the side mirror, seeing the wide smile on Tracy's face. She wasn't expecting her bike to be at the alpha's house, but once she realized it was, she was more than ready to go. Following the dirt road to the highway, his pulse raced with thoughts of how their night would end. *No more cold showers or sleeping on the couch!*

Pulling onto the paved road, he glanced back at Tracy. It was hard to believe the most gorgeous girl in the world had chosen him. He slowed his bike and waited for her to make the turn. Mesmerized by how seductively her body moved as she maneuvered the motorcycle, he pushed open his leather jacket, allowing the cool night air to chill his dirty thoughts. It was too cold to be riding motorcycles at the early morning hour, but Randy could say the same about stripping naked and running through the woods. He glanced back at the grin plastered on Tracy's face. She was having the time of her life—he would have his later.

Tracy had never driven to Berkley before, but she was an excellent driver so Randy felt confident she could handle the road. She was in her element and could ride all night given the chance, but that wasn't part of his plan. He chuckled and clicked on the turn signal, and her pretty, little pout reflected back at him through the side mirror. She now knew they were headed to Tucker's cabin, but had no idea why.

Randy slowed to make the final turn. The moon was high, casting the area in a soft, silvery glow. The worn gravel road ran alongside the river until it crossed a wooded area at the backside of the property. Driving around to the front of the cabin, activating the motion-sensor lights, he pulled up next to the front porch and shut off his bike as Tracy joined him, a frown replacing her pout.

"Why are we here?" she asked when he got off his bike and removed his helmet.

"I thought we could hang out for a little while." She narrowed her eyes, not trusting that's what they were really doing. "Let me help you with that." He unfastened her helmet, and she pushed it off her head, glancing up through the large front windows where candles burned, lighting the room. Her eyes widened with understanding and she stepped off the bike.

"Are we staying the night?" she asked excitedly before squealing when he grinned and wrapped his arms around her waist.

"You can thank Jesse; it was her idea." Randy had yet to tell her they would spend the next five days there. *All alone.* He grabbed her up in his arms and carried her to the front door.

"I can walk, you know." She wiggled, but he wasn't about to put her down.

"You had the gown, now I'm carrying you across the threshold." He held her against his chest and pushed open the door. "Are you hungry?" he asked once he placed her on her feet. She looked over at the small table where various dishes sat covered. "Or would you rather go straight to the dessert?" Her ears tinted with a blush and he cupped her cheek, his thumb brushing over her lip. "I love it when you blush." He drew her into a gentle kiss. "I was afraid tonight would never come."

Tracy slowly blinked up, a sultry glimmer in her eyes. "I'm not really hungry," she said in a soft country drawl that nearly brought him to his knees. When she laced her fingers with his, playfully pulling him over to the large red sofa, his heart jumped into his throat. She had a dirty mind, matching his, which promised it would be a night they would both remember.

He sat down beside her and inhaled through his nose to stifle the desire rippling beneath his skin. To distract his mind, he scanned the room, stopping at the small fire burning in the fireplace. To his left was a small table with two crystal wine glasses and a bottle of grape juice, half submerged in a bucket of ice. "Would you like something to drink?" he offered while glancing up at the various candles lighting the room. Then he looked over his shoulder when Tracy chuckled and stretched her body the length of the couch. Her jean-clad legs were so long and slender... he quivered and shoved the bottle back into the ice bucket.

"Mr. Grayson, are you stalling?" Her fingers trailed beneath his jacket, causing goosebumps to appear on his arms.

Hell no, I'm not stalling! But he didn't want to come off as an overly excited teenager, ready to jump her bones the minute they walked through the door. He grinned roguishly, and said, "Stalling? That's what you think this is?" With her nod, he stood, yanking off his jacket and pitching it onto the matching chair. "Baby, I never stall. I might sputter from time to time, but I never stall." He pulled her off the sofa and, with one hand on her lower back and the other holding her hand to his chest, he moved her around the room. "You're creating a monster here."

"By dancing?"

"No, this is me stalling." He rolled his eyes. "Because you're rushing me and I want everything to happen naturally, not just because we can." He pulled her closer and rested his chin on top of her head to hide his grin. If she bought that line, he had a bridge to sell her.

"Ooh, I like the way you think." She swayed in his arms, her hips pressing and moving against his. She knew exactly what she was doing, and it had nothing to do with buying a bridge. A low moan worked up his throat.

"Fine, have it your way," he caved, releasing her to adjust his jeans. All night he had struggled to distract his mind, but now, it was in the fast lane, heading straight for her. He quickly scooped her up onto his shoulder, smacking her bottom and making her squeal.

"Put me down!" Tracy laughed as he bounded up the stairs to the large master bedroom and dropped her in the middle of the king-sized bed.

"I hope you're ready for The Beast because once I rev the motor, there will be no stalling."

"Are we talking about you? Or your motorcycle?" A smile appeared when Tracy added, "Maybe I should make out with your bike." Her tongue darted out to wet her lips, her face glowing beneath his gaze. Her dirty talk definitely turned him on, and he had just the cure for that sassy mouth.

"No, maybe you should make out with me, on my beast!" The cool air coming in through the open balcony doors couldn't douse the fire burning through his veins, and within seconds, he had her stripped of everything but her smile. He slowed his breathing and yanked his shirt over his head while kicking off his boots. There was no hiding the desire in his eyes as he slowly scanned the soft contours of her body. Mapping every detail to memory, down to the tiniest freckle—which happened to be on her right thigh—he intended to lick every single one before the night was over. His smoky eyes met her brilliant green orbs. "See something you like?"

"A whole lot of something," she replied in that slow country drawl that weakened his knees. Her eyes darkened with unmistakable heat as his jeans fell open, and he shoved them down until they were a pile of denim at his feet. Ever so slowly he loosened the tie and pulled it from around his neck, tossing it onto her stomach.

"You're even more stunning now that you have my last name." Randy couldn't keep his eyes from drifting down as she slowly pulled the silk fabric across her belly, leaving a trail of goosebumps behind. *So beautiful.* His heart hammered triple-time, and as he moved up on the bed to straddle her hips, she draped the tie around his waist. Tugging him down until they were touching skin to skin, his hands fisted in her hair and he drew her into an explosive kiss. Fire shot through his veins and every nerve ending in his body ignited, melting his control. "Tracy," he whispered fervently as he trailed soft kisses to her ear. "If this is a dream, don't wake me."

Tracy moaned and rocked her hips in reply, her soft whimpers urging him on. "I love you," she whispered as he buried his face in the crook of her neck, breathing in her spicy scent. Her body quivered when he nipped her shoulder and then pulled back, propping up on his elbows. She was so damn gorgeous, lying naked beneath him.

His head dropped down to her chest and he sucked in a deep breath to distract himself from the pressure building below his waist. Settled between her thighs, as their bodies aligned, he squeezed his eyes shut. "Tracy." He held his breath and his hips inched forward, slowly adjusting her to him. "I'd like to introduce my beast."

Thirty-Five

Randy

Their bonding night was a success. The soft sigh as Tracy closed her eyes and snuggled against his side testified to that. She was his world and he planned to show her just how much she meant to him every single day. Watching her as she slept, he fought the urge to wake her with wet kisses and replay the night, if only to feel her body moving with his.

Their first time together was electrifying, different from anything he had ever experienced. With his eyes wide open, suddenly everything became more vivid and real. The incredible sensation of the bond binding them together as they reached their mutual release sent them both over the edge of pure bliss, and he craved more.

Randy twisted a strand of her glorious hair around his

finger as it glistened in the moonlight, a sexy shade of take-me-I'm-yours red. And her tantalizing scent, now stronger with the bond, made his mouth water, tempting him to lick her freckles all over again. His breathing grew heavy and he shuddered, hopelessly addicted to her touch. *Could a man die from too much sex?* He silently chuckled at the thought. *If so, kill me now!* His heart strummed as his hand moved down and rested on her low belly. *So damn tempting.*

He closed his eyes, searching for her emotions through the bond. It was crazy to think he could honestly have that kind of connection with her. Their bond was strong, solid, and she was... *blissfully happy.* He smiled, knowing he was the reason for her happiness.

She sighed contentedly and rolled over onto her belly, the silk sheet slipping off her hips. He lifted up on his elbow, his eyes following the slope of her back to the roundness of her rear. She was perfection, from head to toe, and he wanted to trail light kisses down to the little dimple on her lower back. He groaned inwardly, thinking if she didn't wake up soon, he would spend the rest of the night in a cold shower.

"That tickles," Tracy murmured as she stretched her arms up beneath the pillow. *So damn tempting.*

"Are you awake?" he whispered, scattering light kisses down her spine. Then he froze at the sight before his eyes and glanced up at the moonlight coming into the room.

"No." she sighed as her breathing leveled out. She was asleep again.

Randy stared down at Tracy's lower back while working his bottom lip between his teeth. *It can't be.* He swallowed the hard lump of reality that instantly brought him to tears. His heart slammed against his ribs, and his anger grew. He resisted the impulse to wake Tracy and demand answers. Instead, he carefully covered her with the sheet. The urge to protect her and destroy anyone that dared to lay a hand on her had him quietly slipping off the bed and pulling on his jeans.

His body shook with rage as he hurried down the stairs, his eyes wet with tears. She had lived through hell, and now he knew just how deeply hell ran. Grabbing his phone off the sofa table, he hurried out the front door and across the yard to the riverbank. His mind was one thought away from snapping, and his hands trembled as he quickly punched in Tucker's number.

"Did you know?" Trying not to lose control, his voice came out too gruff when Tucker answered the phone. He could have waited until daylight to call, and probably should have, but his need for answers outweighed all rational thought.

"I don't guess so. What are you talking about?" Tucker's mumbled words sounded like he was in a tunnel.

"Who beat Tracy?"

"What?" Tucker was awake now; he could hear him moving, maybe sitting up in the bed. "I don't know. When did it happen? She never mentioned anything to me."

"It wasn't recent, but she has the scars. I saw them, barely, but they're definitely there. Did Travis beat her?" He sunk down to his knees and glanced up at the open balcony doors, his heart breaking for his wife.

"Give me a minute and I'll call you back," Tucker said and Randy glanced down as the call ended.

Thinking back to the stories Tracy shared about her

childhood, she never mentioned anyone but Travis disciplining her. His jaw clenched as he stared across the river while listening to the birds frantically chirping in the trees. It would be daylight soon enough. "Yeah," he said, answering his phone on the first ring.

"I talked to Trace. He thinks it was Owen, Travis's brother. Is she okay?"

"She doesn't know I saw the scars. I had to get out of the house. I'm so damn mad, I want to rip someone's arms off."

"Don't show your anger. She probably wanted to tell you but feared what you would think. Remember, it's Tracy, and she's very critical of herself. If she suspects you have ill thoughts of her, she'll pull away."

"No! I would never look at her any differently. She's my wife, my mate, and I love her for who she is, not for what she looks like. I'm not angry at her." His voice lowered. "Just the SOB that put those scars on her body."

"You and me both," Tucker huffed and then continued. "Listen, when you talk to her, show her how you feel, and make her want to tell you."

"I will. And thanks for calling me back." Randy ended the call and wiped his eyes. He needed to calm down before he snuck back inside, hopefully, without waking her. He silenced his phone and started across the yard.

After undressing and slipping back into bed, Randy pulled Tracy into his arms, holding her until the sun rose above the horizon. She looked like an angel, so perfect, hiding the devastating life she once lived. He blinked hard to clear the moisture from his eyes as he drew in a rickety breath.

Slowly, he sat up, his fingers tracing circles down her

back, causing her body to twitch—she was ticklish. He rolled his bottom lip, ready to smile and at the same time, cry. "Hey, ginger girl. You awake?" His fingers traced the thin, silvery scars that crossed her rear and she shivered.

"Mmm, yeah," she said. Still somewhat asleep, her husky morning voice was sexy as hell.

"What is this?" His voice now louder, but soothing, roused her from sleep.

"What is what?" she asked, gripping the pillow tighter.

"These scars." *Way to be subtle, asshole.*

Tracy startled awake and quickly rolled over, grabbing the sheet to cover her body. Shame filled her eyes and she pulled away, sitting up on the side of the bed.

"I wasn't criticizing you and I'm sorry if I scared you. I just want to know what happened." He inched over behind her and wrapped his arms around her waist as her entire body trembled.

"I didn't realize they were still visible," she whispered as she tucked the sheet beneath her rear.

"No, don't you dare hide from me! I love you, with or without them." He kissed her shoulder and her body shook with silent tears as she squeezed her eyes shut.

"It was a long time ago. Owen, my mom's bond mate, punished me for something I had no control over."

Randy lay back on the bed, pulling Tracy with him— and she turned into his chest. "How old were you?" he whispered in her hair.

"I was five. My mother tried to leave the pack..." Her words trailed off and she opened her eyes to look into his. "He always hated me."

"I'm so sorry. When you talked about your life, it always sounded horrible, but this? I can't imagine. Are you okay? I mean, emotionally okay?" His hand drifted down to her waist and she shuddered. "I promise no one will ever hurt or abuse you again." A tear slipped from his eye and she wiped it away. "I'm here if you ever want to talk, or vent, or take out your frustration. Use me as a punching bag, but don't hide from me. Please. There's nothing you can do that will ever make me look at you any differently than I do right now. We're bonded, and in my eyes, you are perfect."

She stared at the gold band on her finger as he lifted her chin and placed a tender kiss on her lips. She wasn't very receptive at first but eventually wrapped her arms around his neck as her tears flowed freely. "I love you," he said, pushing the sheet down and lifting her thigh to his hip.

Tracy wiped the tears from her eyes and sighed. "At the time, I thought it was just a nightmare. It wasn't until Trace told me he was my dad that the nightmares stopped."

Randy swallowed hard, thinking maybe he wasn't ready to hear the details after all. "You don't have to talk about it right now. I won't pressure you." His voice cracked and he buried his face in her hair. His heart shattering.

"No, I need to get it out so I can leave it in the past." She sniffled, his shoulder now wet with tears. "Owen told Mom she could leave and go back to her pack, but I had to stay there with him. That was the night he found out I wasn't his daughter, and he beat me with a switch to punish my mother." Randy's breath caught and Tracy pressed her fingers to his lips when he pulled back and stared into her eyes. "Mom cried for weeks, telling me I didn't deserve the punishment, but maybe I did. Not only was I an embarrassment to him, but also his primary leverage. He used me to control her, threatening more harm to me if she ever crossed him. She took him at his word."

His fist clenched as more tears filled his eyes. "He was a coward, bullying your mother by threatening to beat you. If he were alive today, I would destroy him." Randy rolled over and wrapped his body around hers. "Don't ever be afraid to tell me anything. I might not like what you have to say, or want to hear it, but I will listen if it's what you need from me."

"I know," Tracy said, pushing her fingers into his hair. "I should have told you sooner, but when the nightmares first started, I couldn't make sense of them. Funny, since meeting Trace, everything's come together like lost pieces of a puzzle. I think visiting my family in Montana helped me overcome my bad dreams."

Randy laced his fingers with hers and kissed her knuckles. "I'm glad you went, and I'm sorry for being such a jackass. Just tell me who you want me to take out, and I'm on it." He smiled sadly when she chuckled. "Seriously, what can I do to make things better? I want you to always be happy."

"Well, since you're asking..." she grinned, her finger tracing over his tattoo. "Breakfast in bed sounds nice."

Thirty-Six

Jesse

"Life is fickle," Jesse said, staring out over the rooftop. It was their last night in Cloverly, so spending it on the widow's walk was the perfect ending to that chapter in her life.

"What do you mean?" Tucker asked, lying on his back to stare up at the stars. He put his arm out for Jesse to lie down beside him.

"I was excited about moving here and living with Gramma. And when I turned eighteen and moved into the apartment, I thought I was all that and a bucket of jelly beans."

"Jelly beans are good. I like the yellow ones."

"I'll make a note of it." Jesse chuckled. "Then bonding with you and moving to your cabin, I was content knowing we would soon be moving to Berkley to start our own family. It's funny because I always thought small towns were supposed to be leisurely, a walk in the park, but that's not what I got. It's like I've come full circle in barely a years' time."

Tucker furrowed his brows. "And that's a bad thing?"

"Not at all. When Dad and I moved here, my gut feeling said this was where we were supposed to be. But now that everything has fallen into place, and I met you, it has proven to me that my destiny is no longer here. I belong with you and our pack. I belong in Berkley. I know that sounds crazy, but..."

"No, I thought that too. I never understood the pull I felt in Cloverly, but I had to be here. Now I know that was because of you." Tucker groaned as the music started to play, interrupting their conversation.

"Wonder what he's up to?" Jesse asked, rolling over to look down at Seth's cabin. She didn't have to wait long before Seth walked out the backdoor, followed by a tall brunette. "I thought he was dating Mallory." She frowned when Seth pulled the girl into his arms. However, when Mallory walked out the door with Brett, she palmed her forehead. "Guess that answers my question." She chuckled, causing Seth to look over at her grandmother's house.

"So, who's the brunette?" Tucker asked, rolling onto his side. He whistled and Seth looked up and grinned.

"I think she was one of the girls that bought underwear from him at the boutique."

"That's kind of personal, isn't it?"

"Considering she proposed marriage to him that day, I think they're long past personal." Jesse rolled back over and stared at the sky.

"I thought you were joking about the marriage proposals."

"No, it happened." Jesse laughed and pushed up to a sitting position as Brian turned into his driveway. "Look." She pointed and Tucker lifted up on his elbows.

"Quick, get the pea-shooter." Tucker grinned devilishly and bumped her shoulder when she rolled her eyes. Watching Brian and Annie gather groceries from the back of the Jeep, Tucker pulled off his pajama pants and said, "Watch this."

Jesse's jaw dropped when Tucker phased right there on the roof. Meanwhile, down at the curbside, Annie walked into the house, leaving Brian in the driveway. Old Clumsy nudged Jesse with his nose and let out two sharp yelps, followed by a ferocious growl.

Brian jerked around, scanning the tree line as he slowly backed towards the house. "He's going to see you," Jesse whispered, ducking behind the chimney so Brian couldn't see her on the roof.

Tucker's wolf inched forward, careful not to step off the edge of the roof, and snarled. Old Clumsy was very protective of his mate, and no matter how hard Jesse tugged on his tail, he wasn't backing down. His golden eyes flared in warning, drawing Brian's attention to the roof. It was the funniest thing Jesse had ever seen, and she could only imagine what was going through Brian's mind. His mouth dropped open as he stumbled backward, landing with a heavy thud as the contents of the grocery bags rolled down the driveway.

Tucker phased behind the chimney and grabbed hold of Jesse who was rolling with laughter. "Shh, he'll hear you." He chuckled as he pointed. "Look, there's Annie."

Jesse released one last snicker when Annie stepped over Brian and stomped out to the Jeep with a scowl on her face. After locking the doors, she gathered all the cans of food Brian had dropped and stormed back to the house.

"What the hell is wrong with you? There's nothing out there!" Annie fussed as Brian pointed to the roof.

"I swear I saw..." His voice trailed off and Jesse wanted to yell, "Who's crazy now?"

"You saw what?" Annie glanced in the direction of his pointing finger.

"Never mind," Brian huffed as he walked into the house, leaving Annie to shut the door.

"You enjoyed that more than you should have," Jesse said, but even she couldn't hide the amusement in her eyes.

"And you didn't?" Tucker asked, his grin exposing his dimples.

"Sure I did. He once called me crazy," Jesse said matter-of-factly.

"Well, there you have it! That's what happens when you talk smack about people. So, yeah, I may have enjoyed it more than I should have, but I'm not always the nice guy, and well, he is still a wuss."

"Really?" Jesse slowly trailed her finger up his arm before tapping the tip of his nose. "Not always the nice guy means sometimes you're bad?" Her brow arched, and his grin turned wicked. "So what does a girl like me have to do to get on your bad side?"

Tucker jumped to his feet, pulling Jesse into his arms. "I guess that depends on how many of the neighbors you want to wake up." Squeezing her against his rock-hard chest, another growl rumbled in his throat as he stared into her eyes.

A challenge, she thought, and one she was tempted to take until Seth whistled and Tucker turned three shades of red.

"Karma." Jesse snorted as she dropped down into the bedroom, leaving Tucker naked on the roof.

The following morning, Jesse was up with the sun, sitting in the swing like she did on her first day in Cloverly. Glancing down at the corner house when a horn beeped, she felt sad seeing the red truck and not Lori's mother's car in the driveway. *Everything changes*, she admitted, glancing across the street at Brian's house.

Nothing had changed there, other than the circle of friends he kept. And since Annie had moved in with him, she rarely saw him out, and when she did, it was usually in passing. He once asked why she turned against him and ran to Tucker. She just smiled and said, "I didn't run to him, I was waiting *for* him." He didn't understand, and she didn't feel the need to explain.

Then her attention was drawn to the two little girls playing four-square on the sidewalk. She recalled the day when she first met Lori and Megan, swiftly going from best friends to business partners, and oh, the memories they made. But when Lori bonded with Hayden and left Cloverly, she took a piece of Jesse's heart with her to the mountains. They were sisters by choice, and now they were sisters-in-law, sharing the same last name. Jesse smiled.

Life was all about changes. For the boutique, it was all about Tracy stepping up to take over Lori's Lingerie. She was a blast to work with and quite the entertainer. Everyone that came into the store complimented her. She was stylish and always dressed to reflect the image of the boutique. She was a lot like Lori with her snappy comebacks and dirty mind. Lori was the sailor, but Tracy? She was every girl's nightmare. And since bonding with Randy, her whole demeanor changed and her beauty intensified with her smile. She was at peace, knowing she had a mate and a pack that supported her no matter what. Two packs actually. Trace's entrance into her life had provided her with a family as well as the strength to overcome her past.

"This is surreal," Jesse said when Tucker joined her on the swing. Allowing Tracy and Randy to spend five days at their cabin to celebrate their bonding, her grandmother was generous enough to let them stay there since they had moved everything from their cabin in Cloverly to Berkley. At first, she thought it would be awkward, but she should have known better. Tucker spent his mornings with Gramma watching the news, while Jesse picked up around the house and tended to Moose— her grumpy ball of fluff. She missed him the most. She rubbed his head as he lounged lazily in her lap. But the nights were the best. Spending them on the widow's walk because Tucker absolutely loved it, was very entertaining. And scaring the crap out of Brian? Even she had to admit it was funny.

"Yeah, if you had told me a year ago I'd be sleeping under this roof, I'd never have believed you," Tucker said, a gentle smile on his face.

"I know. How crazy is that?" She rested her head on his shoulder while he twirled a strand of her hair around his finger. "I'm going to miss Cloverly, but I'm so ready to settle in with our pack."

After moving with her dad to Cloverly, the last person Jesse thought she would meet there was her husband. She figured she would eventually end up in DC with her mother, if only to attend college. College still wasn't off the table, and when she was ready to go, she would attend one of the local universities in the neighboring county. For the time being, she planned to continue working at the boutique. She still volunteered at the shelter from time to time, but since Dr. Steven's wife returned to work, Jesse had more time to focus on new designs. Business was booming, and thanks to Tucker and his input, she expected sales to be great. Smiling as Tucker pulled her out of the swing, she was content with her life and where she was going. Berkley wasn't the mountains, but it was home.

"I love you guys. You'll have to come visit us," Jesse said. Placing Moose inside the house, she moved across the porch, meeting her dad at the steps.

"We will. And if you need anything at all..." He pulled her into a tight hug, making her laugh.

"Dad, I'll only be twenty minutes away, not across the country," she reminded, making him blush. "Gramma, call me when you're ready to plant the garden." She hugged her grandmother and added, "Take care of Moose for me." Jesse hurried off the porch and across the yard to meet Tucker at the truck.

"Drive carefully," Dr. Williams said, waving from the porch as Tucker backed out of the driveway.

"You ready for this?" Tucker fist-bumped Jesse and grinned. She was more than ready to be living on the river in a beautiful cabin.

"I can hardly wait. Our first night alone, just you, me, and the sunset..." She turned down the radio and seductively smiled. "How long will it be before Brayden and the others join us?"

As the beta for the Berkley Pack, Brayden had restored the small garage behind their cabin, insisting newly bonded couples needed their privacy until the honeymoon phase was over. *Too bad he'll be living in the garage for the rest of his life.* Jesse grinned at the thought.

Kelsey was the youngest female joining the pack and she had a crush on Brayden. She reminded Jesse of Lori, and could often be found sitting under a shade tree, reading a book.

Carter and Miles were the two newest scouts, and along with a crew of Kinsley members, they had actually built two cabins on the backside of the property. One for the males and one for the females.

But Jesse's favorite was Nigel's oldest sister Cecilia. After losing her mate seven years ago, she was finally ready to leave Kinsley and start a new life. She accepted the role of house mother and cook, saying it gave her purpose, but Tucker said she was just lonely.

"Brayden was there this morning to help Tracy and Randy clear out, and the others will be there by the end of the week. They're giving us some private time to enjoy the cabin before they arrive."

Tears filled Jesse's eyes and she smiled. "That is so sweet. We have a good pack, don't we?"

"The best!"

Thirty-Seven

Tracy

Never in Tracy's wildest dreams could she picture bonding with a human, and yet there she sat after five glorious days, still amazed by the fact. Who knew running into Randy in the woods would be the turning point in her life? And having a direct line to her dirty-minded farm boy's thoughts kept her blushing anytime he was near. By officially sealing their bond, it connected their hearts and flooded her with the most amazing feeling. Going from being alone, to having a mate and a large family, she was never happier. Her entire world changed in the matter of a week, and not in a bad way.

Granted, the bond had attracted her wolf, but what attracted Tracy had nothing to do with the bond, and everything to do with Randy's sexy smile and confident attitude. Staring into his stormy eyes, she would swear she glimpsed a wolf buried deep in his soul. Thankfully, though, he was just a human, and that's what she loved about him the most. She pinched herself to make sure she wasn't dreaming. In the shifter world, their connection was called fate; but to Tracy, it was love at first sight.

Sitting on the front stoop of the little cottage, she smiled, enjoying the late evening sun as her mind drifted. As exciting as the week was, having an actual family was probably the shock of the century—a father and brother that loved her unconditionally. Okay, so maybe being kidnapped wasn't the greatest ordeal she had ever endured, but the reason behind it was something you only read about in storybooks. Trace was smart to handcuff her and take her to his cabin, giving her time to think about the evidence he presented with no one around to interfere—like Randy who absolutely hated him at the time. But even with all the pictures, DNA report, and her birth certificate, it wasn't until the pack showed up and Randy punched Trace that she realized Trace really was her father. He was more than willing to take a beating for her, and his wolf was ready to let it happen. And because of that, she trusted him, his wolf, and his word.

Thinking about how much her family had grown, she could honestly say she was blessed. Not only did she have Randy's family and her family in Montana, she also had the pack in Cloverly. And it wasn't until Randy referred to Seth as the brother he never had that she noticed the close relationship between the two. They fought like brothers, cut-up like best friends, but in the end, always had each other's back. That was when she realized family wasn't just blood kin, but the people you looked forward to spending your time with on a daily basis.

Tucker was the perfect example, and she would definitely have to do something nice for him and Jesse after they were gracious enough to let them stay at the cabin. As sad as she was to leave what Randy now dubbed *the love shack,* she was glad to be back on the farm. She could officially say she had a home—and a new name. *Tracy Grayson* had a nice ring to it, and no longer would she use the Hudson name. Not because she was bonded with Randy, but because Trace insisted she change her name to Tracy Riley Grayson and she gladly accepted.

"Don't tell me, let me guess," Randy said, shoving his hands into the pockets of the navy pajama pants, hanging low on his hips. He waggled his brows suggestively. "You've been fantasizing about my sexy body."

"Mr. Grayson, you seem awfully sure of yourself," she said sweetly while trying to push his naked image from her mind. *Definitely sexy.* She rolled her eyes at his grin.

"No, I just recognized the smile." He took a seat beside her and pulled her into his lap. "You've been wearing it since the ceremony. I like knowing I put it there."

She traced her fingers over his tattoo, something she did anytime she was close enough to touch him. "I still can't believe you let Seth ink your chest."

"Yeah, he's pretty good with the details." Randy looked down at the wolf's head over his heart. "I figured if you can have a wolf, so can I. I'm going to call him *The Beast.*" He tweaked her nose, and she chuckled.

"Well, if that was your beast I heard growling this morning, the name fits."

"Keep it up, and you're going to hear him growl again. And soon." He tugged at the spaghetti strap of her nightgown. "He likes you better without clothes."

"As tempting as it is... and it really is tempting... we need to get supper before we both collapse from lack of nourishment."

"So you admit you were thinking about my body?"

"That and I was trying to figure out how you pulled it off. I mean the bike, the ring, the cabin, the dress. You even got a tattoo without me knowing. I don't know how to thank you for everything you've done."

He pulled her into a scorching kiss and whispered across her lips, "You don't need to thank me." Tracy moaned when he deepened the kiss, her whole body tingling to her toes. She licked her lips as he pulled back and said, "That's what I'm here for. I will do everything I can to give you the life you deserve."

Tracy snuggled against his chest, his hand moving to her lower back. "But this isn't a one-sided relationship, and I want to make you happy, too."

"You already did by taking my name. Do you know how many times I've said Tracy Grayson in my head? Like a million, and now it's true. I only ever wanted you to be my wife."

His words touched deeply in her heart. She really didn't deserve him. She glanced up at the mischief in his eyes and grinned. "I thought you only ever wanted my body."

"Well, there is that too." He laughed when she squealed and tried to wiggle away from his tickles. She knew better than to tease because it always ended with her being pinned beneath him. "But..." he finally said, allowing her to catch her breath. She snickered one last time and pulled the satin straps back up on her shoulders. "Before you distract me, I have one more surprise but it will be a few weeks before I can actually give it to you."

"No, I can't allow you to do anything more. You've done enough and if I lived a thousand lifetimes, I'd still never be able to give you back all that you've given me." Her heartfelt words made him smile even more, and he lifted her hand to his lips.

"Just this one last thing and I promise no more... at least for a little while. It's as much for me as you."

His pleading eyes broke down her barrier, and she caved. "Okay. Fine. What is it?"

"I've made arrangements for us to spend the summer in Montana."

Tracy squealed and jumped out of his lap, bouncing on her toes. "You didn't! How did you know?"

"Well, I had a man-to-man talk with TJ before our bonding ceremony. And it seems you mentioned scouting with him and Papaw, but because you were so busy with everyone else, you didn't actually go scouting. So he thought you might want to come back so he could take you on a tour of the mountainside. Of course, Trace was egging him on. I think he also wants to spend more time with you."

Tears filled her eyes and she quickly wiped them away. "I loved meeting the Montana pack, but I hated that you weren't there. You don't know how much it means to me, to have you actually meet my family."

"Yeah, I think I do." Randy stood, taking hold of her hand. "It's written all over your beautiful face."

Acknowledgements

Thank you for reading the final installment of the Cloverly Wolves series. If you enjoyed the story, please consider leaving a review so others may find my books.

And thanks to Teri at editingfairy.com for editing my stories.

About the Author

B. S. Todd lives in a small western Kentucky town with her husband, son, two dogs and a ferocious feline. A nature enthusiast, she has always drawn her greatest inspiration from the natural world around her. Her hobbies include reading, writing, and on certain nights throughout the calendar year, she can be found watching meteor showers or lunar eclipses conveniently from her backyard.

.

Other books by this author

The Cloverly Wolves Series
Book One- Looking for Ginseng
Book Two- Paisley Wolf
Book Three- Always Hayden
Book Four- Seeing Red

www.ingramcontent.com/pod-product-compliance
Lightning Source LLC
Chambersburg PA
CBHW020336180626
46812CB00001B/227